NADINE LITTLE

Homecoming

The Faction War Chronicles 4

LITTLE PUBLISHING

Cover design by Serifim.com

This book is written in British English.

First edition

ISBN: 978-1-8380884-2-2

This book was professionally typeset on Reedsy.
Find out more at reedsy.com

Sign up for my mailing list to get a free and exclusive prequel to *The Faction War Chronicles*. Discover the explosive origins of the Faction War ten years before the events of *Captivity*. Members of my mailing list get other bonus stuff and behind-the-scenes material.

Members are also the first to hear about my new books and discounts.

Join at nadinelittle.com

'Home is where somebody notices
when you are no longer there.'
Aleksandar Hemon

'War does not determine who is right,
only who is left.'
Bertrand Russell

1

The civilised world is a little more battered than I remember, and that's only the small part I saw from windows as I was ferried from vehicles to buildings and back again.

But no one's tried to rape or kill me, so that's an improvement.

I cross my arms and glare at the sweat-shiny man across the table. The crumples in his brown suit turn it into a landscape of ridges and furrows.

"I want to see Blake."

"Now, Miss Carmichael, be reasonable." His hand smooths his tie in a quick, darting movement. "Mr O'Riley is busy with his own processing. We only need a little more information then you can go."

"It's Anita or Carmichael, lose the Miss. And I've already answered your questions. The same damn questions I answered in Denmark three weeks ago. It's all getting a bit tedious."

Government drone number two frowns, his watery blue gaze never leaving my face. He hardly blinks, his attention fixed on me, as though I'll disappear if he looks away.

It's getting creepy.

"We have procedures we must follow, Miss—Anita. I'm sure you can appreciate our caution. We've had no communication from anyone in Scotland for almost a decade."

"How is that possible?"

The two men share a glance.

"We are still investigating," Drone-one says. "Granted, we had to focus on our own recovery. We haven't had the resources for much else."

"And you all seemed content to hide behind the fence you built."

I raise my eyebrow at Drone-two. "Are you saying we got what we deserved?"

"I'm simply saying we suffered losses when we tried to approach that quickly became unacceptable given the escalating global situation at the time."

"What happened to the Scottish refugees who made it past the border fence before Soldiers of the Lost weaponised it?"

Drone-one tugs at his tie, the material concertinaing towards his Adam's apple as soon as he releases it. "Many were conscripted."

Refusing our war to be forced into another. How unlucky.

"Those who survived have resettled," Drone-one continues. "Some emigrated following the re-stabilisation."

"Will Blake and I be resettled? We're UK citizens."

Drone-two's eyes roll like he's trying to view the inside of his skull.

I've learned it's one of the many expressions people adopt when they access their neuralnet—the world's solution to the internet collapse. They drilled implants into people's brains and the internet transformed into every single living, breathing human being.

They may not have had the resources to infiltrate Scotland but god forbid they go without cat memes.

A young intern in the marbled government office of Denmark delighted in showing me the wonders of the neuralnet, transferred wirelessly from his excitable brain to a nearby screen.

Anything that involves bore-holing into my skull is not going to happen.

I have too many scars.

My fingertips stroke a long pink line on my left forearm, shiny and healed with no weakness in the muscle.

"Your family have yet to return our communication but their last known address is in New London," Drone-two says.

"What about Blake's mum? Is she alive?"

Please let her be alive. Blake has lost enough family.

Twenty-five percent at my hand.

Drone-two shifts in his chair—a plastic contraption of white curves and chrome legs. It looks fancy but mine seems intent on realigning my spine into a shape no normal person can possibly withstand.

"Yes, Mrs O'Riley still resides at her last known address in the Republic of Ireland. She has also been contacted."

I release a breath and steal a minute to compose myself, meeting the gaze of my reflection in the screen behind my two interrogators/interviewers. Tired green eyes stare back.

It's been a whirlwind three weeks since we landed our stolen jet in a field in Denmark, two refugees from a country that was no longer their home. The end of a perilous ten-day journey through no man's land. I fled the war because it took everything from me.

But it gave me the one person I needed.

"I want to see Blake."

Drone-two sighs and raises his eyes to the panelled ceiling.

"You're both lucky you have family who can vouch for you. Some spend years in processing centres. This world may be less welcoming than you remember—"

"Why don't we go through the questions one last time then we'll take you to Mr O'Riley's room?" Drone-one interrupts, sliding a glance at his comrade—sorry, colleague—while a bead of sweat gathers above his eyebrow.

"Where I believe he is being as intransigent as you," Drone-two mutters.

I smirk.

You bet your ass he is.

"Let's start again then, Miss Carmichael," Drone-one says after another fondle of his tie. "How many factions were involved in your war?"

I swallow a huff.

Blake's absence aches in my chest and prickles in my skin. It's the longest we've been apart since I was captured by Unification Army during our attempt to steal one of their warships.

A short but horrific space of time when I thought he was dead.

"Ten," I say.

Drone-two's watery eyes meet Drone-one's, which are the same colour as his awful suit.

"Rather a lot of you."

"Yeah, it was a great big party."

"What factions were left when you chose to escape?"

"Embra, Revolutionary Front, Rebel State, Soldiers of the Lost, Saorsa, Unification Army and Alba gu Brath."

"And how many of them have nuclear or other weapons of mass destruction?"

4

"I already told you—I don't know the full details of what each faction has. It depended on what we could initially steal or trade."

Drone-two's palm slaps the table. "But Nationless built this dragon machine, you said. Powerful, amazing, capable of ending the war and dominating the world."

"She's gone."

A bead of sweat trembles on the end of Drone-one's nose and plops onto the polished silver tabletop. The silence stretches, footsteps clicking down a corridor through the door behind me.

Drone-two slicks his blond hair back with a long-suffering sigh. "You told us you spent time in four separate factions, including your own. Are we to believe you gleaned nothing on their capabilities? Just tell us which ones have nuclear weapons."

I must not bare my teeth and snarl. I must act like a normal woman.

Demure and shit.

"Since I was a prisoner in three of the four, they hardly shared their secrets. The People's Republic didn't have nuclear, that's all I can tell you."

"But your People's Republic is gone so that doesn't help us. Who is likely to possess nuclear or other weapons of mass destruction?"

My fingertips rub the two pairs of dog-tags beneath my t-shirt. "How about you get off your ass and go find out yourself?"

"Now, Miss Carmichael—"

Drone-two thrusts forward, the edge of the table digging into his chest. "I think you learned more than you're letting on during your captivity. What happened in Nationless? You tense up whenever you talk about the place. Where was it, Livingston?"

I leap to my feet and my chair clatters to the floor. The drones recoil.

"Take me to Blake. Right goddamn now."

"But, Miss Carmichael—"

I plant my fists on the table and lean close to the drones. "No more fucking questions. Replay the damn footage on your fancy neuralnet."

I straighten and stride to the door. Drone-one flutters at his tie and skips over, his key jittering into the lock. The door opens on a long, white corridor.

"F-follow me then, please."

Drone-two stays behind, which is for the best since I want to punch his smug face.

No one gets to hear about those days. My torture.

No one but Blake.

2

Another door opens into an identical room—silver table, grey floor, spine-killing chairs and a shiny screen on the far wall reflecting the gathered people. A hulk of a man stands in the corner, his dark suit perfectly tailored to his large frame. Blake sits with his back to me, his slim figure as familiar as my own hand. The way his navy t-shirt hugs his shoulders, the choppy fall of his black hair.

The ache in my chest spreads to my gut and I stop myself from barging Drone-one out of the way.

I've been in the same buildings as Blake the last three weeks—the same vehicles with tinted windows, the same ferry to London since the whole world is a no-fly zone—but never really together. They questioned us individually and locked us in separate rooms at night, the spartan, echoing halls of the processing centres identical whether we were in Denmark or England.

We stole moments in passing, practically sitting in each other's laps during meals, the brief touch of a hand, a breathless kiss in a bland corridor.

I struggle to sleep without the thud of his heartbeat under my ear.

And Jesus-fucking-Christ I miss the sex.

"Sorry to interrupt…" Drone-one says, his wheedling voice fading as he steps into the room and leaves me framed in the doorway behind Blake.

A woman perches on the edge of the table next to him, too close for politeness, one tawny leg inches from the side of his body. Her charcoal skirt rucks up to mid-thigh, the top buttons of her shirt undone to flash her cleavage. She laughs and touches his arm, his bare skin, and a growl rumbles in my throat.

He is *mine*.

She doesn't appear to notice his body leaning away from her, the tension in his shoulders, his hands clasped tight in front of him.

I slide into the room, moving sideways to see the reflection of Blake's face in the screen. The woman glances at me, a slight frown between plucked crimson brows. Blake meets my gaze in the glass. My heart somersaults from my chest to my throat, as it always does.

All he has to do is look at me and I turn into a babbling idiot.

He thinks it's endearing. It's embarrassing but I wouldn't change it for the world.

Blake's expression shifts from closed and blank to a tenderness that weakens my knees. He jumps to his feet and the legs of his chair screech scuff marks on the floor. The woman gasps, a hand flying to her mouth.

I can't blame her for being attracted to him.

Still do, though.

"Woman, where the hell have you been?" Blake says, his dark and sexy smirk not helping the weakness in my extremities. "I missed you."

He halts inches away, exactly my height, and I stare into

eyes of deep cobalt-blue tinged with violet. My trembling fingers brush his cheekbone and trace down his jaw to his pouty bottom lip.

My hand moves too slowly for the longing tingle in my skin, the desperate need to press myself against him.

"They wouldn't shut up with their stupid questions," I say.

He smiles and kisses my fingertips, destroying what little control I have around him.

Which is none.

I throw myself at him and replace my fingers with my lips, fisting my other hand in his t-shirt. He smells of sunshine and earth. I swallow his chuckle, concentrating on climbing into his mouth and trying not to faint at the taste of him. My back hits the wall, my fingers gliding upwards to tangle in his hair. I thrust my hips into his, the feel of his erection driving all thoughts from my brain.

"There's my wanton little hussy," he moans against my lips. "I fucking missed you."

The desire in his voice sizzles between my legs and demands I rip off his clothes.

"Where did you learn such language?" I manage to stutter past the pulse in my throat.

"From some woman with a very bad mouth."

"Blake, please—"

'Fuck me' would've been the end of that sentence but the sounds in the room finally penetrate.

Drone-one flaps his hand and squeaks, "Miss Carmichael, Mr O'Riley this is most improper! We are government officials. We—"

"Oh, give it a rest, Jones," the man in the corner says, shoving away from the wall to loom above us, "before you sweat through the whole of your suit."

My respect for him immediately increases.

No Drone-three, this one.

The woman's heels clack on the floor and she clomps past us to stand nearer Jones, who flutters next to the doorway like a panicked moth. A scowl reddens her face. Blake and I finally release each other, standing far enough away that the heat of his body doesn't tempt me to ride him to the ground.

"I'm sorry we've kept you here so long," our supporter continues, holding out his hand. "I'm Quintin. Quintin Sall."

We shake his palm in turn, our slender hands disappearing in his grip.

"Are we done for the day? Can we go?" Blake says.

"And don't even try to separate us again. We're staying in the same room—same bedroom, same interview room—or I swear to god, I will shag him whether you're standing there or not."

"She's not kidding." Blake tangles his warm fingers in mine.

Quintin folds his lips. "That shouldn't be necessary."

The woman stalks from the room with a sniff and a, "I have another appointment. A date."

It's refreshing to have a jealous female who snipes about it but doesn't try to kill me.

Though, give her time.

"Our questions on weaponry still need addressed—"

Quintin chops his hand through the air. Jones's mouth flaps but no more words come out. Quintin shuts his eyes, which flick rapidly back and forth beneath his lids.

"You'll need to be satisfied with the footage you have, question time is over."

"But—"

"Check the memo. We have new instructions."

Jones's left eyelid droops as though he's having a stroke. Both hands smooth his tie, one after the other.

"Oh. Very well then. Miss Carmichael, Mr O'Riley..." He bows stiffly, his forehead slick under the lights, and scurries out of the room.

"What new instructions?" I say.

"Instructions from a level above my pay grade. You've been granted permission to enter New London. Your publicist will meet you at your accommodation for a short briefing. One room," he adds quickly in response to my scowl.

Blake frowns. "Why do we need a publicist?"

"The news of your arrival has leaked."

Blake's gaze meets mine and he squeezes my hand. "That sounds ominous."

"You're something of a celebrity in these trying times. A fresh excitement from the drudgery of rationing and austerity. There's been increasing pressure on the Prime Minister to act now that our country has stabilised. You could be the impetus he requires."

The last thing I need is to be a pawn in another leader's game. That's part of the shit I escaped from.

"Come. A car has arrived to take you to your quarters." Quintin sweeps his hand out. "That location is secret from the public. For now, at least."

We walk where Quintin indicates through branching corridors of white, past rooms of people who peek at us. Blake's hand keeps me steady, the reassurance of his footsteps matching mine. Quintin guides us to a rear exit, short steps leading down to a squat black car parked in an empty square of concrete. A single security light bathes the courtyard and bounces my reflection from the tinted windows of the vehicle. The door of the car hisses open.

I stop on the bottom stair. "All the windows are tinted. How can the driver see?"

"There is no driver. It's automated and electric. Safer and more sustainable than human-operated vehicles."

"So we'll be totally alone?" A smirk grows on Blake's face and speeds my pulse.

His thumb strokes my palm in a lazy circle, the tiny motion expanding heat low in my belly.

I clear my throat a couple of times. "How long do we have—how long does it take to get into New London?"

"Thirty minutes," Quintin says, the muscles twitching in his cheeks. "Your car has been cleared through the gate so you won't have to stop."

Blake grins. "Challenge accepted."

3

Two orgasms later—the guy is a fucking genius—we arrive at a townhouse in a street of townhouses. The silent, self-driving car eases to a gentle stop, the world darkened through the tinted windows. The door pops open while we wriggle into our clothes. I wobble out of the vehicle and Blake joins me on the pavement, sliding his arm around my waist and pressing me into his side.

"We should do that again sometime," he whispers in my ear.

"We should've asked Quintin if the car has cameras."

The door thunks shut and the vehicle pulls smoothly into the light traffic, disappearing down the street.

"If it does, they just got one heck of a video."

We stand for a moment to enjoy the summer night, the air thick with the smell of hot concrete. The facade of the townhouse rises three levels high, hidden by vegetation in a fluffy green wall, more plants and shrubs spilling from pots on each balcony. The streets are hushed, almost empty, and quite unlike the London I remember when my sister dragged me on a trip to see the House of Commons.

Though New London is further north than the old London. What's left of it.

We enter through a panelled door into a circular lobby in

shades of bronze and cream. Two women occupy a short desk, their blonde hair in tight ponytails.

Dread fists into my gut. I swallow a few times in case it tries to spill out my mouth.

No reason to panic. They're professional women not twins who looked like pitbulls and strapped me—

Don't think about it.

"Good evening ma'am, sir. Can you show me your credentials please?" says a man in a bulletproof vest over a black shirt, his broad shoulders blocking the rest of the lobby.

He cradles a Heckler & Koch MP5, the cord of an earpiece spiralling into his ear.

Not quite the welcome I expected.

"We're actually meeting someone—" Blake starts.

"Hello! Yes, they're with me." An elfin woman swoops from behind the armed guard and holds her slender hand out to me, a silver charm bracelet sparkling on her wrist. "So nice to meet you Miss Carmichael, Mr O—*wow…*"

Her mouth drops open. She's still gripping my hand but her gaze locks on Blake. I mean to share a knowing look with him and end up staring, as awestruck as the woman.

Dark hair, so black it has purple and emerald highlights like a magpie's wing, kisses his cheekbones and flops over his forehead. Violet eyes and smirking lips, the fascinating hollow of his throat. Sleek and slim but muscled in the right places—

Oh, for fuck's sake.

I shake myself and the woman yanks her hand from mine, her cheeks flushed brighter than the abstract patterns on her dress. "I am so sorry! I'm so embarrassed."

"Don't worry about it," I say, instantly liking her. "He has that effect on everyone."

Blake raises an eyebrow. "Hardly everyone."

I tilt my chin towards the desk where the two women titter behind their hands. They see us watching and immediately bow their heads.

"*Everyone*," I say.

The elfin woman straightens her shoulders and thrusts out her hand once more, the colour slowly fading from her face.

"Let me start again. I am very pleased to meet you Miss Carmichael, Mr O'Riley"—tiny wobble when his hand takes hers but she gamely powers through—"and welcome to the Townhouse. I'm Felice Huffman and I'll be your publicist for the duration of your stay."

"Nice to meet you, Felice. And please, call us Anita and Blake. We had enough of the Miss and Mr crap from the government drones."

She laughs, her hand fluttering to her throat. "Not a problem, Anita. Blake. Follow me and I'll show you to your room."

She whisks away on towering red heels—god, she must be tiny—and we trot after her to a lift at the back of the lobby, next to a large, curving staircase. The doors ping open to a mirrored interior, Blake and I scruffy in comparison to Felice's stiff outfit and silvery-blonde hair. She presses the button for the top floor and the lift glides upwards, classical music piped from hidden speakers.

"As it's getting late, I'll leave you to acclimatise to your room and collect you at 3pm tomorrow for a proper briefing. You have a press conference scheduled for 9am the following day. But it's nothing to worry about," she says, glancing at my face.

"Do we have to stay in our room or are we allowed to leave?"

"Oh, you're not confined to your room. You can explore the Townhouse, the surrounding area. My only advice would be to remain close. The public don't yet know of your location or have a picture of you but that will change after Thursday's conference. Be prepared to become very popular."

The doors slide open to a cream corridor with mahogany side tables holding decorated pots of marigold and helleborine.

"What is this place?" I say, trailing my fingers across slick wood. "It's like a fancy hotel."

"It's for visiting dignitaries. One of the few buildings of opulence we have here in New London."

She leads us to a room at the end, her heels hushed on the carpet. She flashes a black keycard through a reader and pushes the door wide, holding it open.

"Holy crap."

"Holy shit," I say at the same time as Blake.

Felice smiles. "Yes, it's somewhat extravagant but everything is made from recycled materials or sustainably sourced. I admit I'm a little envious."

The room is a palette of honey, bronze and grey, diaphanous curtains billowing around a glass door onto a balcony, bringing the purr of tyres from the street below. White daisies cover every surface—bedside tables, chest of drawers, tables in the separate seating area. The bed appears wider than I'm tall, bedecked with gold pillows and a grey runner trimmed in more gold.

"Blake," I shout from the bathroom, "look at the size of the bath!"

A claw-footed tub sits in the middle of the floor, a colourful array of potions on a cabinet next to it—lavender, jasmine, almond and honey.

I almost climb into it right there despite Felice hovering in the doorway and smiling at our childish wonder.

Blake wraps his arms around me, his chin on my shoulder. "I think we'll both fit comfortably. Lots of space for squirming."

Okay, maybe not so childish.

"Is there enough hot water for us to use it?"

"Oh, yes," Felice says. "Thankfully, we're past the worst of the rationing. August can be a bad month so there's usually some limits to prevent water shortages. There are clothes for you both in the cupboards. You can order food from the kitchen and there's a laundry service. In fact, you have full use of the amenities, including a spa. I am very jealous of that one."

"Who's paying for all this?" I say, sticking my head into an annex off the main bathroom leading to the toilet and a glass-enclosed cubicle with a showerhead as large as a dinner plate. "And can we stay forever?"

Felice laughs. "Courtesy of The Union Party and Prime Minister Bursey himself. And yes, for the foreseeable future, anyway."

Now, why would the Prime Minister splash the cash on two refugees from a country that's caused his so much strife? What's he after?

Cynical, who, me?

"Well, I'll leave you two to rest and knock on your door at 3pm tomorrow. Have a good night." She leaves, placing the keycard on a table in the sitting area.

Blake cups my face as soon as the door shuts. "Oh, we're not going to be resting."

His lips meet mine, the teasing glide firing heat straight to my fingertips.

He kissed me like this the very first time—tender and gentle and skillful enough to make my eyes roll back. One kiss and I was already half in love with him. The glorious sex and the perfect, beautiful person he is sealed the deal.

He slips his hands under my t-shirt and plays his fingers up my ribs, his thumbs lightly stroking my bra. I arch against him, devouring his mouth and dizzy at the taste of him. He pulls away, smirking at my whimper.

"God, I love you." He fists his hand in my hair and tugs my head back, exposing my neck to his teeth. "You run the bath and I'll order food. Let's get you all slippery."

He nibbles along my jaw and bites me over my thudding pulse.

"Blake—"

"Mmm, that'll do for a start. You'll moan it a lot more later. After our bath, we're going to have sex in a bed for once. I want you spread out all naked and wet."

Each word throbs through my body and pools between my legs. He releases me and I sit hard on the edge of the bath. He grins, one finger stroking my cheek, a soft expression on his face.

He loves me. Of that, I have no doubt. And I love him. Him and only him until the day I stop breathing.

Maybe by then, I'll finally deserve him.

4

A polite tapping on the door jerks me from a particularly hot dream about Blake.

Being a light sleeper comes in handy when you're surrounded by enemies.

In a townhouse in the centre of New London, not so much. It seems people like to be out on the streets early rather than late.

A groan rumbles under my ear. "What time is it?"

I raise my head from Blake's chest and squint at the glowing silver contraption that has more buttons than any normal alarm clock should.

"Crap," I sigh, "it's 8am. That'll be Felice again."

I bury my face in the warmth of Blake's neck, his pulse fluttering against my cheek. His arm presses me to the side of his body, both of us naked in a tangle of sheets and comfortable pillows.

We didn't do much resting. I almost fainted from happiness in the bath that first night, cuddled with Blake in the almond-scented heat. His clever fingers stroked my slick skin, avoiding the places aching for his touch until I writhed and begged for him.

His self-control is amazing, though he wouldn't let me touch him. Then he'd lose himself.

He's so damn adorable.

We stumbled, dripping and flushed, from the bath to the giant bed. I climbed onto the cool sheets and propped myself on my elbows, my legs splayed, wet hair curling over my shoulders. My dog-tags danced over the heavy thud of my heart.

"Fucking hell, Anita," he whispered, standing at the foot of the bed, water glistening on his body.

A throb of pleasure flared deep.

I love it when he swears.

Black spikes of hair stuck to his face and framed eyes tinged violet. Two pairs of dog-tags hung between the planes of his chest, one his own, the other his brother's. My gaze drifted downward to the bunch of his abdominal muscles and the tantalising line of his hips.

"Fucking hell, yourself."

Cue his dark, sexy smirk and my sudden trouble breathing. He joined me on the sheets and continued where he left off in the bath, all hands and mouth and teeth. I lost count of how many times I said please and screamed his name to the ceiling.

I hope there are no other dignitaries in residence because quiet sex with Blake is an impossibility.

We collapsed into sleep and made up for our three abstinent weeks by shagging on every available surface yesterday morning. The wall, the floor, me straddling Blake on a bouncy couch that tried to swallow us.

Felice seemed worried we were coming down with a fever when we staggered flushed and bright-eyed from the room at 3pm for our briefing.

The polite tapping on the door returns.

I huff and burrow deeper into Blake's neck. "Can I just stay here forever?"

"I'm all right with that." He pulls me closer, my hand sliding across his chest to play with the beaded chains of his dog-tags. "Who knew such a mouthy pain in the arse could be so soft and snuggly?"

I nip him over his pulse, and he shivers.

"Less of the soft."

"But you're okay with the snuggly?"

I wriggle until I'm on top of him. "I'm definitely okay with the snuggly."

The gentle tapping becomes a fist hammering on the door. "Anita? Blake? Are you ready?"

God, Felice is loud and insistent for someone so tiny.

"I'm coming," I yell and shove myself up.

Blake rolls and pins me beneath him, the familiar weight frying my synapses.

"I'll see what I can do, baby," he says, shifting to nibble my collarbone.

A giggle bubbles in my throat. "Have mercy. You know I can't refuse you. She'll burst the door down and there's no way I'm letting her see you naked."

"Good point. She'd drool all over the floor."

I slap at his chest and he releases me, chuckling while I fumble on a robe tossed to the carpet. He yanks the covers to his shoulders and settles into the pillows, his hair mussed, lips swollen.

The guy screams sex and danger.

No wonder I'm obsessed.

"Blake…"

"What? She can't see I'm naked."

Shaking my head, I tie the robe shut, smooth my wild hair and open the door. Felice stands on the other side, her fist raised in preparation for another pounding.

She's perfectly made up, her hair gathered in a complicated series of twists, a charcoal dress and silver belt highlighting her slight frame.

"I'm so sorry. We slept in. Give us ten minutes?"

"Oh, right. Where's Bl—"

I follow her wide-eyed gaze to Blake sprawled in bed. He waves and she steps backwards so fast she almost hits the opposite wall.

"T-ten minutes, you said? No problem. Take all the time you need. No, don't. I'll, ah, see you in the boardroom. For breakfast. Ten minutes."

She scuttles towards the lift in a puff of sweet perfume. I shut the door and sag against it, my laughter bursting out.

"The poor woman. You're going to give her a heart attack."

Blake sweeps the covers off and stalks towards me, his hands lifting my hips, my legs wrapping around his waist.

"Who cares about her?" he says. "I owe you one spectacular orgasm before breakfast."

He carries me into the shower where my laughter quickly turns to moaning agreement.

5

Felice has composed herself by the time we reach the board-room, her brisk professionalism a shield against her attraction to Blake.

"Please, help yourselves to some breakfast," she says. "We'll head down to the conference from here but I wanted to refresh what we discussed yesterday and see if you had any questions."

"Are the press here yet?" I say.

"They've been arriving since early morning."

"How many?"

"Representatives from the main affiliates, plus a few select local offices. Four hundred or so."

Jesus.

I fill my plate with pastries and fruit despite the nerves tangling my stomach.

The food is all British grown. Sustainable. That's the buzzword in New London. I was a little put off by the menu in our room. A New Londoner's diet seems to be heavy on invertebrate and plant protein. No beef or lamb, though there was chicken and pork.

Blake and I claim the same seats we sat in for our briefing the day before, facing the floor-to-ceiling windows offering a view of New London in the sunshine. The buildings are mostly squat and utilitarian, solar panels winking on roofs not covered in greenery. Wind turbines grace the taller structures and line the wider avenues of the streets below.

I asked Felice if they rebuilt the London Eye but she said they only recreated Big Ben, the Houses of Parliament and Downing Street.

We finally explored the rest of the Townhouse after yesterday's briefing, not quite brave enough to strip off in the spa and show our scars. None of the other rooms appeared to be occupied. The staff we met were always courteous and impeccably dressed, compared to Blake and me in jeans and t-shirts.

I'd ignored the gauzy skirts and low-cut tops in the cupboard in our room. They may be made from recycled plastic bags but they're still a little flashy for me. Same for the make-up.

It's been so long since I wore any, I wouldn't know what to do with it.

"How am I supposed to run in these?" I'd said with a sniff, holding up a delicate pair of pumps, a glittery bow decorating the toe.

"Who are you expecting to run from?" Blake took the shoes and tossed them into the bottom of the cupboard, his arms sliding around my waist. "We don't need to run anymore."

Always the optimist.

We'd left the Townhouse for a stroll in the gathering dusk, the pavements mostly absent of people. Those who were out sat on benches or leaned against walls, their eyes glazed and staring at nothing.

The zombies of the neuralnet.

It's the only entertainment they seem to have in New

London.

We found a small park a few streets away, the grass freshly mown and bordered by trees. Streetlights flickered on in the surrounding residential areas.

"Let's go back before it gets too dark."

"Wait," Blake said. "What's that?"

I followed his extended finger to the other side of the park, the black outline of trees barely visible. A luminescent red shone from the leaves of one in the middle. As I watched, every second tree flared the same colour, painting the landscape a subtle crimson.

"It's beautiful," I breathed, spinning on the spot to take it all in.

A man approached us down the path, a small puff of fur that could be a dog prancing on the end of a leash.

"Look—the trees are glowing!" I said, too excited to notice his lack of wonder.

He frowned, stepping onto the grass as if he might ignore me and keep walking. English politeness won out. "Yes... Where have you been the last few years?"

"But how do they do that? Is it algae?"

"Nanoparticles embedded in the leaves. Wait." The man stopped edging away from us, his posture stiffening, the little dog hopping at his feet. "Are you Scottish?"

Shit. I was about to blow our last few hours of anonymity.

"No," I said quickly. "We're from Ireland, to be sure. Arrr."

"You sound like a pirate," Blake mumbled out the side of his mouth.

My muffled laugh became a sneeze. The dog cocked its head, peering up at me through tiny black eyes. The man frowned again, as puzzled as his pet.

"Well, top of the, um, evening to you!" I said, grabbing Blake's hand and towing him away down the path.

After a pause, the man kept walking, casting glances over his shoulder until he left the park. Hopefully, he thought we were crazy rather than Scottish, though he'd learn the truth if he watched the news.

"That was deeply offensive to my heritage," Blake said, a smile tugging at his mouth. He pulled me off the path and pressed my back against a glowing tree. "I'm going to have to teach you a lesson."

The reddish light tinted his hair and sparked in his eyes, the rest of his face shadowed.

"Yes, please."

He captured my mouth and we proceeded to do something that would've gotten us arrested for public indecency had we been seen.

I keep forgetting there are laws and police and rules of social etiquette.

Felice claps, yanking me back to the boardroom. "Now, as I said yesterday, try to keep your answers light. Avoid anything too graphic and detailed, we've had enough of that ourselves. Give them a feel of what you survived. Scotland has been a black hole of information for years. And something to fear. I want you to show them the human face of your war. Remind them people are still being hurt. Decent people."

I cough. "We didn't run away because most of the people are decent, Felice."

Some offered brief glimpses of kindness, like bursts of light in the dark. Fiona, a member of The People's Republic who never believed I was a traitor. Emily, a doctor who tended my injuries in Soldiers of the Lost. And Blake, a glorious sunrise who banished the dark.

"No, I don't suppose you did," Felice says, dabbing her mouth with a napkin. "But the hope is their humanity can be restored. War forces us to be brutal but there is always hope when it ends."

"Good luck with that," Blake mutters into his hand.

We finish our breakfast in silence, the chatter of people drifting through the windows. Felice glances at her watch, the slim, silver piece complementing her bracelet.

"Time to head down."

Suddenly my food decides it wants to return to the plate. I swallow hard, one hand soothing my belly.

Christ, how can I be nervous about this? It's not like heading into battle. What happens if the press conference goes badly? People may not like me.

Boohoo. I'll take that over death.

I run my fingers through my hair as if that will be enough to tame the wildness.

Do I have pastry in my teeth?

Blake stills my hands and kisses my knuckles. "You look fine. Beautiful. They're going to love you."

Felice sighs then catches herself. She brushes at her dress and feigns immense interest in the carpet.

"I don't care if they love me," I say.

"Good, because the women are going to hate you."

I roll my eyes. "What else is new? Let's get this over with."

We troop into the lift and Felice presses the button for the ground level.

We peeked into the meeting room the day before—a huge space with a high, arching ceiling and a burgundy carpet swamped by the number of chairs laid out in rows.

A stomach-churning number of chairs.

"I'll head in first to introduce you then you can have a bit of an entrance," Felice says, checking her make-up in the mirrored lift panel. "We've been very secretive about you so they're coming into this relatively blind. They're wriggling with anticipation."

That does not make me feel better.

Blake's hand squeezes mine. "This is nothing. We've been through worse than having people curious about us."

I suck in a breath and blow it out, keeping a hold of his hand.

No way am I letting go.

"You're right," I say. "No one's going to hurt us. Well, not physically. They might call us names and hurt my feelings."

"If they do, I'm sure Felice will let you curse at them."

"No cursing, please," she says.

"You're definitely going to struggle with that," Blake smirks. "Best say nothing at all."

"Asshole," I grin.

The doors slide open into the lobby, the meeting room accessed through a corridor towards the back. A buzz of noise greets us around the corner. Through the open half of the double doors, a narrow strip of carpet separates the front row and the raised dais. Clusters of cameras on tripods aim at the front of the room.

"What's with the video cameras?" I say, keeping my voice hushed to avoid alerting the buzzing multitude. "I thought people could record on their neuralnet. You know, using their eyes?"

"That's true, yes, but only the most expensive models produce decent video."

"Doesn't it creep you out that every person looking at you could be uploading your image to the net?"

"Oh, no one records everything," Felice says, waving her hand, her nails the same colour as her dress. "There's a data limit and most people want to star in their own videos. You should get one installed then you can see what's out there and contribute content."

I shudder. "No thanks."

"Blake?" She flushes but her gaze stays steady.

Strong woman.

I empathise. I blushed every damn time those cobalt eyes met mine.

Still do.

"Nope. Not for me, either."

Felice clicks her fingers. "I'll arrange a tour of one of our implantation facilities. You might change your mind when you understand the process."

Not likely.

She ushers us against the wall next to the doorway, out of sight of the media gathered in the meeting room. I try to ignore the rumble of their voices and the sweat pooling in the small of my back, Blake's hand warm in mine.

"Wait here until I announce your names then come and sit beside me on the stage. Take a deep breath. The press will be on their best behaviour, don't worry."

Her face breaks into a beaming smile and she sweeps into the meeting room, leaving Blake and I quivering against the wall.

Or maybe that's just me.

The sound increases to a roar for a beat and fades to the shuffle of bodies and muffled coughing.

"Good morning, ladies and gentlemen," Felice's voice peals out, amplified by the room's built-in speaker system. "Thank you so much for your patience and your indulgence, although some of you were most insistent. I'm talking about you, Linda." Cue a swell of laughter. "Well, let me finally satisfy your curiosity. The rumours are indeed true. Two people fled the Faction War, the only ones to do so in its history, and they are here to answer as many of your questions as they can. Please welcome Anita Carmichael and Blake O'Riley."

"Let's make a run for it," Blake says in my ear, and I jump.

My laugh shakes. "You go in ahead of me."

"She said your name first."

"Coward."

He smirks. "At this, I am. Give me a stronghold to infiltrate any day."

I straighten my shoulders and drag him into the room beside me. A wave of whispering, clapping and mumbling greets our entrance. One guy whoops. A million cameras flash and blind me. My hand flaps at my waist.

"No more guns, remember?" Blake whispers. "We're civilised people now."

God, I miss my Glock, the weight of it on my hip just another part of my body.

I fix my dazzled gaze on Felice and step up onto the stage, collapsing into a seat behind the sheet-swathed table, a bushel of microphones aimed at my face. Blake takes the chair next to me with a little more grace, his hand clutched in mine.

"No more pictures until the end of the conference, please," Felice says.

I blink the white afterimages away. A man on the opposite side of the room waves at me, his face florid in his too-tight suit. As soon as I look at him, a bulb goes off, searing my retinas.

"Flash that in my eyes again and see what happens," I growl.

"We're trying to be friendly," Blake murmurs out the corner of his mouth, suppressed laughter shaking his body.

"What? I didn't swear."

"Who would like to ask the first question?" Felice says, her voice a touch higher. "Yes, Valerie?"

A woman unfolds herself from the seat. "Valerie Marsh, *The Guardian*. What faction did you come from and why did you leave?"

Two questions, the cheat.

Blake and I glance at each other in the hush that follows.

"We're from different factions. I'm from Nationless and Anita is from The People's Republic."

I fist my hand in my lap to stop from rubbing my dog-tags.

Best to keep it simple. No need to go into how I was forced out of one faction and accepted into the other after stealing the weapon I'd used to destroy Livingston.

An excited babble echoes in the arch of the ceiling, the bright eyes of hundreds of people fixed on us.

"We left because we wanted a life," I say. "People trying to kill you gets a little tiresome after a while."

That's light, right?

A skinny man jumps to his feet. "Peter Arthur, *New London Daily News*. Are you saying you're a couple despite coming from enemy factions?"

"Yes, we're a couple." Blake's thumb skims my palm, sending tingles even under the scrutiny of the multitude.

All the women in the room groan.

"Shoshanna Finch, *Islington Gazette*," says a woman, her

dress crinkling as she stands. "Can you tell us how that happened; how you first met?"

Blake fidgets in his seat. "Ah, well, I jumped on her back and pinned her to the ground."

"I called him a purple-eyed freak."

"I tied her to a tree and left her for dead."

"So, you know," I say, "the usual romantic crap."

I try not to laugh at their stunned expressions, Blake's shudders transferred through our linked hands. The room becomes an uproar of shouting voices, everyone yelling questions.

Felice jerks towards her microphone so fast she almost swallows it. "Please! One at a time or this press conference is over!"

The questions continue, the names and affiliations blending into meaningless words. They focus on our relationship rather than details of the war or what conditions were like in the factions. They really are desperate for positive entertainment but it's a nice change from being quizzed about nuclear weapons. We're like bugs to dissect—Blake a butterfly to pin to a board and say, "Look how pretty!" I'm some kind of parasitic wasp.

Or a dung beetle.

A couple of reporters ask meaningful questions. Shocked silence follows the news that the majority of Scots have no idea the rest of the world is normal, or normal-ish. I avoid answering anything about the war's origins.

I'm not quite ready to admit it was all my faction's fault.

"I think that's a good place to stop for the day," Felice says, rising from her chair. "My clients have had a tiring morning. Thank you, everyone, for your time. You can direct any other enquiries to my office."

She holds out her arm and sweeps us from the room, riding a wave of noise and camera flashes.

"That went very well," she says brightly in the blessed hush of the lift.

Blake and I grunt. She herds us to our room and waves us inside, flitting off to do whatever she does when she's not mentoring us. We collapse on the bed, as exhausted as if we've completed a fitness test rather than sat on our butts answering questions.

"Thank fuck that's over," I groan into the pillow.

"Baby," Blake says, "I have a feeling it's just getting started."

6

I wake to Blake spooned against my back, both of us naked.

There's something freeing about being able to sleep with no clothes on. Back in Scotland, when Blake and I journeyed through no man's land, we mostly slept dressed and ready for anything.

Okay, so we were naked lots of other times.

I wriggle in his arms. "Blake, we have to get up. Felice'll be here in an hour."

"Mmm, keep doing that." His hand slides up my belly towards my breast.

I arch my spine and moan.

I can't help it. The guy has wonderful hands.

"Stop that," I say, my voice already shaky. "We can't be naked every time Felice comes to the door."

"Why not?"

Laughing, I roll out of his hug, my bare feet sinking into the carpet. A shaft of sunlight paints my skin golden, blazing through a gap in the curtains. I turn back to Blake, the warmth caressing my shoulders. He pouts at me, his hair falling into his eyes, and my resistance crumbles.

"You son-of-a-bitch," I sigh, climbing onto the bed.

"I love it when you sweet-talk me."

I kneel on the mattress and he sits up, his hands skating around my waist. His dark eyes start a burn of anticipation in my stomach. I lean down to capture his pouting mouth and a light tap comes from behind me. Blake's hands freeze on my butt. A hooded figure stands on our balcony and stares at us. The buttons of his jacket tap gently against the glass.

"Mother-*fucker!*"

I leap across the floor but the man tugs on a wire around his waist and disappears towards the roof before I can open the sliding door and introduce him to the pavement three storeys below. I jerk the heavy curtains, plunging the room into darkness.

"Lights, forty-percent," Blake says.

Lamps bloom on around the room.

"Do you think he was recording on his neuralnet?"

"Better call Felice. There has to be some law about uploading images without your consent, especially naked ones."

"Good point. This is supposed to be civilisation after all."

I tap the little screen embedded in the surface of the bedside cabinet.

Felice showed us how to use it and the other technology throughout the room.

The call rings over the speakers in the ceiling, dialling direct to the private phone application of Felice's neuralnet. I climb into bed and cuddle into Blake.

"You okay?" he says, kissing my temple.

"I guess. It's just… I don't want them to see all of me. They don't deserve to know everything. Only you do."

His arms tighten, his cheek pressed to mine.

Safe and warm.

Is the footage already up there in the amorphous, mystical

space of the neuralnet? Or maybe the man was your typical creep and came to gawk, not film.

Felice's voice sings through the speakers. "Anita? Blake? Is everything all right?"

"Someone was at our window, Felice. They caught me—us—naked. We're not sure if they recorded it."

"That's impossible! We have security on the roof. Let me call you back."

The line clicks, leaving nothing but the hush of the air conditioning.

I dress in a pair of forest-green combats and a t-shirt shorter and tighter than I'd normally wear, unable to stop glancing at the window. No gaps, a faint glow of sunlight bordering the curtains.

Blake orders food and joins me at the cupboard. "Nice trousers."

"What? Oh, for god's sake. Do none of these people have plain clothes?"

Swirls of gold and silver thread flow down the side of my thighs. I twist to look in the mirrored door, the pattern arching over my butt to meet in the middle. Kind of like wings. From my ass.

I bet the thread is made from recycled cans or something.

"Well, I like it." Blake strokes the thread.

I smile and slap his hands away, perching on the end of the bed. "Of course you do. I have an awesome butt."

"Can't argue there."

I watch him pull on navy combats and a t-shirt. No underwear.

He's the only man who makes taking clothes off and putting them on equally sexy.

Though taking them off is more fun.

The speakers trill. I jab the screen.

"Hi, Felice."

"Guys, I am so sorry. There was a commotion at the rear of the Townhouse and it drew security away from the front of the roof. I know exactly who it was and they'll be severely fined for it, don't you worry. The footage was uploaded but it's been removed. However, there were some views."

"How many?"

"A hundred and fifty thousand."

"Jesus Christ! In the two goddamn seconds it was live?"

"You're the hottest topic out there. People will have your names on alert. That's part of what I was going to discuss with you this morning. I'm heading right over. Thirty minutes and we can talk properly. Until then, sit tight. And again—I'm sorry. It's my job to protect you from this kind of thing."

"It's okay, Felice. We'll see you when you get here."

She hangs up and I sigh.

"A hundred and fifty *thousand*. I was hoping maybe ten. Ten people, not thousands."

Blake sits beside me, his arm across my shoulders. "It'd be easier to punch ten people. A hundred and fifty thousand might take me a while. The fuckers."

"Such language." I touch his face. "Now I know you're mad."

"Damn right. No one gets to see you naked but me. No one gets to hurt you."

I rest my head in the crook of his arm and we sit in silence for a while.

He said a similar thing in no man's land, the day I surrendered to him. He promised he wouldn't let anyone hurt me again.

And he kept his promise.

The guy stormed the stronghold of Unification Army single-handed to rescue me.

"When do you think they'll let us see our families?" he says. "I'm sure my mum is calling every hour now my name has been released."

Shit. I haven't thought about my family since the government drones told me they hadn't responded to their communication.

What a selfish daughter I am.

"We can ask Felice when she arrives. You nervous about seeing your mum?"

"Yeah, but excited, too. And sad." He glances at me. "She must already know. Part of her will know Dylan's gone. If he's not with me, he's not alive."

I fiddle with the elaborate decoration on the side of my combats. "And you still plan on telling her the whole truth of how he died?"

"She'll forgive you," he says, catching my hand in his, "like I have. And if she doesn't... I've lived this long without her. I'm not living without you."

I duck my head to hide the tears but he places his fingers under my chin and tilts my face to his.

"I love you, Anita. Every bit of you."

"I know," I sniff. "I love you, too."

I climb into his lap and he holds me while I cry.

7

We've finished breakfast by the time Felice bustles into the room, a tiny whirlwind in a white blouse and turquoise skirt matching her towering heels.

"Screen on," she says as soon as the door shuts. The large screen flickers on the wall opposite the seating area. "Let's get the unpleasant part out of the way before I show you the positive side of yesterday's press conference."

Blake and I sit on the couch, me still curled in his lap, the need to be close to him an ache in my chest. Felice drags one of the honey-coloured chairs beside us to face the screen, sinking delicately into it in a waft of woody perfume.

"I'm going to stream my neuralnet onto the screen for you to see. I can also grant you temporary control so you can have a look around, though it only works if I'm nearby." Her eyelids twitch, more seizure than blink. "Here's the uploaded footage."

A frozen picture of our balcony appears on the screen in full colour and glorious definition. The gap in the curtain is a strip of black, sunlight reflecting off the glass. Felice wrinkles her nose and the video starts. The view zooms in to me, totally naked, facing the camera.

How did I miss the little bastard?

Pixelated bands cover my breasts and crotch.

"Oh, well, I'm practically decent," I say.

The scar on my stomach immediately jumps out, running from below my sternum to past my bellybutton.

Emergency surgery after I was almost beaten to death.

The chains of my dog-tags disappear into the pixels, the bullet scar on my left shoulder hidden behind the spill of my hair where it sweeps forward and trails over my chest.

The only consolation is, apart from the scars, I look great. Long legs, curvy hips, taut stomach. Slim and muscled.

On the video, I turn towards the bed, Blake now visible, the sheet pooled at his waist and protecting his modesty.

I bet a few women will have wet dreams featuring that body stretched out and quivering beneath them, his ribs heaving under silken skin, the hollow of his throat begging to be tasted—

Shit. How did that happen?

Blake's arms tighten around me, drawing my eyes to the screen and the horror show of ridges striping my back.

Whip scars from my five days of torture at the hands of Wick, the leader of Nationless. Alive only in my nightmares since I obliterated his face with a metal bat.

I shiver. Blake trails kisses along my jaw.

"He's dead and gone but you're still here," he whispers.

I nod, not trusting my ability to speak. The video continues, me climbing onto the bed, blocking the view of Blake until his hands slide around to cup my butt (which they choose not to pixelate). Then, spotting the camera, my furious expression. The video jitters, jerking backwards as I stalk to the window. The balcony drops and the video cuts to black.

I release a breath.

So thousands of people saw it. Screw them. They've no idea what I suffered. Let them sneer at the scars.

I'm proud of who I am.

Felice shifts in her chair. "Anita, I had no idea. I know you've both come from a terrible place but this really brought it home to me. To a lot of people who watched it. Our war was devastating, we lost so many, but we weren't brutalised. Most of the comments, ah, if you ignore the obligatory explicit ones, are empathetic. They think you're a kick-ass warrior-woman."

Blake's smile curls against my jaw. "Oh, she is."

"Thanks, Felice. I appreciate you saying that."

"Anyway, the content has been erased and security has been increased on the roof. We can't stop people trying to get a glimpse of you but I'm pushing for at least an electromagnetic barrier around the Townhouse, like there is at Downing Street."

"What will that do?"

"Stop any camera from working."

"What about the neuralnet? That's what he used to record us."

"They have protective shields of plastic and aluminium." She runs a hand through her hair, lingering at the back of her head. "The main concern was a cyber attack on the neuralnet. No one wants a repeat of the internet collapse."

"Is that what started it?"

"I believe several of our domestic intelligence agencies are still piecing things together. Obviously, it wasn't a priority during wartime." She rises to her feet and crosses to the screen, planting her hands on her hips. "Let me show you the results of the press conference. I hope you'll feel better once you see how popular you are."

The monitor divides into several news articles, all with slightly different photos of the three of us sitting on the raised stage in the meeting room. The text scrolls, the articles changing, on and on.

"Most of the coverage is very positive. They want to know more, express awe at your escape. This is a taster of their main focus."

One article stretches across the screen, the photograph banner of Blake and I with our heads turned towards each other, our bodies leaning in, a secret smile on our lips. The headline reads 'Love Conquers All,' and I swallow a gag.

"They're calling you a modern-day Romeo and Juliet." Felice sighs, her hands clasped to her chest. "Two enemies falling in love. It's so sweet. They're really taken with your relationship."

I snort.

"What?" Blake says, easing me forward. "You don't think it's sweet?"

"Romeo and Juliet killed themselves in the end."

"Oh, yeah. Guess we'll have to write our own story. Maybe they'll make a movie about us."

"And Romeo's too soft and whiny to be you."

Heat fills his eyes, his hips rubbing where they press against me. "Well, I'm definitely not soft."

My breath catches.

Felice clears her throat. "And look, here are some of the comments from people on the forum we created."

I drag my attention from Blake.

Felice has already seen me naked but I'm not about to subject her to the live sex show.

The screen splits in half, bubbles of text on each side under

42

a column for me and a column for Blake. New bubbles appear constantly, shunting the others out of the way.

"Anita, your comments want to find out more about you or compliment you. Terrifyingly beautiful was one of my favourites and—"

"They're not wrong," Blake says.

"—they also ask for more information on Blake, ah, what he's like."

"I've got a pretty good idea of what they'd want to know." I roll my eyes and he grins.

"Blake, well, the vast majority of your comments are women asking you to marry them or declarations of a, um, romantic nature."

I scramble off his lap. "Are you serious? Most of them? Show me."

Felice flushes but pulls a slim remote out of a compartment at the bottom of the screen. She squints at the monitor and my column disappears, leaving only Blake's.

"Here, I've granted you temporary control. Use this to navigate around the page and scroll through the comments. I'll give you two five minutes to, ah, play around." She hurries out of the room, tossing an apologetic glance at Blake.

I stalk closer to the screen and jab at the tiny buttons on the remote.

"Christ, she wasn't exaggerating. All of these are marriage proposals." I keep my thumb pressed on the down arrow. "Okay, not this one, that's gross. I'm pretty sure this is anatomically impossible. And if this bitch ever touches you, I'll punch her face in. For god's sake, they know nothing about you other than you're fucking beautiful or, in the words of this drooling stranger, 'darkly angelic'. How is that enough for them?"

Blake's arms wrap around me, his chin tucked over my shoulder. "It wasn't enough for you?"

"You know I was ridiculously attracted to you from the start, but no," I say, my voice quiet, "it wasn't enough."

I need more than a pretty face. Actions matter. How you treat people. Blake and I share similar experiences—Wick, loss, pain. He is too damned beautiful but he also understood and forgave the most awful thing I could have done to him.

How could I not fall in love with him?

The screen keeps scrolling. "Proposals. More proposals. Invitations for sex. Oh, nice, here's some from men."

His lips trail up my neck to nuzzle my ear. "Are you jealous?"

"No. That would be ridiculous."

I cross my arms and duck my head but he spins me around to face him, gripping my shoulders.

"I don't care if every woman in the world proposes to me, they're not you."

I suddenly find it harder to breathe.

And if I propose to him, what then?

Holy shit. Must not think of marriage.

"But they're gentle, feminine women who didn't destroy your home and kill your brother with a war machine."

"So? None of them are you."

"But—"

He buries his fingers in my hair and traps my head. "Woman, what have I told you about that mouth?"

"But I—"

"One more word and I'll have to find a way to shut you up."

His eyes glitter. Desire curls in my stomach.

"Purple-eyed freak," I say in a rush, a laugh trapped in my

throat.

His growl plays havoc with my heartbeat. He yanks me against him, his mouth crushing mine. My knees collapse and we stumble backwards, sinking into the couch, the kiss an unbroken delight of teeth and tongues. I straddle his hips, desperate to be closer, the need to have him inside me scattering all rational thought. My hands slip under his t-shirt, his skin hot and smooth beneath my fingertips, my thumbs brushing each glorious curve of his abdominal muscles. He rolls his hips, his stomach tensing, his erection rubbing against the most intimate part of me, separated by frustrating layers of cloth. I moan but his grip in my hair pins me to him and he swallows the sound.

We definitely have to get naked.

My hands fumble with the button of his combats. His lips curve into a smile but he shows no mercy, deepening the kiss until everything falls away but him. The taste of him, the feel of him. It reduces me to nothing but aching, throbbing need.

The button pops free. My fingers long to touch him, to make him writhe and watch me through dazed, half-lidded eyes.

Jesus, I'm so close to coming already. One caress and I'll explode.

He's done it before.

The door beeps. Felice's strangled, "Oh!" barely penetrates.

Blake eases me away and I whimper, squirming in his lap at his fierce grin and hungry eyes.

"Baby," he says, the strain in his voice pooling heat between my legs, "we have company."

His words take an embarrassing length of time to register. I blink at Felice who stands half-in and half-out of the doorway, as if she can't decide whether to run screaming or ask to join in.

I scramble off Blake, my knees wobbly. He casually places a tiny, honey-trimmed pillow in his lap while I try to remember how to speak.

"Felice. Um, I think we're finished looking at the comments."

Blake chuckles. I force myself not to look at him.

It won't help my intelligence.

Felice hovers for a beat longer but shuts the door and reclaims her seat, her fluttering hands smoothing her skirt. The screen blinks off, replaced by black.

"Good. I wanted to go over our schedule for the next few days and record some press releases to feed to the media. But first, I have exciting news—I've made contact with both of your families." She shifts in her seat, one leg crossed over the other. "Actually, Blake, I believe your mother has called my office incessantly since your name was released."

He smiles. "We O'Rileys are a stubborn bunch. No use trying to stall her."

"And Anita, your parents are living in New London, in Belgravia. We've kept all the street names though the layout is quite different. A bit of nostalgia. Now," Felice continues, her voice bright, "I appreciate visiting your families is your main priority but it will take me a few days to arrange travel, visas, security and press barriers. Shall I plan the visits to happen concurrently to minimise the time spent apart or—"

"No." Blake squeezes my hand. "We'll do the visits together, one after the other."

My heart skips.

I love that he wants to introduce me to his mother but I

can't imagine a scenario where she doesn't hate me. A female version of Blake who'll screech at me and tell me she wishes I were dead.

"Wonderful! In that case, I'll arrange your visit first, Anita. Give me a second to get the ball rolling." She jumps to her feet.

"Wait," I say before I can change my mind. "Do Blake's first."

"But your parents are closer—"

"Blake gets to see his mum. As soon as possible."

Felice nods and slips into the bathroom.

My breath quivers a little on the way out. "Are you sure you don't want a private reunion first? I can meet her another day. Or decade."

"I want you there, always," Blake says, Felice's chattering echoing through the closed door. "I'm nervous about meeting your parents, too, you know."

I twist to face him. He stares at our joined hands, his head bent. I curl my legs into his lap and brush his hair out of his eyes.

"You have nothing to be nervous about. They'll love you. Be prepared for my mum to flirt shamelessly and my dad to slap you on the shoulder and grill you on your family history. They'll probably talk more about Ailsa than me. She was their favourite."

He raises his head, his expression tender. "Then they're idiots. No offence to your sister."

"I love you."

He smiles. "I know."

Felice sweeps out of the bathroom. "Right, schedule! The rest of today, we'll prepare some press releases. Nothing too strenuous. Short interviews and articles to post on the neuralnet. We'll focus on your journey through no man's land together to start, but I'd like to do some pieces on describing a typical day in each of your factions contrasted with preparing for battles. We can have a series on people you knew, people like you. Normal people trapped in a bad situation. Tomorrow, I've organised a tour of an implantation facility in Kensington. You can learn more about the procedure and, if you wish, get your own installed. It only takes an hour. I'm sure your growing number of fans would love to hear from you direct. And it would speed your integration into society. Everyone has one."

I glance at Blake. He gives a tiny shake of his head and I tangle my fingers in his.

We like our brains exactly as they are.

"Sunday, you have a day to yourselves to do whatever you want, although I'd advise staying within the Townhouse. Now the public know who and where you are, the streets may become a bit swamped, I'm afraid."

Great. Imprisoned by a mob who want to stare at us.

Isn't there anything more exciting in post-war Britain?

"Monday is when things get really interesting. Prime Minister Bursey is throwing a gala dinner in the Townhouse and you're the guests of honour!" Felice's face glows, her hands clasped to her chest. "The official meeting of our Scottish refugees and the Prime Minister. All of The Party will be there."

Huh. I didn't expect anything to be scarier than the press conference. Guess I was wrong.

"Anita, I've already got the perfect stylist booked to help you get ready. Hair, make-up, the works."

I swallow a groan.

In a society of rationing and bug-eating, why do they still care about make-up and glitz? Eye shadow and lipstick don't quite fit into the austere country I've seen so far.

Blake wriggles underneath me and I scowl at his delighted face.

"And Blake, don't worry, I have someone for you, too."

I flash him a wicked smile.

"Don't you laugh at me, woman. We're both going down."

I cup his face and kiss him.

"Wouldn't have it any other way," I say.

8

The implantation centre looks like a giant glass cube set back from the street in a landscaped area of drooping trees. Bushes of waxy, pink flowers line the driveway, the air hot and thick with the scent of honey. A man in a white lab coat over a grey suit hurries towards us as soon as we slide out of the sleek, driverless car.

He grabs Felice's hand, pumping it up and down, his eyes on me and Blake. "Miss Huffman! Delighted to finally meet you. I'm Cornell Hoyes—Doctor Hoyes—the director. I'm so glad you selected our facility for this special tour."

"Thank *you*, Doctor Hoyes, for accommodating us at such short notice." She extricates her hand and gestures towards us. "And this, although I'm sure they need no introduction, is Anita Carmichael and Blake O'Riley, our star-crossed Scottish refugees."

"Star-crossed?" Blake mouths at me and I duck my head to hide a smirk.

This Romeo and Juliet crap is ridiculous. Romeo didn't hate Juliet and march her around at gunpoint.

"Yes! No introduction required, indeed. I watched the press conference with avid interest." Pale eyes fix on me, darting downward. "Very informative."

Seems he watched something else with a little more interest.

Doctor Hoyes swivels back to Felice. "If you'll all follow me. My staff are very excited to meet you."

He strides off towards the entrance, the tail of his lab coat flapping in his wake. Blake and I trail after Felice, her slight frame a buffer between us and this confusing but strangely familiar world we find ourselves in.

We sneaked out the back entrance of the Townhouse through a private underground garage on the second basement level. A crowd of people were gathered in the street, metal barriers keeping them clear of the front door. They screamed our names as the car emerged from the ramp, their bodies pressing against each other, heads craning to catch a glimpse through the tinted windows.

Crazy. We're not pop-stars or actors but two soldiers who deserted a war. They must have their own deserters and refugees. But all the public want to hear is when Blake told me he loved me.

In a field of reeds after he was almost eaten by a genetically engineered snake, if you must know.

Polished granite stairs deliver us into a shining foyer of glass and chrome. My boots squeak on the floor, every surface buffed and sterile, the sting of disinfectant catching in the back of my throat. Padded chairs the colour of butter line the wall opposite a long reception desk manned by a beaming woman in pink scrubs.

Dr Hoyes leads us towards a glass cabinet to one side of the desk. "Here's what you've come to see—the neural implants themselves. This is the selection we offer at this facility."

I lean down to peer into the case, still curious despite having no desire to affix one to my brain.

Three shelves contain a single acrylic block, a silver contraption about the size of a teardrop balanced on each. Hair-like fronds droop from the sides, more numerous from the implant on the top shelf.

"It's tinier than I expected," I say, straightening, "but why do you have different ones? Doesn't everyone get the same kind of implant?"

"Excellent question!" Doctor Hoyes says, brandishing an enthusiastic finger and pointing at the bottom shelf. "This is the model anyone can get. Subsidised by the NHS. The other two offer increased functionality and speed for those who are willing to pay a little extra. I'd recommend our most advanced model for you, considering the amount of traffic you'll generate."

The woman behind the reception desk inches towards us, her broad smile creeping me out. She pats at her wispy red hair, the colour clashing with her scrubs.

"Sure, Doc," I say, trying my best to ignore her, which is difficult since her squat body takes up most of my peripheral vision. "I'll just head back to Scotland where I buried all my money."

The skin around Hoyes's eyes tightens but his grin doesn't falter, his white teeth flashing under the lights. "Well, I wouldn't want that. Oh, no. I'd be honoured to implant it on the house as it were. With some additional publicity from you, of course. Think of the number of people who'll want upgraded to the same model as our hero refugee!"

He manages not to rub his long-fingered hands together.

The woman hovers behind the desk, a piece of paper clutched in her fist. "Anita—oh gosh!—I can't believe it's you, can I have your autograph?"

Doctor Hoyes's expression folds into a frown. The woman's eyes flick between him and me, her face blazing red.

"You want my autograph?"

This is too weird.

The woman practically throws herself across the desk. "Oh, yes, please!"

She smooths the crumpled paper, leaving a smear of damp, and thrusts a pen at me. I pluck it from her fingers and scrawl my name on the sheet, trying not to touch it, the pen hot from her hand. She snatches the paper as soon as I finish and hugs it to her chest.

"Thank you so much!"

She scuttles to the other end of the desk under the glare of Doctor Hoyes and hunches over the piece of paper, stroking it like a beloved pet.

Doctor Hoyes meets my eyes and his smile returns. "I can rearrange my schedule to fit you in this afternoon."

It takes me a second of blinking at him to remember what he's talking about. I open my mouth to tell him absolutely fucking not but Felice gestures at me around his shoulder, her hand making sharp chopping motions at her throat.

"Let me think about it," I say instead.

Felice drops her hand and fixes a smile in place in time for Doctor Hoyes to spin towards her.

"Excellent!" he says. "Let's continue our tour."

A door at the rear of the foyer opens into a long, steel-blue corridor. People in lab coats or pink scrubs bustle between rooms, faltering when they see us but too polite to stop.

Or Doctor Hoyes drilled them more severely than the woman in reception.

"If you come this way, I'll show you what the implantation

procedure entails."

He speeds off towards the end of the corridor, his staff ducking out of his way, bobbing their heads as we pass.

"I get the feeling the good doctor is pretending I don't exist," Blake says at my shoulder.

I smirk at him. "You jealous?"

"You bet."

"If he tries to show us a live surgery, I'm out of here."

"But you can't leave before he's fiddled around inside your skull with his long fingers."

I shudder. "Not going to happen."

"This is where all our patients are prepped," Doctor Hoyes says, ushering us into a brilliant white space.

A screen faces a couch the same colour as the chairs in reception, posters extolling the virtues of unlimited neuralnet uploads lining three walls. A hospital bed sits flush against the fourth wall, a white privacy curtain folded away at the foot. Blake and I claim the couch, Felice perched on the arm. Doctor Hoyes points a remote at the screen and a fanfare announces the words 'Chenesitone Implantation Facility' in swirling silver script.

"Chenesitone? Is that another name for Kensington?" I say.

He claps. "What a clever observation! Chenesitone is the first ever reference to Kensington in the Domesday Book—a survey of English holdings in 1086. Not many people make the connection but it's important to preserve our history, after we've lost so much."

The words on the screen fade to a still of the lobby, a posh female voice describing the benefits of the implantation facility and the wonders of the neuralnet.

"Oh, you're so *clever*," Blake murmurs under the blare of the video. "Please, oh-mighty-hero-refugee, please can I fondle your big brain?"

I snort and turn it into a cough at a glance from Felice. "Shh, I'm trying to watch."

"Yes, it's all very informative."

I elbow Blake in the ribs. He wriggles, grinning at me, and drapes his arm across my shoulders. Doctor Hoyes looks at us for a heavy beat, before turning back to the video, which shifts between the different implant models.

"I don't like him," Blake whispers.

"Me neither. Even if I wanted one of the things, I wouldn't trust him anywhere near my skull."

A computer graphic neatly summarises the steps of the implantation procedure. No blood or throbbing cerebral tissue to put off the squeamish. No whine of a bone saw. Another blast of trumpets ends the video.

"There we are then," Doctor Hoyes says. "Absolutely nothing to worry about."

Felice hops off the arm of the couch. "I can attest to that! This is where I got my implant. Before your time, Doctor Hoyes. I can't quite remember the name of the director…"

"Your video didn't mention any complications," Blake says as Felice trails off, his expression perfectly serious.

Doctor Hoyes's curled lip smooths into a smile. "That's because there are virtually none. However, there are risks, as there are with any surgery."

"Such as?"

Doctor Hoyes's nostrils flare.

He really doesn't like Blake.

If I'd asked the question, he would've patted me on the head.

"Bleeding. Infection. The typical surgical complications but nothing specific to the implantation procedure. Let's move on, shall we?"

He stalks out of the room and we scuttle behind, barrelling down the corridor to where it turns left out of sight.

"Are you having fun?"

Blake smirks. "Now I am."

The corridor continues around the corner and past glass-enclosed laboratories, robotic arms fixed to tables. Blake slows and moves closer to one of the windows.

"We'll come back to the manufacture of the implants," Doctor Hoyes calls without turning around, "but first I want to show you where the magic happens."

His composure restored, he strolls to a pair of double doors at the end of the corridor and flings them wide. Felice steps to the side to let me go first, Blake's footsteps hurrying to catch up.

Too late.

I walk through the doors and right into a nightmare.

9

He called me girlie.

Wick. Leader of the political party that became Nationless over ten years ago.

He survived a bullet to the head but it made him a monster who turned torture into an art. He had a whole building dedicated to it.

The logical half of my brain knows it's not the same. The operating theatre of the implantation centre is clean and polished. A padded table sits in the centre, a cushioned loop at one end to protect the patient's face while they lie on their front for the procedure. No straps, no daubs of rusty blood, the smell of iodine and pine not the slaughterhouse stink of spilled intestines.

But the shrieking in the rest of my brain drowns the logical part out.

I back up so fast, I stumble into Blake. He catches me in his arms, hugs me to his familiar sunshiny smell, but I fight him in my panic. Huge gasping breaths tear at my chest and my heart races to a humming crescendo.

I slam an elbow into the person holding me.

Is it Wick? Or the Guard-bitches?

A huff of air blasts my ear and the grip slackens. I twist

away, my legs tensed to run.

If I can't escape, I'll force them to kill me. Anything is better than being dragged into the torture chamber, Wick laughing at my feeble struggles, his black eyes pitiless in his weasel face.

He'll rape me and cut pieces off. His guards will join in, slippery with my blood, the smack of flesh on flesh echoing off the walls. Wick will watch, a sneer on his lips, my limbless carcass reeking of him.

A touch on my shoulder sends an icy bolt down my spine. I pivot on weak legs, my fist swinging, a scream lodged in my throat. The person blocks, and hard hands slam me into the wall.

"Anita!"

The panic vanishes in a burst of heat. I slump against the wall, almost too floppy to stand.

Black hair and violet eyes filled with pain. Not pain because he's injured but pain for my pain.

Blake.

I blink at him, unable to speak, dizziness swirling my vision. My hair sticks to the sweat on my face, my quick breaths shaking us both.

"You're hurting her!" a voice bellows. "I insist you release her at once!"

"Don't fucking touch her," Blake growls, planting himself in front of Doctor Hoyes, whose spindly fingers are reaching for me.

Doctor Hoyes snatches his hand away, back-pedalling down the corridor. Felice stands frozen at the door of the operating theatre, her mouth agape.

My trembling fingers brush Blake's shoulder. "Get me out of here."

Tenderness replaces his fierce expression. He scoops me into his arms and lopes for the front entrance. I curl against his chest, burying my face in the soothing warmth of his neck.

My Blake. Slim and strong and dangerous.

Wick hurt him, too.

Hot, sweet-tasting air caresses my clammy skin. Blake's boots thud on the steps, his pulse bounding under my lips.

"Where?" he says, not even out of breath.

"Trees."

He changes direction, his footsteps whispering on grass. Bees drone all around us but I keep my face hidden until Blake stops. He cradles me in his lap and I risk a peek.

Weeping willows surround a bench, the branches trailing into a pond. Water lilies bob on the surface, goldfish circling in the clear water. No people or buildings in sight, though the swish of a car is close. The scrape of a shovel from a nearby allotment.

There are more than I ever remembered in the old London but I'm no expert. It seems to be where everyone goes so bright and early in the morning.

Off to tend the vegetables or beehives or insect enclosures.

Blake holds me, demanding nothing, his head tucked under my chin. His fingertips stroke my arm and my body relaxes, muscle by muscle.

"Good choice," I manage to wheeze past the tightness in my chest.

He cuddles me closer. "Reminded me of a special place."

Willow warblers flit in the branches above us, the pure notes of their song sinking deep.

"What was so special about it?"

"It happened to be where a haughty, green-eyed temptress

shoved all my misconceptions down my throat."

I smile and kiss his neck. "She sounds wonderful."

He didn't recognise me as Wick's last prisoner, the one who stole their secret weapon and razed his home to the ground, burying his brother in the rubble. He remembered during the night, taunted by his dreams, safe in the pod he stole from me. He returned in the morning and marched me to a pool he'd found. A beautiful, secluded area bordered by trees, water lilies the size of my fist in the pond.

A place where he would decide whether I deserved to live.

He shifts me in his lap to look at my face, his warm hands pressed to my sides. I trace his collarbone beneath his t-shirt and he shivers, his sensitivity to my touch one of the many adorable things I love about him.

"She saved me," he says, his voice soft, "from becoming a monster, from loneliness. From grief."

"She caused you the grief."

"She suffered for it. She also made me the happiest I've ever been. Or will ever be."

My breath hitches. "You're going to make me cry."

"Not my intention, though you are cute when you cry." He kisses me once, lightly. "And when you laugh. And when you're mad or embarrassed. But most especially when you can't control yourself around me. When one kiss turns you into a slavering idiot."

He whispers the last against my lips. My brain turns to jelly. I moan and close the distance, claiming his smirking, glorious mouth. His fingers grip my waist, my body twisted in his lap. I squirm, needing to be closer.

Straddling. Straddling is good.

I try to move one leg to his other side—graceful, like a lady—

and knee him in the ribs.

He chuckles. "Woman, would you stop poking me in the ribs."

I brush the spot where I elbowed him in the corridor, so deep in the panic attack I somehow believed he was Wick. "Did I hurt you?"

"No." He captures my hand and flashes a grin. "You can't hurt me."

I slide off his lap and sit by his side, his arm across my shoulders, his fingers resuming their teasing stroke. We listen to the birds and the tinkle of water as the goldfish break the surface of the pond. Sunshine filters through the leaves, dappling our skin and dancing off the water.

"Better?"

I nod. "It was the operating theatre, the sight of the table and all the shiny instruments. I thought this shit had stopped."

"It's only been three months, Anita. You're the strongest woman I know but give yourself some time. It might never stop."

I sigh. "I know. Just as well I have you to snap me out of it."

"Always."

Felice's tentative voice warbles on the air, quieter than the hum of the bees.

Blake stands and holds out a hand. "Come on. Before she thinks we've done a runner."

"Oh god. What *is* she going to think? About me?"

He tugs me to my feet and slides his arm around my waist, guiding me through the trees. "I think she'll understand."

Felice is next to the car, her hand at her throat, spinning in a slow circle. Our steps crunch on the gravel driveway and she sucks in a breath, steadying herself against the vehicle.

"Oh, Anita, I am so sorry."

She hurries towards us but hesitates, her fingers playing with her charm bracelet. Blake eases away to let me stand alone. Her eyes flick to him, a smile flitting across her face. She squares her shoulders and hugs me, her tentative arms circling my lower back. Her head barely reaches my chest.

"I'm sorry for whatever happened to make you react that way. If I'd known, I would never have brought you here."

I pat her back, touched by her concern. "Not your fault, Felice. I just get flashbacks, sometimes. Guess this was an obvious setting for one—clinical, sharp implements. Did we freak out Doctor Hoyes?"

"Who cares about Doctor Hoyes. I didn't like him anyway."

She sniffs and brushes at her skirt. Home-grown hemp and recycled plastic bottles this time.

I asked.

"What?" she says when Blake and I share a laugh. "It's my job to pretend to like people, even if I find them creepy."

We climb into the car, sweltering in the heat. Felice perches on the seat opposite us, the space like the inside of a limousine. The vehicle reverses as soon as the door shuts and our seatbelts fasten.

"It's so much easier when I don't have to pretend. I like you, Anita. And Blake." She blushes at his grin but gamely continues. "I want to see you both settled here. Happy. Anything else I can do to smooth that transition, you let me know. Things you've missed, experiences you've always wanted to have. We may seem a bit 'make do and mend' but I can pull a lot of strings."

"I have something," Blake says, glancing at me.

"Name it."

"Is there a cinema near here? Do movies still exist?"

"What a joyless world that would be if they didn't! There's a lovely cinema near here. The showings are more restricted—very focused on peace and unity—but it's our main form of entertainment. Before you arrived, of course. Give me two minutes." She shuts her eyes and disappears into the neuralnet. Her fingers twitch on the seat. "Melody! It's Felice Huffman. It's been too long since I heard your voice…"

Blake brushes my hair off my cheek, his fingertips skimming my jaw, and her words fade to a background murmur.

"Might be a bit bland for your tastes," he says, his soft smile tingling in my gut.

"I don't care. You're a genius! I hadn't even thought about it." I bounce in my seat. "I hope it smells the same, like popcorn and butter. That's exactly how I want to spend the rest of the day."

"I can think of something else I want to do but that can wait until later." He tugs on my hair, drawing me closer, his lips tracing the path of his fingertips.

"Hussy," I say, my voice rough.

He smirks.

Damn that smirk. Dark and knowing and sexy. It awakens the first longing to rip his clothes off.

His hand fists in my hair, controlling my head and exposing my neck. He licks the sensitive skin, and I shiver.

"Your pulse is racing," he whispers, his breath hot.

"Blake…"

He takes pity on me and his mouth finds mine.

His clever, smirking mouth.

The kissing is amazing but the rest… *God.*

I'd tell him anything, everything, for the promise of his

mouth.

The seatbelt keeps me from climbing into his lap.

And the loud clearing of someone's throat.

"If you two could disentangle yourselves for more than two seconds, I have good news," Felice says. "The cinema is empty anyway so you can have it all to yourselves. You can pick the movie and have any snacks you want from their selection. The car will return you to the Townhouse when you're done."

I hope they've not replaced popcorn with some kind of beetle.

We babble our thanks at Felice.

Every day away from the war—every hour—dulls the memories of pain, loneliness and despair. Turns us into something more human.

This is freedom. This is *home*.

10

Six hours until the start of the gala dinner and the stylist Felice has arranged knocks on our door.

I thought she was joking.

Even in times of zero waste and austerity, pulling something on half an hour prior to the event is not considered appropriate.

Blake stretches out on the bed with an exaggerated wiggle.

He doesn't have to get ready for ages yet.

I yank the door open harder than necessary to reveal a woman tinier than Felice.

"I am Xia Tseng. You come with me." She spins on her heel and her straight, shiny black hair fans out.

"Wait! Xia? It's not going to take me that long—"

"Yes. Not much time. Come."

I throw a pleading look at Blake.

"Oh, you'll get no help from me," he says. "I can't wait to see what's considered suitable for meeting the Prime Minister."

"If she dresses me in ruffles or bows, I'm holding you responsible."

He slides out of bed and stalks towards me, stopping just short of touching. "Don't worry, I'll rip you out of it later. I'm sure they can recycle the rest into a shoe."

He sends me off with a slap on the butt before I can decide if I'm annoyed or aroused.

Who am I kidding? Aroused, always.

I catch up to Xia, who stands in the lift, her finger on the button, one childlike foot in a sequined ballet pump tapping the floor. We travel to the basement in silence while I tell myself not to snarl at her.

Felice likes her so she must be good at her job. A stupid, shallow job but whatever. They want me to look the part— feral refugee to beautiful princess. I'll smile and laugh and pretend I can't kill most of the guests with my fork.

"Come," Xia says, sweeping out of the lift in a waft of bergamot.

I roll my eyes and follow her into a dimly lit space of tinkling water, flickering candles and lush ferns. A soundtrack of birds twitters from hidden speakers.

"Miss Carmichael, welcome to the Townhouse spa." A woman in white cotton bows from behind a short desk, her hushed tones complementing the reverence to all things relaxation. "Ms Tseng, everything is prepared as you requested. If I can do anything else, please let me know."

Xia sniffs and speeds through a stone archway. A warm corridor extends past four woven wicker doors, two on each side, to a double door of fogged glass etched with leaves and flowers. Xia selects the last room on the left—a treatment room containing a padded bed and a waterfall of plants.

"Strip," she says.

I blink and swallow the instinctive, "Fuck you."

"Why?" I say instead.

"Want to see what I have to work with."

"I'm not a goddamn doll."

66

Unwavering black eyes meet mine. "Pretty doll to woo public for Prime Minister."

She has guts, I'll give her that.

"I'm not wooing anyone."

"Truth." Delicate white teeth flash. "Strip."

Crap, now I like her.

I fold my clothes, underwear and all, on a chair next to the door. Xia circles me, her flat face expressionless. I raise my chin and scowl at the wall, hating the vulnerability of nakedness.

Nothing good ever happens if I'm naked in the presence of strangers.

"Strong," she says. "Survived much."

"Truth."

Another flash of teeth. "Take off dog-tags."

My hand curls around them.

I've worn at least one pair for almost ten years. They're part of me, as familiar as the weight of my hair across my shoulders. A symbol of how hard I fought to live. Each plate embossed with my name, faction and encampment. The People's Republic, Calders and (oh, so briefly) Soldiers of the Lost, Fellhill. One dust and rubble, the other fighting on, seeking glory.

What would they think if they saw me preparing for a glitzy party? The calm room a far cry from the stink of cordite and biodiesel, the muffled whump of explosions. Tepid showers and the cold ground for a bed. The possession of moisturiser the epitome of luxury. Will I become as soft as the pillows I sleep on? Maybe I'll rediscover my femininity and start caring about hair and makeup.

How terrifying.

"They will be safe," Xia says, her voice gentle, "but will not suit dress."

Oh god, a dress. How am I supposed to pull that off after years of combats and long-sleeves?

One ridiculous problem at a time.

I slip the chains of the dog-tags over my head, the metal warm from my skin. I tuck them into the pocket of my discarded trousers with a pang of loss similar to when I surrendered my guns.

Xia hands me a fluffy cotton gown. "Go through double doors to pool. Swim. Sauna. I come collect you."

The etched glass opens into a wide, echoing room of glistening white tiles, the sunken pool reflecting the golden lights and arched turquoise ceiling. I flop into the lazy curve of a lounger, the peacefulness settling into my muscles.

This girly crap isn't all bad.

I manage to lie still for twenty minutes.

Having nothing to do, no tasks to complete, no assaults to prepare for, is odd.

This is how normal people prepare for battle. In a few hours, I'll fight off politicians and their glittering spouses.

No doubt I'll have to protect Blake from fawning women.

I stand at the edge of the pool and dip my toes in the silky water.

An extravagance in a post-war Britain only the elite get to enjoy.

I glance around and shrug the gown off, diving in. Bubbles roil past my face, everything blue and quiet bar the rush of my pulse. I surface on a gasp and complete a couple of laps for appearance's sake before I float on my back, cushioned by the blood-warm water.

Xia finds me an hour later, alternating between the sauna and the steam room to see how hot I can stand it, with quick dips in the pool that's freezing in comparison. She hustles me into the shower and herds me into the treatment room, my skin pink from the heat.

She pats the bed. "Up. Time for wax. Too hairy."

"Shaving my legs had to come after breathing in my list of priorities," I say.

I hop onto the padded surface and stretch out, Xia bending my knees to a position she wants while I try to ignore how extremely goddamn naked I am. She scoops a dollop of honey-coloured wax onto a spatula from a tub by the bed. The warmth of it tingles along my skin as she spreads it up my leg and smooths a strip of paper on top.

"Will hurt," she says.

"I think I'll be fine," I scoff. "I've had worse than—*ow!* Sweet-fucking-Jesus!"

She laughs, a rolling laugh too deep for her tiny frame. I grit my teeth and frown at the ceiling. More stinging wax, more paper. The screech and pop as my follicles rip free. Instead of whimpering, I scramble to focus on something else, something pleasant.

Inspired by our night at the cinema, Blake and I spent most of the next day in bed, binge-watching old movies. Ones we actually remembered. The accommodating staff of the Townhouse, who don't blink an eye at the crowds of people gathered at the front every day, had allowed us temporary access to their neuralnets, one after the other as they came and went on their shifts. As long as they were within the building, we could stream wirelessly from the device in their head.

I got to pick what we watched first.

"*Die Hard*," I said, bouncing on the bed and typing in my search using the remote. "But we have to watch them all. Brace yourself, there's, like, ten."

Blake laughed, dragging me down into his lap. "Fine but then I get to pick."

"Ten of my movies to one of yours—deal."

"That's not what I meant."

"No take-backs."

He rolled and pinned me to the bed, his—

Mother. Fucking. *Christ*.

Bikini wax.

Xia plucks me to within an inch of my life but I wave her off from attacking my eyebrows. Too much maintenance. She massages a cooling lavender gel into the smooth, pink areas, switching to vanilla oil for the rest of me, her firm fingers kneading my muscles into wobbling submission.

She doesn't hesitate over the scars.

Taking advantage of my languid lack of resistance, she props me up and trims my hair, taming the wild tumble and tsking over the state of my split ends. I'm too limp to grumble at her, more noodle than woman.

The final step involves her wrapping me in cotton and leaving me alone, drifting and smelling good enough to eat. Too relaxed to care that she'll be back to cajole me into a dress and smear makeup on my face.

I wish I could get used to this.

11

"How am I supposed to run in these. No. How am I supposed to bloody *walk?*"

I wobble and grab onto the bed of the treatment room. Skyscraper heels enclose my feet, the sole and heel black, silver bands criss-crossing to my ankle. Adhesive wraps polished a sparkly grey hide my missing toenails, which are pitted and slowly regrowing.

There is a *long* length of leg before you even get to the dress.

"Why would you run?" Xia tuts. "Walk slow. Swing hips."

She holds out her hands. Muttering, I take them and she guides me around the room while I try to emulate a sex goddess instead of Bambi on ice. After a couple of circuits, I slump into the chair on top of my—comfortable, perfectly fine—normal clothes.

She slaps at my knees. "Close legs! Be dignified lady."

"Xia, I really think we need to reconsider this no underwear thing. Flashing the Prime Minister and all of his Cabinet is not what I want to be remembered for."

"No. Ruins line of dress." Her black eyes sparkle, a grin flitting on her mouth. "Plus, your man will like."

Holy shit.

The thought of Blake's reaction speeds my pulse, excitement

tightening my gut and tingling lower. He'll look at me with the dazed and wondrous expression I love, his hands gliding down the clinging material of the silver dress where it swells over my hips. His fingertips playing along the beaded lace trim that barely covers my ass, skimming up the line of my thigh to—

Goddammit. Arousal and no pants is a dangerous combination.

Potentially messy.

There's a light knock on the door. I lever myself to my feet, Xia tugging to assist and breathing into my bellybutton as I tower over her in the heels. Felice slips into the room, a vision in a floor-length purple gown split to the thigh, a silver beaded pattern on the single shoulder strap and down one side. Loose curls from her artfully pinned hair caress her face and entangle her diamond earrings.

Or maybe they're recycled glass.

"Oh, Anita!" she gasps. "You look... Wow. Absolutely stunning."

"It's not too much leg—"

"It's perfect. Gorgeous. Xia, you are a marvel."

The two women hug, one stocky and dark, the other slim and light but slightly taller.

"Has she seen herself yet?"

"No. Waited for you."

Xia whips away the towel covering the mirror and shoos me towards it. I approach it like I would a snarling abomination in no man's land. My mouth drops open at the woman staring back at me.

"Fucking hell..."

Okay, so I've been beautiful my whole life. I try not to let it define me, ignoring how people react, but it gets me into trouble. The war was not a medium for restrained gentlemen and when you look like I do... People either wanted to fuck me or kill me.

Or both.

The woman gaping at me isn't beautiful.

She's a knockout.

Smoky makeup highlights bright green eyes and glowing skin, a hint of blush on each cheekbone. No dark shadows or bloodshot eyes. Xia tamed and straightened my hair to frame my face and flow in a shimmering golden fall past my shoulders. It smells like apples, subtle waves teased through from handfuls of mousse. The dress starts below my collarbone, a band of sheer, beaded lace a shade darker than the material of the body to a sweetheart neckline, or so Xia informed me. All I know is it hugs my breasts and makes them look huge without an eyeful of cleavage. The beaded lace continues as long sleeves to each delicate wrist, enough to mask the scars.

People will be too distracted by the miles of leg to notice them, anyway.

I raise my arms above my head and the edge of the dress rises to crotch-level.

"Xia—"

She pinches my ribs. "Don't do that. Stand like this, always. Hips and shoulders back, stomach in. Feet together. Bend one leg."

She manipulates my body exactly where she wants it and the woman in the mirror becomes a curvy temptress, all breasts and hips and taut skin.

Felice claps her hands. "Anita, I swear, you could be a model.

This is how we'll make your entrance."

"My entrance?" I gulp.

She glances at her watch. "Perfect, it's half past six now so we're fashionably late. Blake has been ready for ages. I parked him in the foyer with the Secretary of State for Scotland. Wait until you see him. Blake, not David Brokenshire. Lovely man but a bit dull. His position is mostly honorary. Not much to do when the country he represents has no government and cannot be entered."

Her chatter flows over my head. I soothe a trembling hand across my belly, my shoulders hunched.

Xia drills her finger into my arm. "Stand up straight. No slouch."

I bare my teeth, my lips slick with gloss.

"Yes, good. Fierce. Beautiful."

I sigh. "You make it very hard to hate you."

"I know. Am people person."

Xia ignores my snort, brushing at my dress and tugging on my arm until I bend so she can fluff my hair.

"Let's head up," Felice says, polite enough not to blanch at the eyeful she must have gotten of my bare ass. She opens the door and peeks both ways down the corridor as if she expects us to be mobbed.

Sweat pools in my palms and the small of my back.

I don't care about the twenty-odd cabinet ministers Felice imprinted into my memory, plus their respective husbands and wives. What if Blake doesn't like the new me—a perfumed doll, fake and glittery?

Don't be an idiot.

He knows who I am, the real me, under the finery.

All I have to do is open my mouth.

And what have they done to him? Felice is still forming complete sentences so it can't be that bad.

Bad, as in I'll turn into a drooling moron as soon as I see him.

I totter for the lift behind Felice and Xia, concentrating ridiculously hard on placing my feet.

How can women wear these things? You'd think they would've been phased out but maybe women didn't have to run and fight as much in their war as we did in ours.

The genteel receptionist is gone, the soothing space empty.

I want to stay surrounded by the peaceful tinkle of water not parade my nearly naked self in front of England's most powerful people.

But at least I'll be with Blake. Six hours apart, no matter how relaxing, is an emptiness in the centre of my chest.

Felice presses the button to the first floor.

"For your entrance," she says to my raised eyebrow. "I want you to pause at the top of the staircase and stand like Xia showed you. Wait until everyone is focused on you then glide down the stairs and I'll meet you at the bottom with Blake."

"Glide?" I wheeze. "Felice, please. Have you seen me walking in these damn things? I'll fall and make a complete fool of myself."

Huh. I won't beg for mercy during torture but I will beg Felice not to make me walk down stairs in heels.

How times change.

"You'll be fantastic! Every man will want you, every woman will want to be you. The press will love it."

The lift rises past the ground floor, a burst of laughter and violins seeping through the doors.

"Reporters have been invited?"

"Only for the drinks reception. The dinner is guests only." She squeezes my arm, her fingers cool through the lace sleeve, silver beads pressing into my skin. "There will be cameras but they've been warned to stay a minimum of two feet away."

Am I hyperventilating? It feels like I'm hyperventilating.

"I'm not wearing underwear."

She giggles and covers her mouth, her perfectly manicured nails a deeper purple than her gown. "Xia, you are a naughty woman."

"Ruins line of dress," Xia says, flashing her teeth.

"Quite right, my dear. Don't worry, Anita, only the best of the profession have been invited. They're not paparazzi scrambling over each other for a crotch shot."

The lift slides to a stop at a carpeted corridor similar to ours. I press my back to the mirrored wall, my sweaty hands gripping the chrome handrail. Felice somehow prises me out without breaking my fingers.

"Good luck, warrior girl," Xia says as the doors close.

"The dinner is only for politicians and their partners," Felice says to my wide-eyed panic. "I'm lucky to have gotten an invite."

She coaxes me, stuttering and reluctant, towards the stairs. The swell of many voices is muted, the steps turning a corner before they widen into the staircase visible from the whole of the lobby.

"Felice, shit, I'm not built for this kind of thing. I can't schmooze. Can't I just go to my room?"

"You'll be fine! Take a deep breath. Smile. Try not to swear. Everyone will love you."

She shuffles me closer to the stairs, her palm in the small of my back, my mincing steps muffled by the carpet.

"There's one person down there who loves you already. The only one who matters." She eases away from me and I sag against the wall. "And if you give me a couple of minutes to get down there to watch your entrance, there'll be another."

She skips down the stairs, no wobble evident despite her own killer heels.

"I… Felice."

She pauses at the corner, her smile warm. "Knock 'em dead, Anita."

She disappears and I try to breathe slowly instead of panting or fainting. The noise drops for a short beat and resumes, someone shouting her name.

I can do this. Glide, smile, don't swear. Easy. No one is going to hurt me, which is the scale I use to measure the shit I'm in.

And if no one is going to hurt me, everything will be okay.

I practise a few steps on the stairs, my ankles bending dangerously. Up and down, up and down, until I don't have to hold the banister in a death grip. I force myself to stop at the corner instead of scuttling away. A loud rumble of voices punctuates the sweetness of strings.

This is my life now. This is what I wanted. No fighting, no screaming, no slaughter.

The price of peace.

I suck in a breath, my heartbeat drowning out the noise of the crowd, and step around the corner.

12

For a single, glorious second, no one notices me quivering at the top of the sweeping staircase. People cluster around the lobby, streaming to and from the meeting room, drinks in their hands, watched by two armed guards at the front door. The media scuttle about, cameras perched on their shoulders and panning the crowd. Others scribble on tablets and stare too long at the guests, their eyes too wide.

Remembering Xia's postural advice, I throw my shoulders back and stick my butt out, my chin raised.

Attitude is all about pretence.

A gasp. The noise level plummets to zero and I stop myself from running away, whimpering, "Nope, nope, fuck it." Cameras point and flash, people shouldering each other as they fight for space. Every pale face turns to me. Felice beams from the bottom of the steps, her hands clasped at her chest.

I'm glad someone is having fun.

Get your ass down the stairs, you wimp.

Tough words but my fingers freeze to the banister, my knuckles white.

Then I find Blake.

The rest of the party may as well not exist.

His violet eyes meet mine with a physical jolt, his stunned

expression making the possible public humiliation worth-while.

I float down the stairs, cool air brushing my legs, the material of the dress gliding over my hips. Blake abandons whomever he was speaking to—David Brokensomething—and waits at the bottom step next to Felice, the media parting for him. His predatory gaze travels up, up and up, darkening as it goes.

He looks gorgeous. A black tuxedo hugs his slim shoulders and narrows to his waist.

I immediately want to get him out of it.

Someone has cut his hair, styling it so the artfully messy layers frame his face and kiss his cheekbones.

God, I love him. Started falling in love with him the second those eyes captured mine, even though he'd pinned me to the ground and stolen all my stuff. I was his prisoner for four days. Four days where the instant attraction and respect for him combined to doom me further. I hated myself for what I did to him. Didn't deserve his forgiveness.

He gave it anyway.

I surrendered everything to him on the fifth day—my heart, my body, my happiness. If he wanted to hurt me, all he had to do was leave, or die, and I would be nothing.

I wobble on the last step and force myself not to touch him.

Touching would be bad, the desire to wrap myself around him, fuck him, ridiculously strong in the presence of so many people.

He tilts his head up, no longer eye to eye because of my heels. His pulse flutters in the hollow of his throat and begs me to lick it.

"Hey, shorty," I say, softly.

"Baby, you look—"

"Like a girl, I know."

"—fucking amazing."

I bite my lip and he follows the movement. My resistance, feeble to begin with, crumbles under his hungry stare.

Xia has really not thought this no pants thing through. She'd never have insisted on it if she knew of my constant state of arousal in Blake's presence.

I step into him, my hands on his shoulders, the heat of him intoxicating. His fingers skim around my waist to the curve of my butt. I lean closer, my head bent, my mouth at his ear.

"I'm not wearing underwear."

His hands still for a beat before resuming their caress, a strangled noise in his throat. "Fuck this party, I'm taking you upstairs."

I collapse against him and feast on his mouth. His hands are everywhere, sliding down to tickle the backs of my thighs, my hips arching into him. I fist both hands in his hair, frustrated by the extra height and desperate to rub myself over his erection.

I believe Felice has to clear her throat three times before the sound penetrates.

"Remember this is on camera," she hisses, her smile in place, though her eyes dart over the watching crowd.

Blake and I manage to disengage, our faces flushed, my lip gloss shiny on his mouth.

He pats his head. "You better not have messed my hair."

"Narcissist."

He grins and captures my hand. "I warned you this would happen if you kept telling me I was beautiful."

"You are beautiful."

"Woman, what did I just say?"

Felice curtails another snog-fest by marching us through the room, introducing us to everyone. I must look attentive as they all smile and laugh but their faces blur.

The only real thing is Blake's hand in mine, his thumb tracing my palm, the tiny movement feeling as though he strokes some place way more intimate.

I snap to attention at the final introduction to a rotund man in a brown suit and red bow tie.

He shakes my hand, his large, dry paw holding on a little too long. "Miss Carmichael. I'm Wilson Bursey. I see you've settled in well here."

"Nice to meet you, Prime Minister. I trust we have you to thank for our sudden change of fortune."

Ailsa would have loved this. Despite her desire for independence, my sister viewed the Prime Minister as a figure of awe. A power to be respected, as she would be when she became First Minister.

Shrewd blue eyes measure me from behind round lenses the size of a penny.

The leader of a civilised country. Will he act differently to the psychotic leaders of the Faction War or will that casual cruelty be just as much a part of him?

"I hope all will become clear when you join me at my next Cabinet meeting," he says.

He moves to Blake, the shake perfunctory and awkward since I refuse to release Blake's hand. His wife, as delicate and tiny as a bird, twitters over us, her fingers wrapped around Blake's while she barely brushes my palm. Her cream dress, patterned with large crimson flowers matching the colour of Bursey's bow tie, falls straight to her knobbled knees, a red belt struggling to hint at a waist. They disappear into the crowd, her thin frame dwarfed by his.

"Cabinet meeting?" I say into the space left behind before other guests pluck up the courage to come and babble at us.

Felice frowns, her eyelids fluttering shut. "Well, what do you know—I've received a parliamentary memo. Your presence has been requested for a special Cabinet meeting this Friday, a day later than usual to allow you more time to visit your families."

"Requested or demanded?"

"Expected is the terminology they use." She waves her hands. "I'm sure I'll receive more details later. Let's put the press out of their misery and do some interviews. I've never seen such a swarm!"

I glance around. Lenses stare at us from all angles, photographers swirling between their more stationary colleagues.

"Aww, look, your cameras are merging with my cameras."

"You seem to have way more than I do," Blake says, his fingertips playing with my hair. "Being around you is hard on the ego."

"Your ego is doing just fine."

"I wouldn't be so sure. Everyone's gawping at you, not me."

"Then they're idiots."

"You're lucky I'm confident in my overwhelming masculinity."

"Overwhelming is right."

We trail after Felice, who barrels for a gaggle of reporters near the front door. Bursey watches me despite appearing to be deep in conversation with his Home Secretary.

I shiver and Blake squeezes my hand. "What do you think he wants?"

"Nothing good."

"Such an optimist," he chuckles.

"I have you for that."

"It's not like he can do anything terrible to us."

"I'm still waiting for someone to arrest me for war crimes. Or call me a terrorist."

Blake raises my hand to kiss my knuckles, a quick nip of teeth pulling a gasp from my throat.

"Stop that. You're neither of those. Plus, you're too pretty for people to believe half the things you've done."

"Sure, I just batted my eyelashes and everyone left me alone."

What would the civilised masses think if they knew how many soldiers I've killed? My total count isn't quite as high as the population of New London but if you factor in everyone who died indirectly because of my actions, it's probably a few million.

Less supermodel, more Stalin.

13

After forty minutes of talking to reporters, the Townhouse staff finally usher us into the meeting room for dinner, the media dispatched to upload their footage for the greedy public. Round tables swathed in silver fill the room, the ten place settings containing a disconcerting variety of cutlery and glasses. The stage used for the press conference holds a podium instead of a table. Fairy lights on the walls and in the tree-like centrepieces twinkle to life with an, "Ooh," of appreciation from the guests searching for their seats.

Felice leads the way, as usual. "You two are at the central table with the Prime Minister, the Home Secretary, the Chancellor of the Exchequer and the Secretary of State for Defence."

"You're not sitting with us?"

Goddamn, how breathy do I sound?

She smiles at my panic. "I've been relegated to a non-ministerial table in the corner. To be honest, I would've sat in the lobby. It's been a long time since luxury was something to enjoy, rather than wasteful extravagance."

"I'll protect you from the scary politicians," Blake whispers. "Should be easier than rapists and abominations."

Felice settles us into our seats and flits off to her table, murmuring, "Behave yourselves."

We attempt polite conversation while the discreet wait-staff serve us drinks.

"Miss Carmichael, would you like red or white wine?"

"Um, could I just have some water?"

Best not to risk blabbing something improper under the influence of alcohol. Or falling over and flashing my lady parts to the universe.

Another waiter appears and pours the water from a weeping jug, my wine glass whisked away faster than a blink. Ice cubes rattle. My body tenses, goosebumps flaring in a wave of cold. My nails dig into Blake's leg under the table, and he jumps.

I flap at the glass, my throat tight. "I can't—not ice. No ice."

"I'm sorry?" The waiter bends closer to my frantic mumbling.

"Could she have it without ice? *Please*," Blake says, his voice strained, his fingertips stroking my hand where it clutches his leg.

The waiter removes the glass and scurries away. I relax my grip, painfully aware of Bursey's heavy gaze from across the table. Blake twists in his seat to shield me with his body.

"The bath?" he says, his worried eyes intent on my face.

I shiver and nod.

"Do you want to leave?"

"It's not as bad as the implantation facility. I'll be okay in a minute."

Four days into my torture, I was delirious. Battered, filthy, in shock. Weak from pain and hunger. Wick plunged my naked body into a tub filled with water and ice. It was the most peaceful I'd been in days, despite the chill nipping at my wounds.

And it was the moment I tried to drown myself to escape him. Exhausted and hurting and utterly alone.

Who knew something as innocent as an iced beverage could catapult me back there? I hate the clinking, the feel of ice on my skin, both sticky and smooth. Memories of the worst days of my life I'd rather forget.

"Are you all right, Miss Carmichael?"

I flinch at Bursey's impassive voice and suck in air until it no longer trembles. My steady hand touches Blake's face. He kisses my fingers and eases back into his seat.

"I'm fine."

Bursey's raised eyebrow indicates he expects more.

He'll be waiting a while.

I bet he's used to people telling him everything and doing whatever he says.

He reminds me of Buxton, leader of Soldiers of the Lost.

The waiter returns with a glass of water, minus the ice. I accept gratefully and try not to gulp it. Blake places his warm hand on my knee, banishing the last of the shivers.

Starters of poached egg and spring greens arrive at the table, light, meaningless conversation flowing on the quality of the food, the oppressive heat of summer. Mrs Bursey nibbles on a single leaf, her husband quick to scoop the rest onto his plate.

No wonder she's so slight. Starvation will do that to a person.

The man sitting on my right—Phillip Carrbridge, Defence Secretary—dabs a linen napkin to his mouth. "Tell me, Anita— may I call you Anita?—what defences did you have in your encampments? I find the technology of war fascinating."

If he asks me about nukes, I'm leaving.

"I can't speak for all the factions, Mr Carrbridge—"

"Please! Call me Phillip."

"—um, Phillip, but we had the usual particle beam fencing and laser-cameras."

"Ah, yes, from Africa?" The white glow of the fairy lights shines on the silver at his temples. "How wonderful!"

Sure. Who doesn't enjoy getting their face melted?

"They've been banned in the civilised world, of course," he continues. "Too savage."

He keeps talking but Blake strokes the inside of my knee and I almost swallow my tongue. He seems unaware of what his fingers are doing, talking about Ireland with Mrs Chancellor of the Exchequer.

"I'm sorry, Phillip, what was your question?"

Can he hear the desire in my voice? That's embarrassing. Especially if he thinks it's for him.

Christ.

"Oh, I was just wondering if you got to see a laser-camera in action. They're a particular interest of mine. The way they—"

Blake's fingertips tickle my inner thigh. He peeks at me, his black hair falling across one eye, lips half-parted. I squirm and widen my legs, the breath catching in my throat.

God, what a hussy.

His slow, wicked smile tightens my stomach and speeds my pulse.

"So, did you?"

I blink at Phillip. "Did I what, now?"

"See a laser-camera in action?" He tugs at his tie, the white polka dots on blue silk already askew.

"Yes. On two abominations. Stopped them dead."

Blake's fingers skim higher, pausing short of where I ache for him to touch me. I bite my lip to trap a moan.

"Anita? And they didn't activate against yourselves?"

Shit. How many times has Phillip asked that?

Blake draws a long, lazy loop from knee to upper thigh. A cough disguises my whimper.

"Nope. You're safe—if your facial scan—is in the database."

Oh, crap, I'm panting.

The main course arrives to save me. Vegetables fresh from a New London allotment and a slab of something dark drizzled in rhubarb sauce. Blake quits teasing me long enough to cut off a corner and pop it in his mouth. I wrinkle my nose.

"You're going to have to get used to this," he says. "It's really not as bad as you think."

"I can hear you crunching from here."

"What's wrong with a little crunch?" The slow, wicked smile returns and his hand slips under the table. "Maybe if you eat all your bugs, I'll give you a reward."

He starts at the back of my knee, the barest of touches, and trails upwards. My nails sink into the edge of my seat, my muscles quivering with the urge to writhe.

I lean into him and hide my face in his neck. "If you don't stop that, I'm going to get a wet patch on my dress."

His fingers tense on my leg, a pained noise low in his throat.

"That's it," he growls. "Meet me in the bathroom in two minutes."

He stands and mumbles an excuse to the table, heading for the door, his posture hunched. The glittering eyes of women track him. I painstakingly dissect my block of invertebrates instead of chasing after him. Nibble on a potato. Swirl my fork through the rhubarb sauce.

Fuck it.

"I'll be right back," I say to no one in particular, leaping to my feet and almost toppling into the centrepiece.

I stride for the exit, my heartbeat as loud as my footsteps, waving at Felice who aims a quizzical look in my direction.

My body feels swollen and my shaking knees struggle to hold me.

Oh god, one touch from Blake and I'll have an orgasm. He's done it before.

Him and his clever fingers.

I steady myself against the wall outside the meeting room.

Breathe. Smile. Shag my perfect, gorgeous boyfriend metres from the most powerful people in England.

Boyfriend. How normal.

Maybe not the sneaking off to have sex during a fancy dinner part but what do I know?

I stumble down the corridor towards the bathrooms, aiming for the men's. A hand tugs me into the disabled toilet—a wide, lavish space of quartz and lilies. Blake presses me to the cool tile and swallows my small, eager sounds.

"You're going to have to be quiet," he groans, the loss of control in his voice pulsing between my legs.

"I don't think I can."

He braces his hands on the wall, his head bent, his rapid breaths scorching my collarbone. "Jesus, woman. Do you know how close I am to ruining this tuxedo?"

Blake collapses into me, tongue, lips, teeth. I arch against him and the hem of my dress rises. Frustrated by the extra height of the heels, I slide out of his grip to perch on the edge of the sink, trembling too much to stand anyway. I watch him and slowly open my legs.

"Fuck," he whispers and I almost come. "I promise I will do this properly later. Peel you out of that dress. Do the things you love with my mouth."

Dark eyes meet mine, fierce with possession.

"Blake, please."

He closes the distance, his slim fingers unfastening his trousers, the sight of him so hard and straining playing havoc with my pulse. He grips my hips while I blink and pant and try not to faint.

"You're going to scream really loud, aren't you?"

My teeth sink into my lip, the urge already expanding my chest. "Can't help it. Please. I need you."

"I know, baby."

He thrusts himself inside me and his mouth smothers my cries.

I'm pretty sure the people in the next county still hear me, though.

14

"Wait a minute. Your mum lives in a place called Ballyloogy? You're making that up, right?"

"Now you're going to insult Irish towns? Maybe I should have left you in New London."

Blake's fingers slip under my t-shirt to tickle up my ribs. I squirm in his lap, lights strobing through the tinted windows of the car, and stop myself from asking him again, for the sixteenth time, if he's sure he wants to introduce me to his mother.

Apparently, he is and it's non-negotiable.

Smooth concrete hisses under the wheels of the vehicle, spiriting us through the Irish Tunnel connecting Fishguard in Wales to Rosslare Harbour in the Republic of Ireland.

Following the Scottish rebellion, Wales and the Republic of Ireland strengthened their ties with England, while still maintaining their independence. The Irish Tunnel was built to symbolise unity between the countries, and strengthen trade, especially since road and rail are the main transport routes after countries signed the no-fly treaty. Felice gushed for quite a while on the ingenuity of a tunnel over 100 km long beneath St George's Channel, despite having never been through it herself. Powered only by renewable energy.

It can also be used as a bomb shelter.

Felice waved us off from the Townhouse that morning, our journey programmed into the car, bags packed with recycled clothes for a couple of days away.

For all their talk of rationing, I've never owned so many outfits.

No reporters trail us, only security staff, the reunion with our families private. Interviews are scheduled for when we arrive back in the Townhouse on Friday morning, the Cabinet meeting in the afternoon.

It's exciting to finally get out of the city.

I pressed my face to the glass and drank in the green beyond the wall. I miss being surrounded by trees and grass, even when the pretty foliage hid snarling abominations or soldiers intent on dragging me off to their encampments, Neanderthal-like.

The car took a slight detour north-west from New London to circle Birmingham, the distance less than if we'd been in old London instead of what used to be Northampton, the River Nene a narrow substitute for the Thames.

London was not the only city hit by a nuclear weapon.

Our car rumbled on the potted road, our breath fogging the window. Birmingham was a city of ash, the skeletons of buildings poking from the grey.

An uncomfortable reminder that our war and their war were not so different.

Though they had the sense to stop theirs.

The Irish Tunnel gets boring very quickly, unchanging kilometre after kilometre. Lights cast a band across the curved ceiling, spiralling off into the distance, the bulbs merging into a single line broken only by recessed doors. Blake helps to alleviate the boredom, deciding it's only proper to christen our first journey through the tunnel by teasing me out of my clothes and making me forget any name but his.

We staggered back to the dinner the night before, mumbling something about talking to people in the lobby, my screams still echoing off the quartz of the disabled bathroom. Bursey's sharp gaze drilled into us but he said nothing. A damson and chocolate tart followed the invertebrate slab, so delicious I wanted to lick the plate. I got excited when the coffee arrived but had to swallow hard to keep from spitting it out.

"It takes some getting used to," Phillip Carrbridge said, cheerfully, sipping from his cup. "The environmental catastrophe all but wiped out the humble coffee bean. We make do with roasted, ground acorns. It's an acquired taste."

Are Soldiers of the Lost the only ones left with real coffee? Buxton could make a killing if he sold it to the civilised world.

I'd pushed my fake coffee away and Bursey concluded the dinner on a rousing speech about how matters were being put into place to end the conflict in Scotland.

His eyes stayed on me the whole time.

"Hey, look, we're coming to the end."

Blake's voice jolts me from worrying about the Prime Minister's intentions.

Golden sunlight drowns the last few lights of the tunnel, dazzling even through the tinted windows. The car whooshes up a gentle incline into a beautiful summer evening.

"Ah, to be sure, the lovely Emerald Isle," I say in my terrible Irish accent. "How long to your mother's?"

"A couple of hours. The villa Felice booked is about an hour and a half away."

"Thank god. Good thinking on her part to give us the night

to recover." I yawn and snuggle tighter into his lap.

"Getting soft already."

"It's so much easier when you don't have to struggle for everything. Normal life is simple."

"We're not living a normal life yet."

True, but at least we no longer have to fight quite so hard for it.

15

The car turns down an aspen-lined avenue in a tiny village and my heart thumps harder.

Blake's mother owns a smallholding where she produces food for her community.

I imagine caring for goats and chickens helps distract her from her dead husband and missing sons.

I wipe my sweating hands on my jeans.

They look smart but they're quite tight. The pistachio-green top flows loosely over my breasts, slits in the long sleeves exposing my upper arms.

Am I wearing the right thing?

Felice packed my stuff. She knows what she's doing.

Okay, so being nervous about meeting my boyfriend's mother is probably normal but not the way I picture it: "Hi, Mrs O'Riley, lovely to meet you. I'm the person who killed your youngest son but look how well I've treated your firstborn. I hardly tried to hurt him at all. High-five!"

Blake takes my shaking hand and places it on his jittery leg.

His jeans are some kind of fashionably crinkled pair with a thick, black belt.

"I'm nervous, too," he says.

He doesn't have to be nervous, she's his mother, she already loves him. Her surviving son, returning home. It doesn't matter that he broke his promise to keep his brother safe. He did everything he could.

Then I came along.

The car brakes on a cracked concrete drive beside a large stone house. A path leads to the front porch and a turquoise door. Vegetables fill the garden bordered by a wooden fence, netting strung between the planks. The trees continue to a barn and a greenhouse at the back, the soft clucking of hens almost peaceful.

Blake slips his hand beneath his black shirt and pulls one pair of his dog-tags over his head, his thumb stroking the embossed metal. His brother's name. The beaded chain of his own dog-tags hangs through his open collar, framing the hollow of his throat. He bows his head and sucks in a breath.

I lick my lips. "I'll wait in the car for the first bit. She won't want me to see—"

"Don't make me go in there alone." He raises his head, the pain in his eyes hurting my chest. "I know it's going to be awful but I need you there. With me. Please."

"I'm with you. Always."

He relaxes a little but his hand grips mine hard. We climb out of the vehicle into the warmth and the smell of cut grass. No pale face peeks at us through the windows, no twitch of a curtain. Everything is still.

Idyllic.

Is she pacing from room to room, wringing her hands, refusing to look out the glass? If she doesn't see her one remaining son she can pretend they're both alive.

We shuffle to the door, alternating between Blake dragging me along and me pushing him from behind.

What big tough soldiers we are.

"Where's the doorbell? Or do we knock?" I clear my throat, my voice a whisper.

"Maybe it's this thing."

Blake releases my hand and places his palm on a metal plate flush to the wood in the centre of the door.

A computerised voice says, "Unknown caller," and we jump. "Look into the camera and identify yourself."

Blake glances at me then peers at the tiny lens above the palm plate.

"Um, I'm Blake. O'Riley?"

Bolts scrape in the lock. The door bangs open, scaring a woodpigeon from the aspens in a clatter of wings. I glimpse a purple sundress and white, open-toed sandals.

"Mum—"

A sobbing, raven-haired woman flings herself at Blake. He staggers but catches her, her face buried in his neck. She clings to him, her fingers gripping his shoulder blades.

"Hi, Mum," he whispers into her hair.

Tears burn my eyes.

Oh god, I'm going to start blubbering in a second.

I swallow and get myself under control.

Show no weakness. Usually to enemies, not mothers.

Blake coaxes her into the house, not letting go. I tip-toe behind and ease the door shut, feeling like an intruder. An interloper in the grief I have no right to share. Blake guides her into a cosy living room and sits with her on a sagging couch covered in crocheted pillows, holding her quivering body in his arms while she cries into his chest. Silent tears glisten on his cheeks and drip from his jaw, his eyes closed.

I look away before I lose it and drift over to the fireplace, swept clean and stacked with logs that won't need lit for a few months yet. Three photographs in silver frames line the mantelpiece.

A nice, homey touch and a middle finger to the digital age of the neuralnet.

The central photograph appears to be Blake's mother—younger, black hair to her waist—though I haven't seen her face. She stands arm in arm beside a strapping blond man who's grinning wide at the camera. Two pairs of serious, cobalt eyes stare out of the picture closest to me. Two toddlers, one dark, one light.

I slide along the mantelpiece to the last photograph.

Blake and Dylan as teenagers, smiling, their arms flung around each other's shoulders. Dylan resembles his father—blond and already filling out with muscle. Handsome. Blake steals my breath, his black hair completely obscuring one eye and flopping to his jaw, purple highlights bringing out the violet in his eyes.

Teenage girls didn't stand a chance.

Hell, I didn't stand a chance.

Adult Blake is even more stunning.

I return to the opposite side of the fire, slotting myself in the corner behind a rocking chair in case I need a shield.

Terrified, who, me?

I want to stay out of sight of Blake's mum for as long as possible. Let her mourn. I can stand her hatred if it soothes her pain.

But not quite yet. I need to work up to it.

"Are these his?" She sniffs, her voice wet but steadying.

Blake spools Dylan's dog-tags into her hand. Slim fingers stroke the metal, a shining waterfall of hair hiding her face.

Blake's eyes dart to mine, as if making sure I'm still there. My smile wobbles but maybe he won't notice.

"I'm sorry, Mum. I promised to protect him and I failed." Blake bows his head. "I'm sorry."

I dig my fingernails into my palms, shaking with the effort to not respond.

His mum cups his face. "Don't blame yourself. Not all promises can be kept, no matter how hard we try. I'm just so glad you're here."

They hug each other, their faces pale, the tears drying on their cheeks.

"There's so much I want to hear but would you tell me how it happened? Would you tell me how he died?"

Oh, crap.

"I will, I'll tell you everything, but there's someone I want you to meet first."

I tense to run. Blake crosses to me, sadness bright in his eyes and freezing me to the spot. His hand brushes my cheek and his fingertips come away wet. His tender smile nearly undoes me. I scrub my face while his body blocks my view of his mother. He slides his arm around the small of my back and steers me towards her.

Too late to escape.

"Mum, this is Anita."

She jumps to her feet. I twitch towards the door, ready to bolt if she goes to scratch out my eyes.

"Of course I know who she is! I watch the news." The lovely, female version of Blake taps her temple.

Age has not stripped her beauty despite the wrinkles on her face and the silver streaking her hair. She blinks at me with Blake's eyes and I desperately want her to love me.

Another person's love I don't deserve.

She strides across the room and takes my hand in her cold fingers, looking up to meet my gaze. Feminine and delicate despite her core of steel.

"Well, I can see what captured my son. I'm surprised he didn't fall a little bit in love with you at first sight." She squeezes my hand and her smile stabs knives into my stomach. "He attacked you?"

Blake snorts. "I wouldn't say attacked—"

She pokes his chest. "I taught you better than that."

Our world was fight or die. No hesitation, no surrender. Survival justified a multitude of terrible acts.

And Blake had more justification than most to kill me.

Mrs O'Riley waves us onto the couch, flitting into the kitchen to collect a tray of tea in china cups and lightly sugared biscuits. She claims an armchair the same burgundy colour as the couch, dragging it closer and perching on the edge, leaning towards us. Every few minutes, her fluttering hand reaches out to touch Blake's knee. Her bright, beautiful eyes shift between us, as if to look away from one for too long will make that person disappear.

I press myself as close to Blake as possible without climbing into his lap.

Must show some decorum in front of his mother.

Sure, because that's what she'll remember.

Blake holds my hand on his thigh, our fingers tangled together. I take a cup of tea to be polite and cradle it to my chest, chilled despite the sunshine streaming through the multi-paned window.

"It doesn't matter to me how you met. The important thing is you're here. You helped bring my son home. Thank you,

Anita."

Letting her be nice to me feels like trickery.

"Please, don't thank me, Mrs O'Riley—"

"Don't be silly! And call me Niamh. I think you and I should be on a first name basis."

Nausea curls in my stomach and I shoot a pleading glance at Blake.

He better tell his mother how Dylan died before I blurt out the truth.

"Mum, about Dylan…"

She sits back on a sigh. "I want you to tell me, I do, but let a mother indulge herself a minute. I always hoped you'd bring a girl home. You and Dylan both. Did you meet him, Anita? Knowing my sons, I can imagine the fight they must have had over you. There was this one girl—"

Words bubble in my chest, scalding my throat. I try to swallow them and give Blake the chance to explain it his way.

Don't say anything. Don't say—

"I'm the reason Dylan is dead."

Well, shit.

16

I stare at my lap, unwilling to see the expression of either O'Riley. I should have kept my mouth shut.

"I'm sorry—"

"Anita, look at me," Blake says, squeezing my hand until I raise my eyes. "You know that's not true."

"It is. It's one of the first things you said when you didn't know it was me. You hated her, blamed her. Blamed me."

He buries his fingers in my hair, gripping tight and controlling my head. "Do you think I could do this, any of this, if I still blamed you?"

"No, but I don't deserve—"

"Woman, will you never learn?" he growls and claims my mouth as if it isn't already his.

Everything is his. Every living, breathing, beating part of me.

I sag against him. The taste of him dazzles me, makes me forget all but him.

For a moment.

"I don't understand."

The tiny voice rips us apart. Niamh blinks, her face pale apart from two bright spots of red on her cheeks. She clutches Dylan's dog-tags in a fist pressed to her chest, the beaded

102

chain dangling over her knuckles and swinging with her rapid breaths.

"Anita, did you kill my son?"

I open my mouth but shut it again at a glance from Blake. He leans forward, putting himself in front of his mother. Her shimmering eyes meet his.

"I said I'd tell you everything, Mum, and I will. But you have to promise me you'll listen."

Her gaze darts to me, swirling with too much I can't read. She drags her attention back to Blake, and nods.

"The leader of my faction became an evil man who tortured people. Hundreds of people. But one of his prisoners finally escaped and used our own weapon to destroy us. Dylan died in the rubble before I could reach him."

Niamh presses her fingers to her mouth. Tears glisten in her long, black lashes.

"Anita was the prisoner."

"She killed my son," Niamh whispers.

"No, Mum, you're not listening. Wick, my leader, tortured her for five days. She was traumatised. Furious. She thought we were all like him and I don't blame her. Of course she destroyed us. If she hadn't, we would've followed her back to her faction to reclaim our weapon. She had to protect herself. We had to do awful things just to survive. Surely you understand that. You lived through a war."

Niamh shakes her head, her glossy hair trickling over her shoulders. "You're saying she destroyed your whole faction and you justify her actions?"

"Not the whole faction, only Livingston, our stronghold."

"How many people, how many including my son?" Her slim body shakes in the chair, her knuckles mottled around the dog-tags.

Okay, so this is going to sound bad...

"About a hundred thousand," Blake says.

Yup. Pretty bad.

"How—how can you—"

She sits forward suddenly, her fingers digging into the arms of the chair. Blake jerks back to avoid being head-butted.

"She murdered a hundred thousand people, including your brother, and you bring her into my *house!*"

"I'm sorry, Niamh—"

Her head whips towards me and her eyes blaze.

Guess we're no longer on a first name basis.

I try again. "Mrs O'Riley—"

She dives at me, all claws and bared teeth. Instinct raises my hands to ward her off, her pretty, snarling mouth connecting with my fist. She lands hard on the carpet, knocking into the table and rattling the china cups. A bead of red wells on her lip.

A tiny, trembling hand smears the blood on her mouth. "She hit me."

"I didn't mean—"

Niamh pounces but Blake intercepts her, wrapping his arms around her waist and hauling her away from me towards the fireplace. She fights him, but not effectively, her arms and legs flailing and slapping at his hands.

"How can you stand to touch her! How can you call her your girlfriend! How can—how—"

She bursts into sobs and her body folds in Blake's arms. He lowers her gently to the ground.

"Because I know her. I love her. You will, too."

I very much doubt it but stay quiet, fidgeting on the edge of the couch while my presence ruins Blake's reunion with his mother.

The sobs abate. Niamh slowly lifts her head to reveal tear-dampened cheeks, a swollen mouth and lovely eyes glittering with hatred.

"Get that murdering whore out of my house," she hisses.

"Mum—"

"Get her out! I want her out! *Get her out of my house!*"

I jump to my feet. "I'll, um, wait outside."

Blake throws me an apologetic look and holds his wailing mother while she calls me a few more names.

Son-stealing bint is a particular favourite.

I scuttle for the exit and yank at the front door, no locking mechanism visible. A metal plate similar to the one on the outside sits beneath a small screen in the wall to the right. I slap my palm to it and a helpful robotic voice says, "Print not recognised. Consult owner."

I climb out the window in the dining room. A simple catch to release and up it slides.

No stupid palm reader to imprison your visitors.

My ridiculous ballet pumps with the bow (why did I think dressing nice would make a difference?) crush a row of herbs, the scent of mint and thyme marking my escape. Sunlight caresses my icy skin, glorious after the grief-laden chill of the house.

I skirt the cars, needing warmth and fresh air, and walk further down the avenue towards the main road, following the aspens, their leaves rattling in the gentle breeze. One of the security guys follows at a discreet distance. A humpback bridge crosses a small burn, sunlight dappling the surface. I climb onto the stone barrier and swing my legs over the edge.

The burble of the water soothes me.

The first time I realised I'd fallen in love with Blake was in a river after some particularly awesome sex.

It scared the hell out of me.

Loving someone—trusting anyone—made it too easy for them to hurt you.

I understand how his mother feels. I think the same.

How can he touch me, want me, look at me without picturing the face of his brother, pale and cold in the rubble of their house where I buried him?

A shoal of minnows flashes silver beneath the surface of the burn, their tiny bodies undulating against the current in a shaded patch close to the bank. I glance up at footsteps on concrete and scramble to my feet, hesitating with one hand balanced on rough stone.

"Blake, I'm sorry—"

He crushes me against him and buries his face in my hair, holding me tight, a little too tight if I like breathing but I'm not about to complain. I wrap my arms around him and press my lips where neck meets shoulder, the wonderful smell of him teasing me to do more. To slip my hands under his t-shirt to slide over the ridges of muscle and scar tissue—his own whip scars courtesy of Wick.

Not as extensive as mine but another way we match.

"Is your mother okay?" I say, softer than the rustle of the aspen leaves. "I really didn't mean to hit her."

"I shouldn't be surprised. You've set a precedent for accidentally punching us O'Rileys in the mouth."

He eases back only far enough to place a light kiss on my lips, removing any sting from his words.

"I'm sorry, Anita."

"You don't have to apologise."

"Of course I do. I forced you to meet her and it went pretty much as you expected. I managed to calm her down but she does not like you at all right now."

"Well, if she's anything like you, I'll just lob some fish at her and save her from a death-trap tree and she'll love me forever."

"Woman," he says, squeezing my ribs in another hug, "how could she not?"

"Promise me one thing, though? Even if she never forgives me, you have to keep visiting her. I can't... I can't be responsible for you losing your remaining family. You have to fix your relationship with your mother. Pretend I don't exist, if it helps, but at least promise me you'll try."

"Anita—"

"No. You have to. You're the only ones who knew Dylan. I want you to be able to remember him, talk about him, when he was alive not be reminded he's dead every time you look at me."

Blake wraps my hair in his fist, and tugs. "That's not what I see when I look at you."

"What do you see?"

"Just you. The haughty, mouthy, pain in the arse I love." His mouth steadies my wobbly smile. "And if it makes you feel better, I promise I'll continue to visit my mother. Now, I'm looking forward to meeting your parents. It can't go any worse than this."

How true and yet how horribly untrue that turns out to be.

17

"Darling! Your hair! You look like a cave woman."

The first words my mother has spoken to me in ten years.

I accept the obligatory peck on both cheeks, her gardenia perfume the same as always.

Funny how it's comforting now rather than cloying.

"Hi, Mum," I say.

She grips my arms. "Good lord, darling. You're so muscular."

Blake coughs from his hiding place behind me.

The coward.

The front door burst open as soon as we stepped on the pavement, eliminating the worry about being unidentified by snooty palm plates. The green-walled, green-roofed building is quite different from their huge, red-bricked house in Sevenoaks.

The front garden contained a fountain, for Christ's sake.

Still, the terraced structure is fancier than most of the residential areas we passed through. Flats featured heavily, though none taller than three storeys.

I slip to the side on the doorstep, exposing Blake to my mother's feline gaze.

This will be fun.

Her green eyes, slightly darker than mine, widen, her thin hands immediately smoothing her red sheath dress. Her mouth works but no sound comes out. I cough to cover my own laugh.

It's not every day my mother is struck speechless.

She lurches and grabs Blake's hand in both of hers. "Blake, darling! So lovely to meet you. You are even more gorgeous in person, wicked boy."

She wraps her thin arms around him, her head on his chest. He flashes me a panicked glance over her blonde, grey-streaked bob.

She used to dye it every few months but I guess hair dye isn't environmentally friendly. Or necessary.

She reclaims Blake's hand and tugs him into the house, shouting, "Harold! Anita brought a visitor!"

"Oh, you'll get no help from me, wicked boy," I smirk as my mother drags him past me.

The front door opens into a cramped hallway brightened by a potted ivy on a shelf. Warm wind licks my bare legs as I shut the door behind me, my black skirt hitting above the knee and angling to calf level on the other leg.

Last time I trust Felice to pack clothes. I do not wear skirts. Though I have enjoyed the effect on Blake and his wandering hands. It also has certain advantages in places where being naked would be indecent…

Okay, maybe I can wear skirts more often.

My mother is the only splash of colour in the beige living room. She tows Blake towards my father, who levers his long body from a chair. He claps Blake on the shoulder and shakes the hand released from my mother's grip.

"O'Riley, is it? Irish descent?"

"Yes, sir."

"Farming family?"

"Ah, a few generations back. Until recently."

"Right, right. Welcome, welcome. I have to say it's a relief. Anita seemed to have no interest in men, unlike her sister. I worried she was, you know, a lady fancier."

I drop my face into my hand. "Jesus, Dad."

Blake's eyes shine and he presses his lips together.

It's a special gift parents have to somehow embarrass you immediately in any social situation, whether they see you every day or once a decade.

"And there she is." My father folds me in a brief hug, taller than me and much greyer than my mother.

It feels the same but his usual scent of sweet, woody pipe tobacco is absent.

Maybe it, too, went the way of the coffee bean.

"Wonderful to see you, Anita. You remember the Seymour-Bertrams?"

A couple are squashed on the couch. Friends of my parents since I was a toddler. Round, fleshy and unremarkable. The man rolls to his feet and waddles towards me.

"Little 'Nita! How you've grown!" His sweaty hand clasps mine and holds on, his beady eyes roving from my face to my chest, framed perfectly in the tight tops Felice insists on dressing me in.

"Augustus. Can't say I'm surprised you're here."

"Oh, 'Nita, you haven't changed a bit. How many times have I told you to call me Uncle Gus, surely you haven't forgotten?"

I haven't forgotten.

And never in a million years.

I bare my teeth in the semblance of a smile, trying to ease

my hand out of his moist grip.

Blake appears at my side and slides one arm around my waist, his eyes flashing. "Nice to meet you, Uncle Gus."

Not quite a growl.

He sticks his hand out, forcing Augustus to finally release me. Augustus touches it limply and scuttles back to the couch. His wife bobs at me, not bothering to get up. A dowdy woman in an unflattering paisley dress. Ludicrously wealthy, or she used to be.

"And this is… a friend of your mother's."

I narrow my eyes at my father's hesitation. The final person in the room rises to her feet, fingers extended, her nails manicured into talons. The pinstriped skirt and jacket are a size too small, the material straining against the curve of her hips and chest, her breasts almost spilling out of her blouse. She shifts her hand at the last minute to greet Blake first, her hungry gaze barely lingering on his face, devouring his cobalt-blue shirt open at the collar and dropping to his slim waist.

"I'm Courtney Poulson."

A snarl vibrates in my throat. "And how exactly do you know my mother?"

"Marissa and I are recent acquaintances but I think she'll become a dear friend."

She shakes my hand without tearing her eyes from Blake and her claws scrape my wrist. I squeeze her fingers until she looks at me.

"And what is it you do, Courtney?"

Her gaze flicks to my mother and her tongue moistens her lips. "I'm a reporter with the *Daily Mail*."

"What the hell is this, Mum?" I say, wheeling on her where

she flutters next to Blake. "No goddamn media was made pretty clear."

"Language, darling! Can you cut that from the footage, Courtney?"

"Absolutely. Now, why don't we have the ladies on chairs beside the picture of Ailsa and the men standing behind? A poignant reunion. Then we can get started with the questions."

A framed photo of my sister sits on a polished table, a small candle wavering in front of it and reflecting off the glass. She beams at the camera, dressed in her graduation gown, the dome of McEwan Hall arching in the background.

Given the state of Edinburgh these days, I doubt it's still standing.

Courtney watches me, unblinking, and I realise I'm rubbing my fingers over an ache in my chest.

It's been so long since I saw a picture of my sister.

"Get out," I say to Courtney and she finally blinks.

"I'm a guest of your mother—"

I grab her arm and spin her around, frog-marching her out the front door. She staggers on the steps, unable to widen her legs due to the tightness of her clothes. The security guard leaning on the car straightens abruptly.

"Don't let this woman back in. She violated the press ban."

I give Courtney a helpful shove and slam the door on her screech.

"Oh, darling, I wish you hadn't done that. She was going to pay for exclusive rights to record the return of our only surviving daughter."

"Mum, just don't talk to me right now, okay?"

She sighs but retreats to the living room, her voice too loud and bright. "Why don't I freshen everyone's drinks? Blake, darling, what would you like?"

"I'm fine, Mrs Carmichael," he calls over his shoulder, joining me in the hall.

"It's Marissa, darling," trills the response.

I roll my eyes, and Blake grins.

"Your mother is interesting."

"Sure, if by interesting you mean you want to shake her." I take his hand and tow him to a simple wooden door opposite the entrance. "Come on, I need to get away from everyone for a minute before I do something violent."

The door leads into a cupboard, an automatic light switching on since there are no windows.

Perfect.

"How many coats and shoes do your parents need?"

Jackets on hangers line three walls, two shelves with a variety of footwear filling the space below. Heels, boots, brogues.

More shoes than I know the name of.

"One for every day of the year, apparently. I hope they're all sustainable." I pull Blake into a hug and huff into his neck. "Can we go back to your mother's?"

He chuckles, slipping his hand under my top to play his fingers up my spine. "It's not that bad. They love you. Except creepy Uncle Gus. I might have to get violent if he keeps looking at you like that."

"He's an old friend of my parents so I've known him since I was a kid. He's always been touchy-feely. With me, never Ailsa. When I got older, he'd burst into my room without knocking or find any excuse to put his sweaty hands on me. Nothing too inappropriate but—hey, where are you going?"

"To break his fingers."

I slap my hand to the door before Blake can yank it open.

Anger brings out the fierce beauty of his face.

I slide my body between him and the exit.

"While it would be what he deserves, I'd rather not see you arrested."

Blake relaxes and braces his hands on either side of my head. "Stupid civilised world."

"We're not in Scotland anymore, Toto."

He smirks. "Misquoting a movie—how very unlike you."

I fist my hands in his shirt, an eager noise in my throat, and lose myself in the taste of his mouth.

18

Having sex in my parents' coat cupboard was not on the agenda but it happens anyway. The thrill of capture heightens everything—Blake's fingers gripping my thighs where he pins me to the door, the thrust of him inside me, the thundering of my pulse. He cups his hand over my mouth to shut me up, the delight on his face driving me over the edge. He buries himself as deep as he can go and muffles his cries in my throat, his teeth in my skin making me writhe.

It takes an embarrassingly long time for me to open my eyes, our panting loud in the small space.

Blake shifts to lower me to the floor and I groan, "No, wait, I don't think I can stand yet."

He purrs into my neck, such a happy, male sound. I shiver, tightening around him, and the purr becomes a moan. He slowly rotates his hips, whipping my settling heartbeat into a canter.

"Oh, god, Blake, please, they'll be wondering where we are."

"Let them wait." He continues his slow, teasing rhythm and I can't help but respond.

"But what if they come looking?"

Jesus, the lame protest does nothing to mask the trembling, aching need he stirs in me.

He bites me over my throbbing pulse. I convulse against the door, driving him deep inside me. His shaking breath scorches my neck.

"Baby, you are murder for my self-control."

"You're the only one of us who has any," I gasp. "I can't say no to you."

"I know. I love it."

"Please, have mercy. What if my dad—"

He kisses my throat, gentle over the marks of his teeth. "I'm sure he'll clap me on the shoulder and thank me for ensuring you're not a lady-fancier."

I laugh, which doesn't help, my body clenched around him.

He makes a pained noise. "Christ, woman, okay. For my own sanity. But we are definitely picking this up later, where I will get you all flushed and squirmy until you do that little begging thing…"

I chew my lip to keep in a whimper. "Blake—"

"I hope you appreciate how hard it is to stop."

"Oh, I can feel how hard it is."

"Hussy."

He lowers me and my feet touch the floor. I sag against the door, my knees too wobbly to take much weight. He tucks himself into place and zips up his trousers.

"I may need a couple of minutes before I'm decent enough for company," he says.

"Easy for you. I definitely need to go to the bathroom to tidy myself up. You'll have to distract my parents and the awful Seymour-Bertrams."

He grins. "You do look like you've been royally fucked."

Heat throbs between my legs, my eyes rolling back in my head.

Seriously, the guy leaves me breathless.

I manage to blink at him and he smirks at me.

"Aftershock? Flashback?"

"Both."

"This is not helping my erection."

I make my own pained noise. "You have to leave or we'll never get out of here."

"You're kind of blocking the door."

Shit.

I slide to the side and nearly disappear into a rack of coats. Blake steals a kiss, his thumb brushing my cheekbone.

"Don't take too long. I can't promise not punch Uncle Gus."

"I'll be quick. Wicked, *wicked* boy."

Chuckling, Blake eases open the door and slips into the hall. I wait for my mother's, "Blake, darling, there you are!" before I stagger after him and dart up a curving staircase, the carpet muffling my steps. I find a bathroom two doors down. White tiles, white ceramic. No lock but it'll do.

The woman pouting at me in the mirror has just had glorious sex—flushed skin, wild hair, swollen lips. I straighten my dishevelled clothes and run my fingers through my hair. A washcloth soaked in cold water soothes the redness. I stroke a fingertip over the imprint of Blake's teeth in my throat and plonk hard on the closed lid of the toilet, struggling not to wriggle off onto the floor.

He's the only one who gives me orgasm flashbacks.

I take a few, steadying breaths and will my pulse to calm the hell down. I need to rescue Blake from my mother.

Who knows how badly she's flirting right now.

The door bursts open.

"'Nita! I'm so sorr—" Augustus's words die, the greedy light in his eyes dimming when he realises he hasn't interrupted me relieving myself.

I rise to my feet and widen my stance.

I spent most of my childhood avoiding him, disgusted and frustrated at being too small and weak to escape his sweaty grasp.

"Well, I'm glad I've got you alone. I have to say that boyfriend of yours is a tad possessive." Augustus spreads his arms, barring the exit. A yellow stain crusts on the chest pocket of his shirt. "Why don't you give your uncle a proper hug?"

"You're not my uncle."

"Same old feisty 'Nita!"

I clench my teeth, my hands loose at my sides but ready. "Stop calling me that and get out of the way."

"There's no need to be rude. What would your parents think?" He closes the door, a calculating gleam in his eye. "Give your uncle a hug, there's a good girl."

A nasty smile stretches my face. "Come and get it, *Uncle*."

He hesitates for a second but steps closer.

"You really are being a naughty girl. I'll have to tell—"

I move to the side, one hand grabbing his wrist and pressing it to my chest, the other circling his flabby bicep. I pivot and use his own weight to slam his stomach into the edge of the sink. His breath huffs out and fogs the mirror. I twist his arm behind his back and he yelps, his wide eyes meeting mine in the misty reflection.

"You try to touch me one more time and I'll break every bone in this arm." I shove it higher, forcing his mewling bulk onto his tiptoes. "In fact, call me 'Nita again and I'll start with your fingers."

"You—you can't do this! I'm—"

118

I yank his arm. He squeals, beads of sweat slicking his wrinkled head.

"You're not my uncle. You're a sick, sad little man who fondles children," I say, swinging him around, his skin mottled under my grip. "Open the fucking door."

He reaches out with his shaking free hand. I propel him into the wall opposite the bathroom. He heaves his body around to face me, his back pressed to the silver- and white-patterned paper. He cradles his arm. A bubble of snot glistens on his lip.

"You—you're a savage!"

"No, I'm just tired of being pawed at by perverts."

Movement catches my eye. Blake bounds up the stairs, his fists clenched.

He pauses at the top and the tension eases from his shoulders. "Bastard sneaked out while your mother showed me her art collection."

"Weird, isn't it? I don't get her fascination with random shapes and bright colours. Looks like they're drawn by kids."

Augustus's incredulous gaze flicks between us, his jowls an unhealthy puce. Blake leans against the wall, his casual posture hiding the predator beneath.

"You into art?"

I shrug. "I prefer landscapes."

"Me, too. Trees and stuff."

My heart does a slow roll at Blake's tender smile. I focus on Augustus. He meets my eyes, and flinches.

"Go collect your wife, and leave. You won't see my parents for a while. If ever. Got it?"

He nods, rapid enough to scatter droplets of sweat on the carpet.

I jerk my chin towards the stairs. "Then get the fuck out."

He scuttles along the wall, hesitating at Blake on the top step. Augustus cowers past, as if Blake is a wild animal he's trying not to provoke.

A jaguar—dark, dangerous and terribly beautiful.

Augustus thuds down the stairs and out of sight.

Blake hugs me in the middle of the corridor. "You okay?"

"Yeah. Didn't give him the chance to touch me." I shudder. "God, I really wanted to break his arm."

"You showed amazing restraint. And I like that you're a little bit scary."

"You're not normal, you know that, right?"

"Baby, neither of us is."

We wait for the hurried sounds of departure to cease, the muttered excuses in a high-pitched voice, before joining my parents in the living room.

"Darling, the Seymour-Bertrams had to leave, Augustus looked awfully peaky. It must be his heart, poor man."

Blake and I share a smirk. My mother waves us onto the couch and flits around serving drinks, squeezing onto the seat beside Blake. I slurp from my glass to hide a snort and choke, liquid burning my nose.

"Mum! This is vodka!"

"When you said you wanted water, I thought you were joking, darling."

"It's two in the afternoon!"

"Would you like a cocktail instead?"

"Jesus, god, no. Water. Just water. You know, from the tap?"

My mother sniffs and flounces into the kitchen. "Honestly, you're no fun. I've been stocking up. Rationing is dreadfully dull."

Blake eyes his glass of coke.

120

"Yeah, that's definitely got rum in it," I whisper.

He places it on the coffee table. My mother returns and thrusts a cold glass into my hand. A tentative sip confirms it's water. She reclaims her position next to Blake, curling her slender frame close to him.

My father finishes his drink and switches his attention to us. "What are your plans for when you're released back into the general public? Are you thinking of moving to Ireland to be closer to Blake's mother?"

"Um, no, probably not Ireland," I say after a glance at Blake.

"You're welcome to stay here, of course. We've already vouched for you."

My mother grips Blake's knee. He jumps and fists his hand in my skirt.

"Oh, Blake, darling, that would be wonderful if you lived here! And you, too, of course, Anita."

"Thanks for remembering I exist, Mum."

She tuts, patting Blake's leg. "She always misinterprets what I say."

"Anyway, Dad, I don't know when we'll be able to go where we want. We have a meeting with the Prime Minister and his Cabinet tomorrow. Maybe we'll find out more then."

Or be dragged into some political scheme.

"Ooh, the Prime Minister! What are you going to wear? Who's going to do your hair?"

"Mum—"

"You must look the part, darling, he's the most powerful man in the country. Sit up straight, legs together, no swearing."

Blake coughs into his palm and grins at my narrowed eyes.

"I'll make sure she behaves, Marissa."

"Of course you will, darling boy!"

Oh god, gag me.

"Whatever happened to Alan Marshall?" my dad says. "Did he not escape with you? An intense chap, but good for your sister."

"He's dead," I say flatly.

My mum's hand flutters to her mouth. "Oh, how tragic! First my darling girl then her husband. How long was it after her death?"

"Too long," I say.

My mother cocks her head but jerks on the couch before she can ask anything else. "Hello? Yes, this is Marissa Carmichael. Yes, she's here. Let me transfer you to our screen. One moment please."

My mother sits, spine rigid, one eyelid fluttering. She blinks and snaps back to herself.

"Anita, there's a Felice Huffman on the phone for you. Let me show you where you can take it."

Blake and I follow her into the hall past the coat cupboard—my knees only wobble a little—and up the stairs to a tiny study. She crosses to a screen the size of a notebook embedded in the wall behind the desk.

"I can't believe you haven't got a neuralnet installed yet, darling," she says, tapping at the screen, a glowing blue handset symbol winking in the centre. "This is positively medieval."

"I just don't fancy someone drilling into my head, Mum."

"Oh, don't be morbid, darling. There. Touch this icon to connect the call." She shuts the door behind her.

I tap the screen. "Felice?"

"Anita!" Her voice peals from a hidden speaker. "Is Blake with you?"

"Yes, he's beside me. Is something wrong?"

122

She says nothing and unease slithers into my stomach. Blake's hand slides into mine.

"Felice?"

She sucks in a breath. "Anita, what happened at Blake's mother's?"

19

'She's Stolen BOTH my Sons!' screams one headline. 'She MURDERED my Son!' shrieks another.

Felice sends a photo of each article to the screen in my parents' study and summons us to the Townhouse. We make our excuses and leave, though my parents will discover the real reason soon enough.

The neuralnet is buzzing, apparently.

Courtney Poulson, evicted reporter, positively beams where she stands at the end of the street, one of our security detail glowering at her. She follows the departure of our car intently, panning her head and not blinking. I lower my window and give her the finger.

Felice will have a fit but it's not like my reputation can be saved.

The headlines aren't lying.

I fidget in the car, alternating between touching Blake for reassurance, staring out the window and frowning at my lap.

"You know I don't care what anyone thinks, right?" he says after my tenth nervous circuit.

"I know. Turns out I care."

"I can't believe she talked to reporters."

I shrug. "I don't blame her. She's angry and upset. People

do crazy things when they're grieving."

"That's true." Blake captures my hand and tucks me into his side. "I tried to kill you, took you prisoner, decided to keep you alive then fell in love with you. *Insane.*"

I manage a laugh, and curl in his lap. "I'm still waiting for you to come to your senses."

"Not going to happen."

A crowd waits for us outside the Townhouse, held at bay by police and metal barriers. The roar of their voices penetrates the car, their faces twisted. Several women brandish placard screens flashing the words 'Save Blake O'Riley' and 'We Love You, Blake!'

"You have your fan club, at least," I sigh.

"I'm sure they'll turn against me when they realise I'm in complete control of my mental faculties."

The car brakes sharply and Blake's arms tighten to hold me in place. A woman slams her hands on the bonnet and attempts to circle around to the door. Two burly policemen haul her away.

I shudder. "I was hoping my days of angry mobs were over."

The vehicle aims for the opening to the underground garage, the barriers and police penning the crowd. The wave of humanity ripples and spills into the road behind us. The police and security guards manage to hold them back but our support car gets trapped in the furore, separated by a wall of bodies. The furious shouts diminish as we descend into the garage, my body relaxing into the quiet.

"Should we wait for our security guys?"

Blake shakes his head. "Let's just get into the Townhouse. It might take them a while to get past the crowd."

The car parks and we collect our bags from the boot.

"Shit. I left the room key on the seat."

"I'll get it," Blake says.

"Okay. Give me your bag, I'll wait at the lift."

It happens in the space of a few heartbeats.

A woman steps from behind the last car. Young, blonde and too much makeup. She carries an open bottle in her hand.

"You evil witch," she hisses and pulls her arm back.

I lob a bag. It catches the rim of the bottle, tilting it so the liquid splashes into the woman's face. Her skin reddens and starts to blister. She howls and collapses to the concrete, a horrible froth covering her cheeks. I spin towards running footsteps and raise my fists. Blake stutters to a halt, the woman's screams bouncing around the garage.

"That's it," he gasps. "You and I are surgically fucking attached from now on. Get to the lift."

"What about her?"

"Fuck her, I want you safe."

We hustle for the lift and Blake watches our retreat. The doors close, classical music replacing the girl's frantic cries as her skin bubbles away.

The tremors hit as soon as we're alone. Blake catches me before my legs collapse, and we cling to each other.

"She—tried to throw—*acid*—in my *face*."

He shivers and squeezes me tighter. "Wait. Did any splash you?"

He shoves me to arm's length and runs his palms over me, his eyes a little wild. I capture his hands and kiss his fingers.

"I'm okay. It all went on her."

"Good. Goddamn fucking *cunt*."

I hug him, hard, whispering, "I'm okay, I'm okay," over and over until he stops shaking.

126

Violence isn't anything new to us. Hell, we come from a country where someone is more likely to shoot you in the gut than wish you good morning. But attempting to disfigure me, to turn my face into a weeping, melted nightmare?

That's a Wick level of sadism.

The doors ping. Blake growls and shields my body with his. There's a delicate yelp. "Blake! It's... What's going on?"

I peek around his shoulder.

Felice has one hand at her throat, her eyes wide. Her black silk skirt and matching shirt are impeccable, which somehow makes me feel better.

A woman who deals with a crisis without falling apart. Or who invests in some serious anti-wrinkle fabric softener and anti-perspirant.

"Someone tried to attack Anita with acid in the garage."

"But that shouldn't—"

"The woman is still there," Blake says, his voice low. "Screaming. You might want to get an ambulance."

The doors start to slide shut. Felice's hand shoots out and her eyelids flutter.

"Let's talk in the room—yes, hello. This is Felice Huffman. There was an attempted acid attack on my client in the garage. The female assailant remains on site. She needs medical attention." Her gaze darts to me. "No, my client is not hurt. I want to know how this happened. The garage should have been secure!"

She waves us out of the lift while she berates the poor soul who accepted her neuralnet call. Blake scans both ways down the corridor before he lets me leave, his warm hand on my lower back guiding me at a trot to the safety of our room.

I don't complain. I like the protectiveness. I can defend

myself, as can he, but it's nice knowing he has my back. Always. He'll fight for me, whether it's giant snake abominations or a psychotic woman intent on scarring me for life.

I shudder.

The scars I have are plenty. What if I hadn't been quick enough? I'd be the one writhing on the concrete, blinded, my skin dissolving.

Ruined.

I've experienced a lot of pain in my life, am even missing some body parts—spleen, a few teeth, part of my liver—but I'm still me, still mostly whole.

Who am I without a face?

The door bangs shut, and I jump. Felice continues to yell, pacing in a tight circle. Blake searches the room to confirm we're alone. He takes my hand and leads me to the couch, pulling me into his lap and stroking my hair. I curl against him, intermittent shivers shaking us both.

Felice huffs. "After your car was blocked, internal staff were distracted by a fire in the lobby. A waste receptacle."

"So there's someone else in the Townhouse who wants to hurt Anita?" Blake's hands clench.

"The man who started the fire was caught. Security are searching the building to make sure. You're the only ones authorised to be here at the moment." Felice perches on the chair opposite us, crossing her legs and smoothing her skirt. "They're going to update me on the situation in the garage."

Is there anything left of her face?

I hope not, the little bitch.

Felice leaps to her feet. "I'm going to make tea. It won't change anything but it'll make me feel better."

She busies herself at the kettle and serves three cups. I

accept mine with steady fingers, inhaling fragrant steam.

Hey, I do feel better.

How quickly we get used to home comforts—tea, warm beds, hot running water. People not trying to kill me all the damn time.

Excluding today.

"We can discuss the negative press in the morning," Felice says. "I don't want to show you something that may cause further distress after what's just happened."

I blow on my tea. "It's okay, Felice. We'd rather get it over with."

The screen on the opposite wall flickers. Felice cocks a hip against the cabinet, the petals of a daisy brushing her bare arm as she sips her tea. Niamh O'Riley's living room appears on the screen, the woman herself sitting in her burgundy chair, pale, tearful and lovely.

"She talked to the *Irish Independent* this morning," Felice says. "This is what they uploaded."

The video plays, the view panning out to include a female reporter on the couch, her sad, concerned face turned to Niamh. Her pink suit clashes with the settee, her heels taller than the ones Felice likes to wear. Niamh is in a simple white blouse and black skirt, a silver heart pendant sparkling at her throat.

"Mrs O'Riley, I know this is difficult for you but can you tell us what happened yesterday?"

She nods and stares at her lap, her silken hair falling forward to caress her cheek. "I saw my son for the first time in ten years."

"And what was that like?"

"It was wonderful. He's still my beautiful boy. But of course you know that, you've seen him."

They share a demure chuckle.

"And it was devastating."

The reporter leans closer. "Devastating? How so?"

"Because my youngest son, Dylan, wasn't with him."

"Did you know Dylan had died before yesterday?"

Niamh dabs her eyes with a crumpled tissue, Dylan's dog-tags swinging in her hand. "I knew. I knew as soon as I heard one of the refugees was my Blake and the other was a woman. My son would never have returned without his brother, if he were alive."

"That must have been upsetting."

"Yes. But I was glad to have one of my sons returned to me. He seemed happy—infatuated—with the woman."

"And this woman is the second refugee, Anita Carmichael? The Juliet to his Romeo?"

Niamh raises her head, her violet eyes blazing into the camera. "She's not who she's pretending to be. She's not a wounded warrior hero. Do not be fooled by her pretty face. Do not—"

She drops her gaze to the fists clenched in her lap and her shoulders shake with the force of her panting. The camera zooms on the dog-tags, the words 'Dylan O'Riley, Nationless, Livingston' revealed to the background chorus of her harsh breaths.

"Sorry. I'm sorry. It makes me so angry. I was taken in by her, too. I would've welcomed her as my daughter."

"What changed your mind?"

"I learned the truth of my youngest son's death."

"Mrs O'Riley, thank you so much for sharing this with us. I know our viewers will be as shocked as I am at what

130

you're about to say, especially as Anita has become the nation's sweetheart in the short time we've known her."

I was my faction's sweetheart, once.

That didn't work out so well, either.

Niamh squares her shoulders and I try not to be annoyed by her performance.

I deserve this.

"That sweetheart is responsible for killing a hundred thousand people, including my Dylan. A hundred thousand people who did nothing to her. My son—Blake—he…" She sniffles into her tissue. "He justified what she'd done. Like it wasn't her fault. He expected me to forgive her."

"Do you believe he's forgiven her?"

Tears shimmer in her eyes, highlighting the cobalt. "No. My Blake loved his brother. He would never forgive the person responsible for his death. *Never.*"

"So how do you explain the love story he presented to the world? Why does he act like they're a couple?"

"Because she's brainwashed my beautiful, trusting boy. He's lost in his grief and she's a black widow, sinking her claws into him. She is a siren, an evil temptress, poisoning him to the truth."

She's really mixing her metaphors.

"What would you say to Blake, if he's watching?"

Her lip trembles and her hand presses the dog-tags to her chest. "Please, come home. That woman doesn't deserve you. Come home. It's what Dylan would have wanted."

Blake sits very still underneath me. I fix my eyes on the screen, afraid of his expression.

What his mother said is true—I don't deserve his love, don't deserve him.

But I can't live without him.

My breath hitches.

Fuck, I'm going to cry.

"And what would you say to Anita?"

"You should be *ashamed*," Niamh hisses, flashing perfect, white teeth. "You are a *criminal*. You do not deserve to be free while my son is dead."

Oh, shit. Will I be arrested? They can't separate me from Blake. I won't let them.

Maybe Romeo and Juliet is chillingly accurate after all.

A pressure expands in my chest, too high to breathe past. A single, hot tear splashes my cheek and drips onto Blake's hand.

"Anita?"

He twists to look at me but I bow my head and hide my face.

"I'm sorry," I wheeze, wanting to say more but the words can't get past the obstruction in my throat.

Destroying Livingston is something I'll regret for the rest of my life. In the ecstasy of my escape, it felt like my only option. Revenge against the faction that broke me. A way to bury the worst memories of my life.

But only Wick and his depraved torture guards deserved to die. The rest of the encampment lived in fear under his rule, suffered his punishments. They survived as best they could, which was all any of us could do in the mess we made.

The mess The People's Republic made.

Though if I hadn't destroyed Livingston, I wouldn't have met Blake.

Is that worth a hundred thousand lives and his pain at losing his brother?

Yes.

Guess I am an evil witch.

Blake slides out from under me, his hand pressing on my spine and forcing me to bend at the waist.

"Breathe, Anita," he says. "Just breathe."

Oh, yeah. That's what the pressure is.

I suck in air before I faint. Blake rubs my back in soothing circles. No sound from the screen so maybe the video has ended or Felice has decided we've seen enough. I focus on breathing until it and my vision stop wobbling.

"You mean it's true?" Felice says, her voice soft. "You really killed all those people?"

I lift my head enough to stare at her through the curtain of my hair. She flinches and her eyes dart away.

"It was a war not a goddamn party." Hey, look at that, I can talk. "You people should know unless you exchanged flowers instead of bullets. How is it any fucking different from one of your jets bombing a city? How—"

"Anita," Blake says.

I scrub my face, and sigh. "I'm sorry, Felice. That wasn't fair."

She nods but the wariness stays.

It hurts but what do I expect? Her world wasn't fight or die, even during their war. She didn't need to slaughter thousands of people just to live.

Soldiers did that for her.

She clears her throat and pushes away from the cabinet. "Well, the video was the worst of it. The other newspapers took up the story. And the forums are inundated with 'Save Blake' posts."

"Sure. Who wouldn't want to save the beautiful brainwashed boy from the murdering harpy?"

Blake cups my chin and turns my face towards him. "When are you going to stop blaming yourself?"

"For what I did to you? Never."

He rolls his eyes but leans in for a kiss. "Such a stubborn pain in the arse."

The screen fades to black, removing the image of Niamh glaring at me. Felice places her cup beside the kettle and straightens her shirt, busying her hands instead of looking at us.

"I'll tell you what I told my mother, Felice," Blake says to the top of her head. "Anita was tortured in my faction—you saw her scars. She destroyed us to protect herself and because we deserved it. Our leader abused hundreds of people and we did nothing to stop him. She's suffered more than any of you can understand. But I understand, even though my brother died in Livingston. And I'm not fucking brainwashed. Tell the world that. They should goddamn love her, like I do."

Felice blinks at him then shakes herself, meeting my gaze. "I'm sorry, Anita. Blake. You're correct. I have no right to judge. I know what war is, though not as intimately as you, and for that, I'm thankful. I made an assumption based on how you look, which was unprofessional. You were a soldier, of course you've killed people."

"Thanks, Felice. I wouldn't worry about it, you're not the only one."

"Mostly to their detriment," Blake whispers, and I elbow him in the ribs.

"I'll see what I can do to salvage the situation, minimise the backlash, but we'll be curtailing travel until the furore dies down, excluding tomorrow's meeting with the Prime Minister."

Damn. I forgot about Bursey and his secret agenda disguised as a Cabinet meeting.

Felice pauses with her hand on the door, her head cocked. "Hello? Ah, yes! What—oh. Okay, thanks for letting me know. And it's all on the video? The fact my client was attacked and defended herself? Good. Forward a copy to my office, please."

Blake and I stand up, his hand in mine.

Felice takes a deep breath and faces us. "The woman who attacked you died from her injuries."

Whoops. Add another body to my kill count.

"I'll put out a statement but it's a clear case of self-defence, as the security footage will prove."

Felice pulls open the door but doesn't immediately sprint away from us.

Strong woman.

"I'm glad it wasn't you, Anita," she says.

The door hushes closed before I can reply.

20

My answer to the media's call for a press conference following Niamh O'Riley's revelation is a firm, "Hell, no."

I'm not going to answer questions on my torture. On what happened, what it was like. How it made me *feel*.

Felice doesn't insist, spending the rest of the journey to Downing Street staring out the window, her fingers flicking rhythmically as she surfs the neuralnet.

A blank-faced liaison in a dark suit ushers us straight to the Cabinet meeting room. Pale faces turn towards us as the door shuts, every seat around the table full. A carriage clock on the fireplace ticks loudly in the silence.

"Miss Carmichael, Mr O'Riley. So glad you could make it." Bursey rises to his feet from the middle of the green-felt-lined table, a burgundy suit impeccably tailored to his portly frame.

And what does that mean? Did he expect me to hide in the Townhouse, too ashamed to show my face? Maybe he'll question me about it or arrest me as soon as the Cabinet meeting ends.

"The purpose of this meeting is primarily information-gathering. It's taken us a long time to reach this level of stability. As you'll no doubt agree, your war puts that in jeopardy." He sits slowly, one hand twiddling his bow tie.

"So, let's start at the beginning."

I glance at Blake. We hover near the doorway like two schoolkids forced to give a presentation. Felice was waved to the only empty seat crammed in beside the fireplace next to the Chief Secretary of the Treasury, her slight frame vanishing behind the gathered ministers.

"Our beginning or your beginning?" I say.

"What do you know about the internet collapse?"

"It happened about the same time as the debating chamber assassinations," I say with a shrug. "We were a little preoccupied to give it much thought. Was it some kind of virus?"

"Amber, if you will?" Bursey says.

Amber Dundas, Home Secretary, leaps to her feet from her position on Bursey's right. Her steel-grey hair is pulled into a bun that accentuates her narrow face. She flaps at one of the heavy gold curtains framing the two floor-to-ceiling windows and drags a screen mounted on a stand to the end of the boat-shaped tabletop. Eight pictures replace the blackness, eight men scowling out at the room from passport photos or stills of security camera footage. I find myself walking forward as Amber reclaims her seat.

"Someone you recognise, Miss Carmichael?"

Buxton's arrogant grey eyes glare at me from the centre of the screen. Current leader of Soldiers of the Lost. There are fewer lines on his face in the photo, a diamond earring sparkling in his left ear. Immediately below him—a position reflected in the hierarchy of Soldiers of the Lost as I left it—is a man with mussed hair and expressive, chocolate-brown eyes. His broad shoulders barely fit in the small frame of the picture.

I stab my finger at the screen. "Buxton. Gizzy. I don't

recognise anyone else."

"Ah, yes, Scott Buxton and Gareth 'Gizzy' MacKenzie," Bursey says. "A most interesting duo."

"That's Gizzy the twat-nozzle?" Blake whispers at my shoulder.

"Twat-nozzle?"

"Any guy who believed you destroyed the weapon you loved then abandoned you in favour of his leader is a twat-nozzle of the highest order." Blake raises his voice and taps the photo of a smirking man with ginger hair and bright-green eyes. "Michael Simmons. Party leader of Solidarity then faction leader of Soldiers of the Lost, removed when his methods became too bloodthirsty, even for them."

"Very good, Mr O'Riley," Bursey says. "The men you are looking at are—or were, as the case may be—the reason for the internet collapse."

"Well, weren't they busy fu—" I clear my throat. "Weren't they busy little bees."

"Nice save," Blake mouths.

"Oh, you do not know the half of it, Miss Carmichael. The internet collapse was a meticulously planned attack. At first, we believed it was a virus, which was what they wanted us to think. It triggered a protocol to rebuild the damaged database. Karen, would you explain the technicalities?"

Karen Rutlidge, Secretary of State for Digital, Culture, Media and Sport clasps her spindly fingers on the green felt. A gold watch a shade darker than her hair flashes on her wrist under the light of three brass chandeliers.

"The virus attacked the ICANN database—the Internet Corporation for Assigned Names and Numbers. When the rebuilding protocol was triggered, the terrorists captured the seven key-holders and unlocked the safes scattered around the world to obtain the master-key, which allowed access to the ICANN database. Control of this meant control of the internet. And they shut it down."

Karen relaxes in her seat and straightens her plum-coloured suit.

"Thank you, Karen," Bursey says, turning back to me. "A devastating and complex attack we were unprepared for, given the environmental emergency the world was facing at the time. What do you know about that?"

"Did Soldiers of the Lost do that, too?" I say with a sardonic smile.

"Not quite, Miss Carmichael."

"From what I remember, there were weather extremes—flood, drought—mostly in the southern continent, making it uninhabitable. People fled north and triggered unrest. Last I heard before you all went silent on us, there was rioting in most major countries."

"Yes, escalated by the United States, who built a wall along their border with Mexico." Bursey mirrors my sardonic smile. "Not quite as barbaric as your border fence but effective all the same. South America launched missiles. The Middle East launched missiles. Europe tried to intervene. Then a nuke hit London."

The gathered ministers give us grave eyes, haunted by remembrance.

"No offence, but why did you go so quiet? I understand your war being a bit of an attention-grabber but there was nothing. No static, no sign of life. Not until a couple of years ago."

"Now, *that* you can blame on Soldiers of the Lost."

"Oh, Christ, what did they do?"

Buxton held a grudge when most of us blamed Soldiers of the Lost for the assassinations that started our war. Considering all the goddamn things his faction did, it wasn't a wild assumption.

"They bought jamming technology from China and ringed the coast, blocking all communications into the country."

My eyes meet Blake's and he raises a brow.

Is that what the black, alien monolith was on our way to the coast? One of them must have stopped working for Emily to hear the emergency broadcast from England.

No wonder she said Buxton had looked worried, the bastard.

"China were fond of the technology, before the neuralnet," Bursey continues. "That can't be jammed, though they have limited its implantation to senior government officials. These days, China are more secretive than North Korea, who have fully embraced the neuralnet. But I digress."

The photos of the core Soldiers of the Lost group disappear, replaced by a map of Scotland, a blinking red dot centred over what used to be Inverness.

"What do you know of Alba gu Brath?"

I blink at the topic change. Blake shakes his head at me.

"Means 'Scotland Forever,'" I say, helpfully.

David Brokenshire, Secretary of State for Scotland, coughs into his hand. He's a plain, bald man in a plain, brown suit. Bursey eyes me and I smile at him.

He removes his glasses and polishes them on a red handkerchief. "What do you know of their capabilities, weapons, leader? I need information, Miss Carmichael."

"You're kidding, right? This is where I'm from." I jab at the

140

central belt of Scotland on the screen then circle an area north of Glasgow. "I know nothing about Alba gu Brath except they used to be the Scottish Libertarian Party."

Oh, and Weir, Marshall's second, assassinated their party leader with a garrotte, probably around the same time Marshall was putting three bullets in my sister's chest.

"Mr O'Riley?"

"I know the same as Anita. It's not like we could drive up and visit."

The silence of the other ministers is getting a little disconcerting. They shuffle in their seats, blink and breathe but look to their leader to speak for them, obedient in their muteness.

"Are you saying the Lost's jammers also stop you from using satellite imagery or drones?"

"Yes, Miss Carmichael, that is what I'm saying, much to the vexation of the MOD. Phillip, I believe you have some photos to prove my point?"

Phillip Carrbridge twists to squint at the screen from his position on Bursey's left. He's wearing a yellow tie with white polka dots this time; an interesting choice next to his charcoal suit. A grainy black and white picture replaces the familiar map of Scotland, covered in blobs and lines of grey.

I tilt my head as if that will help. "I've no idea what I'm looking at."

"This is the clearest shot we've managed to take of what was once Inverness, now the stronghold of Alba gu Brath as I understand it," Bursey says, slipping on his glasses. "I've had this image analysed by a variety of experts and their interpretation is alarming. They believe it indicates the possible construction of an underground launch facility."

How the hell can they tell from a bunch of splodges and

squiggles?

"For ballistic missiles?" Blake says. "Are you worried about nuclear?"

No wonder the government drones in the processing centre kept asking us about nuclear weapons.

Bursey spreads his hands. "We cannot risk another nuclear war, Mr O'Riley. We barely survived the last."

"I would've thought you'd be more interested in Soldiers of the Lost, then," I say. "They bombed London once before, I wouldn't put it past them to have nukes and no qualms about using them."

Something passes over Bursey's face and twitches his mouth into a grim smile.

"Soldiers of the Lost have already used nuclear on us, Miss Carmichael."

21

Blake and I gape at Bursey, his words dropping like one of those nuclear bombs he keeps talking about.

"But none of us had nuclear," I say, glancing at Blake. "Right?"

Blake shakes his head. "We didn't. Wick would've used them."

"Trust me, Miss Carmichael, Mr O'Riley, Soldiers of the Lost had nuclear. We thought they came from the Middle East. We thought there was a glitch in our tracking systems, which is why we couldn't pinpoint where they were fired from." Bursey clasps his hands on the table, his skin mottled. "But they weren't fired. Soldiers of the Lost delivered thirteen bombs to the centre of our cities, including London, and set them off."

"Jesus," Blake and I whisper.

"We were merciless in our response," Bursey says, almost as quietly. "It was only later, when it was safe to analyse the debris, that we discovered the true origin of the missiles."

Silence hangs over the room, every eye fixed on Bursey. The clock on the mantelpiece ticks the solemn seconds.

"They were Trident nuclear missiles," he says, "stolen from Faslane by the same group who caused the internet collapse."

Soldiers of the *fucking* Lost.

They may have played no part in the debating chamber assassinations but they were never the good guys.

"Do they have more?" I say, afraid to hear the answer.

Is nowhere safe from the goddamn war?

"It is not Soldiers of the Lost you should be worried about, Miss Carmichael. They used all of their nukes on us."

"How do you know that? Didn't the Trident submarines have over a hundred of the damn things?"

"I may not have a reliable eye in the sky but I have eyes on the ground," Bursey says with a hint of smugness. "Like I said, Soldiers of the Lost couldn't jam the neuralnet."

"You have spies in the factions?"

A still image appears on the screen, slightly blurred as if clipped from a poor-quality video.

"That's you," Blake says, softly.

I'm standing in chains next to John Anders, my tatty combat jacket mud-stained and dappled by rain. His annoying mouth is frozen mid-word. The person films from the crowd facing us.

The day I was captured by Revolutionary Front.

The photo changes.

Night. More rain. The flank of a machine, silver and beautiful, half-buried in crumbled houses.

Felice gasps.

I'm lying on the ground, my face battered, blood on my clothes.

I look dead.

The day I stole the dragon for Soldiers of the Lost.

The picture switches again to piles of rubble and smudges of smoke. A hulking black Raider-3 tank perches in the ruins like a spider, more vehicles and a crowd of people gathered around it.

"And there's me," Blake says even softer, trailing his finger across to a pale face peeking behind shattered brick on the edge of the clear area occupied by soldiers.

The aftermath of my escape—Blake in the wreckage of his home, the body of his brother interred nearby, witnessing Revolutionary Front burying the rest of the survivors of Nationless in their bunker. He fled into no man's land that day.

Alone, lost and grieving.

"That's enough," I say to Bursey. "You've made your point. You have eyes on the fucking ground."

"Anita!"

"Sorry, Felice."

Bursey smiles a small smile. "Just so you know there should be no secrets between us, Miss Carmichael."

I meet his gaze without flinching.

If he wants to imply he knows everything about me, fine. Have at it. I don't care how many times he spied on me and Blake, he'll never understand who we really are.

Bursey's eyes flick to the screen. "Let's get back to Alba gu Brath."

"Are they the only faction you haven't infiltrated?"

"Unfortunately, yes. Every team we've sent has gone missing. No call-ins or mayday signals. One has to presume they're dead. We received a snippet of video on the neuralnet. Phillip?"

The still of a room appears on the screen, the view quite low as if whoever recorded it was on their knees.

"Is that a throne?" Blake says, his eyebrow raised.

A great slab of stone sits on a plinth, polished to a gleam, threads of white running through it like capillaries. A fan of iron spikes creates the backrest, an eye-poking hazard if ever there was one. Saltires hang on both sides of the throne. A woman stands next to it, her black hair cut in a severe bob and straight fringe, dark eyeliner making her look like an Egyptian princess.

"Meet Morrighan or The Morrigan, real name Dorothea Nadir. Incumbent leader of Alba gu Brath. Morrighan is a warrior goddess from Irish mythology who foretells death in battle and is a guardian of the territory and its people."

I snort. "She couldn't find a Scottish warrior goddess to name herself after?"

Ah, the pride of all leaders, so swollen with their own importance.

"Much of Gaelic mythology was imported to Scotland because of the movement of people," Bursey says, snapping the sleeve of his suit into place. "Play the video, Phillip."

The video jolts, the perspective swaying and interrupted by quick, flickering sweeps of black. The rapid blinking of the person recording the footage. Dorothea—no way am I thinking of her as Morrighan—nods to someone out of sight. A quiet beep, a sharp intake of breath and a loud bang.

Static covers the screen.

I widen my eyes at Bursey. "That's it?"

"That is all we have, yes. Ten different teams—SAS, MI5, other government agencies and even the Ministry of Defence Police—and this is all we recovered to understand their fate. As you can imagine, we are getting desperate. We *cannot* risk another nuclear war, Miss Carmichael. Alba gu Brath must be neutralised before we can pursue an end to your war. I

146

believe we are running out of time."

His shrewd gaze bores into mine. A horrible weight expands in my stomach and crushes my chest.

"The next team may be our final hope of avoiding more deaths. We have already lost millions to the First Nuclear War. We cannot lose more. The team must be familiar with the landscape, the war, the politics. Trained through years of experience—"

"No."

The single word crackles through the tension in the air.

Bursey cocks his eyebrow. "I didn't ask you a question, Miss Carmichael."

"You are not sending us back there," I say past the rapid bounding of my pulse.

A restless shuffling and whispering rises among the gathered ministers.

"Now, I don't believe I could compel Mr O'Riley to return. For all intents and purposes, he conducted himself honourably throughout his tenure. But you, Miss Carmichael"—the screen changes to the photograph of a destroyed Livingston—"you appear to have violated the principle of proportionality. It would be a shame for you to refuse to serve your country and be arrested for war crimes."

"You son-of-a-bitch."

"Anita!" Felice squeaks. "You can't call the Prime Minister a-a..."

I plant my fists on the soft felt of the table. "You. Goddamn. Son. Of. A. Bitch."

Since punching the Prime Minister won't improve my situation, I grab Blake's hand and storm for the door. Several Cabinet members leap to their feet.

Bursey remains seated, a smile on his wide mouth, his eyes following me the whole way.

22

The replicated Number Ten Downing Street is the most elaborate prison I've ever been in. The police officers in the black- and white-tiled lobby refuse to open the iconic door, sunlight mocking me through the semi-circular fanlight window.

"The Prime Minister has requested you stay inside ma'am, sir. For your own safety."

Funny how the Prime Minister's requests resemble demands.

"I don't think we'll be able to climb out a window like you did at my mother's," Blake says as we head back down the carpeted corridor towards the Cabinet meeting room, his hand still gripping mine.

We jog up the main staircase past a huge globe, the wrought iron balustrade embellished with a scroll design and a shining handrail. Photographs of former Prime Ministers hang on the pale-yellow wall. Voices from an upper level force us to duck under the rope barrier at the top of the second bend. We listen at doors and creep around corners, eventually ending up in a grand dining room with oak-panelled walls and a vaulted ceiling. Sconces cast a cheerful orange glow, the heavy drapes drawn against the day.

Being the leader has many perks, whether it's in the dark depths of a Scottish encampment or here, in a battered but civilised England.

Blake shuts the double doors and slumps into a wooden chair at the long table, his slim fingers turning a silver candelabra round and around. I pace behind him, too restless to sit.

"This can't be happening. This can't be goddamn happening."

"He can't force us back there. It must be against some human rights law. Felice would know."

"You heard what he said." I spin on my heel for another pass down the table. "If I refuse to be his personal spy, he'll throw me in jail."

"The accusation would hardly stand up in court. We'll get you a lawyer—"

"With what money? Everything we have, everything we've been given, has come from Bursey. I fucking *knew* he wanted something. Why else would he move us from the processing centre to the fancy Townhouse?"

"What about your dad?"

Oh, yeah. I have family again.

I cross to one of the screens beside the door, embedded in the wall like the one in my dad's study, but punch it in frustration after tapping on it for a couple of seconds.

"It's password protected."

Blake huffs and runs his hands through his hair. "So we have no choice. What else is new? Normality was nice while it lasted."

I stop at the far end of the table and frown at my hand on one of the curved chair backs, unwilling to look at his face.

"You don't have to come. Bursey won't force you."

My soft words fall into a pool of silence, the ripples spreading out to drown the room. I flinch at a bang, my startled gaze darting upwards, expecting to be alone, Blake too disgusted to stay.

I can't bear to be apart from him in this country where he's safe and everyone loves him. I can't let him return with me to the most dangerous place on Earth, even if it means driving him away. Making him hate me.

Finally, I'll get what I deserve. My only consolation will be knowing he's alive.

A chair lies on the carpet, Blake on his feet, his fists clenched.

"If you think I'm going to let you go back there alone, you have no fucking idea who I am, Anita."

"I won't let you—"

"Let me?" he growls. "Woman, just try and stop me."

He stalks towards me. I want to run away but my trembling knees threaten to collapse if I release my death grip on the chair.

"I can't let you sacrifice yourself—your chance at a normal life—for me. You've lost too much because of me already. Because of my faction."

Blake halts, close but not touching. "Anita—"

"*No.*" I bow my head, a tear shaken loose and plopping on the table. "I thought I'd lost you in Dunbar. I can't go through that again. I can't—"

He gathers my sobbing body into his arms and I bury my face in his neck. He rubs my back, murmuring into my hair until I quit being such a girl.

"What makes you think I could have any kind of life here without you?" he says, easing me away, his thumbs brushing the tears from my cheeks. "You are my life, Anita."

"Do you want me to keep crying?"

"I like that you cry when you're worried about me."

He kisses a fresh tear from my face and moves to my lips. I drink in the taste of him, the feel of him. I hug him tight, the kiss deepening to the glide of tongues and hot breath. His hands slide down to cup my butt, pressing me against him.

I gasp and pull away. "We are not having sex on the Prime Minister's dining table."

"Why not?"

Blake tilts his hips, his erection scattering all my perfectly good reasons for why not. He kicks a chair out of the way and lifts me onto the polished surface, easing his body between my legs. I suddenly remember I'm wearing a dress, a pale-blue, long-sleeved lace number that falls to above the knee, with underwear this time. Felice pouted when I refused the heels and some frothy thing she called a fascinator.

All recycled materials, of course.

Blake runs his hands up my thighs, teasing the edge of the dress higher. He nibbles my neck and my pulse bounds under the scrape of his teeth.

Valiantly, I try again. "Blake—"

Voices chatter outside the double doors. Blake freezes, his breath tickling my throat. I wriggle off the table and shove the chair into place.

Too late to do anything about the one Blake tipped over.

I tug him towards a door beside the windows. It opens into a narrow cupboard smelling of dust. We squeeze inside and ease the door shut as the entrance to the dining room swings wide.

"You know they're going to find us eventually, right?" Blake whispers, his lips on my ear.

"Yes, but I want to have as long as possible before I see that bastard's smug face again. Now, shh."

"Don't you shush me, woman."

He fixes his teeth in my earlobe, and tingles shiver to lower places. His lips curve against my skin at the eager noise in my throat.

He is definitely smirking at me.

Footsteps thud on the carpet on the other side of the door. A pause, a click. We wait a few more minutes before peeking out. The room is empty, the chair righted and tucked under the table.

Blake pats the tabletop. "Where were we?"

"I'm sorry," I say, swallowing hard.

He cocks his head.

"I know who you are. I know you won't let me go alone but I had to register my protest."

He skims a finger over my raised chin. "Futile protest noted and ignored. Besides, I haven't forgotten my promise."

He promised me several things while we were in Scotland—to never do anything I didn't want him to; to never let anyone hurt me again—but the one that resonated the most was after I blurted out I loved him.

"You promised me the same thing." He cups my face and kisses me, his fingers buried in my hair. "The thought of your death kills me, too."

We hold each other until the world steadies and the sick dread fades from my stomach.

If Bursey forces us back to Scotland, I'll worry about Blake every second we're there but I'd die to save him.

And so he'll live.

Hell, we escaped the war-torn cesspit once, we can do it again. After we rescue the world from Alba gu Brath.

Screw Scotland forever. It's Blake and I forever.

Always.

23

David Brokenshire's round head bobs between the double doors of the dining room.

"Blake, Anita, there you are! The Prime Minister requests you re-join him in the Cabinet meeting room."

"The Prime Minister requests a lot of things he has no right to."

David smooths the lapels of his suit and his throat bobs. "I admit it is a—dangerous task he has assigned to you but you are citizens of Scotland. Your actions could save the country and the rest of the world. An honourable venture."

"Why are we the only ones who can save the world?" Blake says. "You're Secretary of State for Scotland, David, why don't you act as our emissary?"

David sputters for a good few seconds, his cheeks red. "I, well, um, am not trained for such a highly technical assault as would be required to infiltrate Alba gu Brath."

Hard to argue there.

He motions for us to follow him and we comply, Blake's fingers tangled in mine.

A united front against the might of The Union Party and its tyrannical leader masquerading as a civilised human being.

The Cabinet meeting room is mostly empty when we

reach it, only Amber and Phillip standing beside Bursey, who remains in his chair. David ushers us inside and closes the door, bumbling across to join his colleagues.

"Where's Felice?" I say.

Bursey steeples his fingers beneath his chin. "I have sent Miss Huffman home. Her services are no longer required."

My stomach clenches at the thought of never seeing her again. I like the tiny, elfin whirlwind of a woman.

Typical leader tactic. Isolate and undermine.

"You will be pleased to hear she argued quite ferociously in your defence. She believes it is monstrous to send you back to Scotland."

Go, Felice.

I level a glare at Bursey. "She doesn't deserve to be punished for her opinion, which is correct. She did an exemplary job while she was assigned to us. She's the reason I'm in a goddamn dress right now. You should be congratulating her."

"Miss Huffman will not be negatively affected by today's events. She is, as you say, an exemplary publicist. And, for the record, if there were another way to neutralise Alba gu Brath that didn't require your involvement for its success, I would take it."

I open my mouth. Close it. Blake shrugs when I glance at him.

Threatening one minute, placatory the next. Bursey could be Buxton's brother.

"If I still refuse?"

Bursey spreads his hands. "Then I would have to initiate a war crimes tribunal."

"I could hire a lawyer and fight it. My family is rich."

"And perhaps you would win, Miss Carmichael. I hope the victory will be some consolation after Alba gu Brath drag us into another nuclear war and we all die in the ashes."

"All of us seems a slight exaggeration," Blake says.

Bursey gives him a steady stare. "You may have come from war, Mr O'Riley, but you were not here for ours."

"Okay, for argument's sake, let's say I agree to go"—Blake squeezes my hand—"let's say *we* agree to go. There will be some conditions."

When I was in The People's Republic, our motto was 'we didn't start the war but we *will* finish it'. Turned out the first part was a lie. Now, it looks like I'll get to fulfil the second part.

"Such as?" Bursey says.

"Such as we will be pardoned for all acts, war crimes or otherwise, committed up to and during the war and including anything we have to do while we're in Alba gu Brath. We will be allowed to live where we want with a yearly—"

"Monthly," Blake says.

"—monthly stipend from the government to keep us in the, ah, lifestyle you have so recently accustomed us to. And you can never ask us to do anything like this again."

"And you will give a speech to the media exonerating Anita for the revelations my mother made to the press. In fact, you will give her a freaking medal of honour or something."

"Blake—"

"Okay, I'll take one, too."

He grins and I grin back.

God, I love him.

"I'm sure I can meet all of your demands," Bursey says mildly, levering himself from his chair.

"Requests," I say, my smile so sweet it hurts my face.

David has another coughing fit into his hand.

"I want it all in writing. Signed, stamped, official. No way for you to wriggle out of it."

Bursey raises his eyebrow. "I do not wriggle, Miss Carmichael. But I will have my lawyers draft a document as requested, of course."

"Great. I'm glad we understand each other."

"Oh, we do. Now, if you will both follow me?"

He leads us into the corridor but away from the front door, his Secretaries of State trailing behind. Past the main staircase, another corridor ends in a steel door as thick as my leg. Metal steps head down, lit by domed lamps fixed to the brick walls. The basement level opens into a blue-carpeted corridor, the ceiling a maze of ducts and pipes. Potted plants add a splash of greenery next to the industrial-sized vents disappearing into the floor. Bursey bustles through the twisting corridors, moving deftly for a man of his bulk. He opens another armoured door wide.

"Miss Carmichael, Mr O'Riley," he says, sweeping his arm out, "welcome to our war room."

24

A bank of blank screens forms the far wall opposite the door, an oval table crammed between. Maps cover the remaining oak-panelled walls, zoomed in on sections of Scotland. Two men face away from the door and talk in quiet voices, their heads bent together. The taller of the two clasps his hands behind his back, not a wrinkle on his crisp military uniform. The other man is wearing a navy suit.

"This is Major-General Forrest Lamb, the Director of Special Forces," Bursey says. "I believe you've met my other guest."

I glimpse a rugged face and shorn grey hair before I slam to a stop and Blake walks into my back.

His arms immediately curl around me. "Just say the word and I'll get you out of here."

I shake my head and suck in a breath then let it out slowly. "What the hell is he doing here?"

"Cornell has graciously agreed to undertake your implantation procedure despite the short notice and his busy schedule," Bursey says.

Doctor Hoyes folds his long-fingered hands on his belly, his pale eyes drifting from my face and lingering on my bare legs. Blake's arms tighten, a growl rumbling in his chest.

"Seriously, I'm going to punch the guy."

I soothe him with my fingers and relax into him, his heartbeat against my spine.

"No implantation procedure."

I keep the 'no fucking way' part to myself.

"Now, Miss Carmichael, the neuralnet is an essential avenue of communication and information-sharing."

"Really? Hasn't worked so well for the other teams."

Major-General Lamb clears his throat. "Ma'am, the model you will receive is different to the ones used previously by my men. A military prototype Doctor Hoyes has been working on. He hoped to fully test it but he has sped the process on our request."

How wonderfully gracious of him.

"You are not putting anything in my head or under my skin. No implants or chips or tracker doo-dads."

Lamb's bright blue gaze shifts to Blake.

"Nope," he says before Lamb opens his mouth.

"Very well," Lamb sighs. "Doctor Hoyes, are you able to swap the rest of my team's models to the military grade prototype over the next two days?"

Hoyes jerks his eyes from me, his puckered lips becoming a smile.

His obvious disappointment increases my determination to never let him touch me.

"Certainly, Major-General, I—"

"We're not taking anyone else with us," I say.

Lamb frowns, the heavy wrinkles collapsing his entire face. "That is quite impossible, ma'am. This mission requires—"

"Let me be clear, Major-General. I don't doubt the skills or experience of your men but something has blown the cover of every team you've sent in there. I'm not jeopardising our survival on the same thing happening again. This time, we're doing it with Blake and me and no one else."

"That's preposterous!" Lamb splutters. "You cannot do this mission alone. You have no training—"

"What do you think we've been doing for the last ten years, fucking crotchet?"

"Baby, stop swearing at the nice military man," Blake whispers into my neck.

I clear my throat to disguise a laugh. "Major-General, we fought in Scotland for a decade. We survived no man's land, missiles and stone-throwing savages to escape. Show me anyone else in this free world who has that kind of experience."

Lamb turns to Bursey, his bushy eyebrows furrowed. "Prime Minister, surely you cannot entertain this suggestion. The success of the mission is critical. I do not have time to argue with some woman who has delusions of military experience. My men are poised and ready for deployment, sir."

I tense to smack the nice military man in his stupid haggard face but Blake's arms pin me. He bites my neck, the pressure of his teeth dissolving my fury and weakening my knees.

"In my experience, Miss Carmichael does not make suggestions lightly, Major-General," Bursey says with a twinkle in his eye. "And we are at the stage where we are desperate, are we not? Perhaps enough to entertain the notion of sending two non-military personnel into the depths of Alba gu Brath alone."

A battle rages across the trenches of Lamb's face. He swallows and his throat clicks but he straightens his spine, his hands clamped behind his back.

"Of course, Prime Minister. Then I must insist on the implantation procedure—"

"Not a chance," I say.

Lamb bares his teeth. "If you are going alone, you cannot infiltrate Alba gu Brath without the neuralnet. We must be able to communicate with you."

"So disable the nearest jammer on the coast. We'll find a way to communicate with you from the inside but I am not letting that man anywhere near me."

Hoyes's mouth turns down. "Miss Carmichael, you are being quite unreasonable—"

"I can get another doctor to complete the procedure," Lamb says, earning a glare from Hoyes.

"I don't care if you get the best doctor in the world, no one is attaching anything to my brain."

"Prime Minister, please—"

I raise my voice. "Since we have no time to argue, Major-General, these are the non-negotiable terms: Blake and I go alone as we are, no implants, though I'd be happy to take some guns. And a couple of knives."

"You know Alba gu Brath won't let us keep them, right?" Blake says, ignoring Lamb's red face.

"I know, but at least I'll get to hold them for a while. I miss my Glock. Damn. That should've been one of our conditions—I get to keep a gun."

"So violent."

"Prime Minister," Lamb says, his words clipped, "you have the ultimate authority here. You can—"

"You force us on these two issues and we don't go at all. We wait here and ride out the second nuclear holocaust."

Lamb's lip curls. "You would sacrifice millions of people to get your way, you stubborn—"

"*Major-General.*"

Lamb's mouth snaps shut, his eyes watering as though he tastes something unpleasant. Hoyes's gaze darts between the powerful figures of the Prime Minister and the Director of Special Forces but always returns to me.

I should have let Blake punch him. The guy gives me the creeps.

"I think that's enough for today," Bursey continues. "Cornell, thank you for your time but we will no longer be requiring an implantation procedure. David will show you out."

Hoyes bobs his way to the door. He hesitates as he nears me but a low, "Keep it fucking moving," from Blake encourages him onward.

"Major-General," Bursey says as soon as they're gone, "taking everything we have discussed today into account, how would you like to proceed?"

Air whistles through Lamb's nose, his cheeks alternating between bright red and dappled white. A vein throbs at his temple, his spine so rigid it threatens to break.

"The briefing will start here as planned at 0600 tomorrow. For them. *Alone.*" A wince ripples across the wrinkles on his face.

"Excellent. Your cooperation is much appreciated."

Lamb nods once, stiffly, and leaves, his eyes fixed ahead.

You'd think a man who's reached his professional level would have better control of his anger.

Bursey removes his glasses for a vigorous polish. "You drive a hard bargain, Miss Carmichael. I hope you know what you're doing."

"Me, too, Prime Minister," I say. "Me, too."

25

"Welcome back, girlie."

The hated voice freezes my breath and stoppers my throat.

Part of me knows it's a nightmare. They all feature Wick and dismemberment and pain. It's a pity I can never wake myself up, forced to endure every horrific, blood-splattered detail.

Just like my real torture.

Wick leans his long frame over the table, my stomach clenching at his rotten breath. A limp strand of brown hair escapes from his ponytail and tickles my cheek. I struggle against the straps at wrist and ankle, my naked body writhing on a cold, hard surface.

Wick's plump lips, too full for his weaselly face, stretch into a smile. "Have you not realised how futile it is to fight? Though, please, don't stop. It will be exquisite when you break."

"Fuck you, Daniel."

I'm getting braver in my nightmares. At first, I mewled and begged, too terrified to do anything else.

Not that it changes a damn thing. No matter how much I swear or fight, Wick always gets what he wants.

My eyes dart around the torture room from the shelves of shining implements to the emergency exit mocking me through a strip of glass in the far door. A chair bolted to the floor sits next to the table, loose straps hanging open on the armrests and legs.

He electrocuted me in it until I soiled myself, spasming too much to control my own body. A hook on the cheerful pink wall is where he hung my bound hands and whipped me, the ridges of scars on my back a constant reminder.

Wick runs his hand down my front, his pointed nails scraping my breast. I gasp before I can swallow it. A wave of goosebumps follows his touch.

"Pay attention, girlie," he says. "You and I have such little time together, I'm loath to waste any of it on your daydreaming."

I screw my eyes shut.

Wake up. *Wake up, wake up, wake up, you masochistic bitch!*

Icy metal presses against my nipple. I flinch and my eyes snap open. Wick raises the knife to caress my face, tracing burning lines. Blood trickles down my cheek and dampens my hair. The knife moves lower, circling my breast and lingering over my stomach.

Wick licks his lips and his black eyes sparkle. "I cannot wait to see what your insides look like, girlie—"

"—and I can't wait to welcome you home, Anita."

Wick's face shifts to the Egyptian-princess features of Dorothea Nadir, her fringe falling into eyes as dark and fathomless as the beady stare of a crow. Bronzed fingers grip the hilt of the knife, the blade pointed towards the delicate flesh beneath my sternum.

"Dorothea, wait—"

The tip slices my skin and sinks slowly. A bead of blood wells.

"Call me Morrighan."

"Screw you, *Dorothea.*"

Her smile flashes, her golden earrings jangling and brushing her shoulders.

The knife bites deep.

A howl reverberates in my skull and off the red-daubed walls. Dorothea jerks downward and the blade catches on my pubic bone. The world explodes in scorching white—white agony, white vision, my pale guts bleached under the harsh light of the fluorescents. The only sounds my shrieking and the splash of blood on the floor.

A new, ripping pain.

Dorothea grins at me, elbow-deep in my abdominal cavity, her face dotted red. An awful, tearing tug and she grips something resembling a giant, glistening bean in her bloody hand.

My kidney.

She tosses it over her shoulder and it splats on the floor. Her cold, cold fingers slip into the fiery hell of my abdomen, the pain too overwhelming to describe. She gnaws her lip, a frown of concentration on her face, her hands searching...

Searching...

"You can stop this any time, Anita," she says, her scorching touch stroking my liver. A jagged pressure increases as she tightens her grip, my connective tissue stretching and pinging. "All you have to do is—"

"Morrighan!" I scream. *"Morrighan!"*

My body jerks.

Is she still yanking on my liver, the lying cow?

Hands hold my shoulders and shake me.

I suck in a breath. "Morri—"

166

"Anita, baby, wake up."

My shout becomes a whine as I blink awake, my heart thundering against my ribs. Blake leans over me, his anxious face a mix of shadows and soft light from a lamp on the bedside table.

My trembling fingers reach for his cheek. "Are you—"

"Real." He smiles and captures my hand, kissing the knuckles. "I'm real. It was a nightmare."

My gaze zips around the antique furniture and salmon-pink walls.

Where the hell am I? This isn't the Townhouse.

"We're in the new and improved Downing Street," Blake says. "Safest building in England."

Bursey decided it made more sense for us to remain in his humble residence than travel to the Townhouse. He'd shipped our amassed belongings to a bedroom on the second floor while we attended his Cabinet meeting. He wanted us close and available at any moment for the intensive briefing and training to prepare us for returning to—

My shivers travel from my hand to the rest of me.

"Don't make me go back," I say, fear like the taste of pennies in my throat. "I don't want to go back there."

It's harder to be courageous in the darkest hours of the night.

Blake gathers me in his arms and rocks me, his heartbeat steady under my ear. "We can run. Sneak out of New London. Travelling through this country will be easy compared to no man's land."

"And what if Alba gu Brath launch a nuclear war we could have stopped?"

He shrugs. "We hide in the Irish Tunnel."

"None of this would have happened without Marshall and The People's Republic."

"Marshall got what he deserved."

"Yeah, but what about everybody else dragged into a war we should never have started?"

Goddamn Marshall. He ruined the legacy of The People's Republic. I have to set it right.

It's what Ailsa would have wanted.

"Ah, fuck," I sigh. "I have to go back."

"Is that what your nightmare was about?"

"Not at first. It was the usual—Wick, the torture chamber, me strapped down. But then Wick turned into the leader of Alba gu Brath and she gutted me."

Blake kisses my temple, the warmth of him and the gentle rocking soothing my nerves. "I hate that we have to go back, too. I just want to keep you safe but I can't protect you from all the arseholes in that damn country."

"You do all right."

"I can't stand it if you get hurt, Anita."

I curl tighter in his arms. "I know. The thought of what might happen to you terrifies me but I couldn't do it without you. I can't do it without you. I love you."

He bends his head to kiss me, a fine tremor transferred between us.

Is it him shaking, or me?

Probably both.

"I love you. I'm with you. Always."

"You're going to make me cry again."

He pauses in the act of wiping his face. "You and your girlish softness."

I laugh and hug him hard. He hugs me back and Scotland

doesn't seem so scary anymore.

That'll change when my boots hit the ground but in this moment, I'm safe and warm and loved.

Blake eases away and fiddles with his dog-tags, unclipping the shorter beaded chain, one embossed metal plate slipping into his hand. He holds it out to me and I take it, brushing my thumb over the words 'Blake O'Riley, Nationless, Livingston'.

"Swap for one of yours," he says. "The People's Republic one. That's who you are to me."

My trembling fingers struggle to unclasp my dog-tags. I drop the single plate into his waiting palm and thread his tag next to mine while he mirrors me.

"Does this mean we're engaged?"

I mean for it to be a joke but my wobbling voice betrays me.

His smirk punches straight to my gut. "Damn right it does."

Holy *shit*.

Before I can hyperventilate or swoon in his arms—been there, done that—he captures my mouth, his slim, perfect body pressing me to the covers.

Everything vanishes but him.

Him and his name hanging next to my heart.

26

I step into the war room and Major-General Lamb thrusts a necklace into my face, a purple stone pendant swinging on a short, silver chain.

"Well, this is awkward," I say. "I didn't get you anything."

A muscle in his cheek twitches. "It's a simple transmitter since you refused a neuralnet implant. Twist and pull the stone at each end to release the mechanism and activate the device. A signal will be pulsed when you press the revealed button."

"You just have these things lying around?"

"You have no idea what we have lying around, Miss Carmichael."

Man, he really doesn't like me.

Blake teases the pendant from Lamb's white-knuckled grip and fastens it around my throat, his fingertips stroking the nape of my neck.

Play nice.

"What does the signal do, Major-General?"

Lamb spins on his heel and strides for the bank of screens, waving us impatiently towards the nearest seats at the long table.

"If we intercept the signal, we know our Intelligence is

confirmed—Alba gu Brath are building nuclear weapons, or other weapons of mass destruction. It will be our cue to mobilise."

The familiar, blurry image of Inverness appears on the screens, Lamb's broad shoulders blocking a tiny portion as he paces in front of it. He folds his hands in the small of his back, the universal posture of all military men (and those who like to pretend).

"Now, let's start at the beginning. Your first objective—"

"Sorry to interrupt, but will the transmitter set off a scanner? I can't wear it if it will immediately warn—"

"No," Lamb barks, his fingers pinching the bridge of his nose. "The transmitter is inactive until you release the mechanism. It will not register on any scanner unless it is activated. The neuralnet implant is the same but you did not give me a chance to explain in your haste to dismiss it. Unless Alba gu Brath routinely submit their prisoners to an MRI scan, there is no way to detect it. We are not bumbling incompetents, Miss Carmichael."

"Didn't say you were but it's still a no."

He huffs out a breath. "Mr O'Riley, I was hoping you could be the voice of reason—"

"Sorry, sir. I'm with Anita."

We grin at each other while Lamb shakes his head and turns back to the screen.

He must hate working with us. We don't do mute and obedient, "Yes sir, no sir," bullshit.

Not anymore.

"Will the signal get past the jammers?" I say.

"We will deal with those. Your first objective is to confirm whether Alba gu Brath are constructing weapons of mass destruction, be it nuclear or some other form of long-range ballistic missile. You will be dropped here, seven miles to the north-east along the Moray Firth coast."

The screens change to a satellite image, the area over Inverness like looking through warped glass, little visible but a swirl of colours. Lamb taps a grey splodge surrounded by squares of yellow and green.

"It's hidden from view of the heavily guarded Kessock Bridge by this headland and is far enough from Inverness to be a drop point that won't alert the encampment whilst close enough for a patrol to pick you up."

"Wait a minute. You're relying on a patrol from the encampment to pick us up? Is that how you did it with the other teams? Maybe it's the reason you've heard nothing from most of them. The soldiers shot them on sight. We have to do it different—"

"They are not soldiers," Lamb says, his blue eyes blazing. "They are rebels and terrorists. Soldiers protect their country, not descend it into chaos for their own selfish agenda."

Can't argue there.

"As for a different method of infiltration, Miss Carmichael? There is none. We cannot fly over, we cannot approach closer than several hundred metres. The only way to get inside Inverness is to be taken in. As a prisoner." Air whistles through Lamb's gritted teeth, bright spots of red flushing his cheeks.

"Great," I say. "That happens to be my area of expertise."

How many men has he lost to Alba gu Brath's defences?

A shit-tonne if his anger and frustration are anything to go by. Phillip Carrbridge must have missed the opportunity to tell him of his delight with laser-cameras and how wonderful they are.

Lamb stares at me in silence for a full two minutes, a slow frown wrinkling his brow. The redness fades from his face.

Blake covers my hand in his. "She's not wrong. Five-time prisoner and still breathing. In our country, that's rare. We're not incompetent either, Major-General."

"No, perhaps not." Lamb runs his hands over his scalp, his fingers rasping through his short hair. "Once you are inside the encampment, do whatever it takes to access this location in the north between the canal and the river."

He circles an area that might be Merkinch but it's too smudged to pick out any detail.

"This is where the analysed images were taken. Confirm if there are underground missile silos. If Dorothea Nadir happens to brag about possessing nuclear warheads then that is also acceptable confirmation. The transmission of the signal from the device around your neck will complete objective one. Your second objective is to disable the power to the defences, allowing my mobilised forces to enter. You will be extracted once Alba gu Brath is neutralised."

Easy-peasy.

Jesus Christ, we're going to die.

Maybe we should take a whole battalion of special forces. How the hell can Blake and I do this on our own?

Okay, he infiltrated Dunbar by himself, stole one of their jets and rescued me from a rooftop while I merrily crumbled the encampment with a rocket launcher. And I've escaped from numerous dire situations, maybe not intact but alive.

It seems woefully inadequate to what we're expected to face in Inverness.

I wait for Lamb to cock his finger and laugh and explain how it's all a joke. No risk of another nuclear war, no need to return to Scotland. Just a quiet, normal life.

"Now, this is what we know about Alba gu Brath's defences," Lamb says, his eye twitching at the screen.

Crap. This shit is real.

I press my lips together to stop myself from begging him to send men with us. Backup would be nice but the disappearance of his previous teams makes me uneasy. They must have done something to trigger Dorothea's suspicion. Talked weird military-speak, acted like professionals, owned shiny new equipment. Or she has a policy of slaughtering everyone picked up by her patrols.

Textbook leader behaviour.

I smother a wave of nausea and focus on Lamb.

What he knows about Alba gu Brath's defences can be summed up in two words: not fucking much.

Okay, three words.

Image after image flickers on the screen until I blink to confirm it's not my eyes that are blurred.

Going by how impossible it is to approach from land or air or sea, I guess a particle beam boundary fence and laser-cameras at a minimum, with a very powerful aerial defence system.

Even ours let something through. And it didn't activate past a certain height.

How is she targeting the drones?

I'd respect her ingenuity if the term 'evil genius' wasn't so synonymous with 'faction leader'.

Lamb describes the operation once more in full—how we'll reach the drop point, what to do when—if—a patrol takes us inside Inverness and doesn't blow our heads off, how to find the power source for the defences, different scenarios we might encounter. On and on until my head swells with information.

At least he's thorough instead of packing us onto a vehicle and waving us off with a smug smile, happy he'll never have to see us again.

A fitness test and medical exam consume the afternoon and evening, Blake and I hooked to exercise machines monitoring our heart rate, blood pressure and lactic acid build-up, plus a hundred other indices that mean nothing to me. Lamb seems surprised at our performance, neither of us embarrassing ourselves despite the sedentary lifestyle we've recently become accustomed to.

No running for our lives or jumping off buildings.

Boring, really.

"Well, you are both in fine physical condition," he finally concedes, Blake and I slumped on a bench in the underground gym. "Although, Miss Carmichael, you appear to be missing your spleen and a quarter of your liver. Your cardiac enzymes are also above normal limits."

"No idea what you're talking about, Major-General."

"Your heart muscle is damaged."

"Oh."

Goddamn Wick and his electric shocks.

"What does that mean?" Blake says, his hand gripping mine tight.

"Nothing for her overall health, which is fine, Mr O'Riley. The levels are not high enough to indicate impairment. I'm curious to know whether the heart injury occurred at the same time as the liver and spleen."

"It did not," I say.

Lamb's eyes drill into me, one brow raised. "You've also

been shot, cut and whipped."

I give him a blank expression. "What's your point, Major-General?"

"You've been in the wars, Miss Carmichael."

"Only one war, sir," I say. "Only one."

27

"What are you *doing!?*" squeaks an incredulous voice. "That's Ministry of Defence *property!*"

I pause on my knees in the act of battering my SA80 A3 rifle with a ball pein hammer. Blake glances up from his cross-legged position on the coated metal of the hanger floor, or the hanger aft bay as he likes to remind me, scraping his knife along the barrel of his rifle.

I raise my eyebrow at the man in his dark-blue uniform. "We're trying to make them look well-used. If we're caught with shiny new weapons, they'll know we're not who we say we are, um, Lieutenant Richardson."

I'm getting better at reading the rank on the epaulette in the centre of the chest of the naval uniforms. This one has a single golden bar below a gold bar and a circle. And his surname embroidered in white on the top left breast pocket.

Handy on a warship carrying over six hundred people but with the capacity for well over a thousand.

The HMS *Queen Elizabeth* is the biggest aircraft carrier I've ever seen.

Okay, she's the only aircraft carrier I've ever seen.

It takes twenty minutes just to walk from one point to the next. *Twenty minutes.* On a hunk of metal floating in the sea.

Yet Blake and I stand out wherever we go, clearly not military despite our boots and combats.

We arrived on the warship yesterday, delivered by high-speed rail to RAF Coningsbay in Lincolnshire then flown in a Merlin helicopter out to the heaving nothingness of the North Sea and the anchored HMS *Queen Elizabeth*. A whirlwind journey from the bright lights of the city to echoing metal corridors and the throb of diesel engines.

Bursey communicated via neuralnet with the other world leaders for a temporary exemption to the no-fly treaty and they were only too happy to sign off, as long as none of them have to go to Scotland.

As well as the no-fly treaty, the rest of the world has decommissioned all its nuclear weapons.

So if Dorothea Nadir starts a nuclear war, the rest will be fucked, particularly as the HMS *Queen Elizabeth* contains the only squadron of planes left in the British Army.

Blake loves it, geeking out on the Lockheed Martin F-35B Lightning III jets lined up on the unending expanse of the flight deck and in the hanger bays. He flew all manner of aircraft as aerial team leader in Nationless but the Lieutenant Commander in charge of the air squadron on the HMS *Queen Elizabeth* refuses to let him take one of the F-35s out for a spin.

The spoilsport.

"You can't just destroy it!" Lieutenant Richardson continues, his wide eyes darting between us.

"We're not destroying it. She told you what we're doing." Blake bends his head and returns to scarifying the surface of his gun.

"We're also going to rub dirt on them when we get back on

land," I say helpfully.

Richardson's mouth opens and closes. He pivots on his heel and marches towards the air squadron complex of rooms, probably to complain about us to his ranking officer. I whack another dent in my rifle and assess it with a critical eye. The diamond-patterned carbon fibre coating is dulled and scratched, the dents giving it a battered appearance.

Perfect.

I yawn and stretch my arms above my head.

Long day, already nearing dawn, but we're staying up late to acclimatise. The mission/assignment/last-ditch-attempt starts at 2300 tomorrow.

Or today.

I've been too busy to dwell on it, which is probably for the best. Thinking about it looses the panic in my stomach to wriggle and squirm and bite at my insides. It reminds me death is highly likely. Mine, or Blake's, or both. And the thought of Blake hurt or dead makes me want to—

Fuck. Quit thinking about it. Winging it saved my ass before. This assignment will be no different to the others.

Alba gu Brath won't know what hit them.

I find myself stroking the dings and scratches on the Glock 17 in my ankle holster and force myself to stop.

I almost hugged the man in charge of the naval stores when he signed it out to me. I hugged Blake instead. He laughed and pretended disappointment that his wasn't a Browning, the Nationless handgun of choice.

Blake sheathes his knife and cracks his spine. I get distracted by the stretch of his t-shirt across his chest and shoulders.

"Your fan-boys are amassing again." He tilts his chin towards a squat doorway opened by spinning a thick, metal wheel.

Four men huddle inside the door, their uniforms snug over broad shoulders and thighs. The shine of their eyes flick our way, a burst of laughter echoing in the airy hanger bay.

"Only because there are hardly any women on this boat. If there were, your fan group would be bigger than mine."

It seems most of the men of the Royal Navy don't care one bit about the encampment I destroyed or how many people I've killed. Not because they're hardened veterans themselves but because they don't believe it. They look at me and see a slim, blonde woman, more beautiful than average. I should be sewing pretty, recycled dresses, not shooting people in the face.

Sexism. It's still out there.

"I doubt it," Blake says. "And please don't call it a boat in their earshot. You know how defensive they get."

I grin. "They make it too easy to wind them up."

"This is why you always get into trouble."

"Hey, you knew I had a mouth on me from the moment we met."

"True." He smirks and crawls towards me, his hair flopping across his forehead, the heat in his eyes playing havoc with my pulse. "I do quite like that mouth of yours."

His lips capture the offending body part and tease it into submission, his hand reaching up to tangle his fingers in my hair. I grip his t-shirt, his dog-tags beneath the material in my fist. My name and his, next to his heart.

A loud wolf whistle forces us to stop.

This is also why we stand out. Apparently, public displays of affection are unprofessional on a working vessel.

"How about we pick this up in our bunk?" I whisper, refusing to glance over my shoulder at the snickering men.

"You mean my bunk? You haven't slept in yours yet."

For some ridiculous propriety, I was assigned a bunk in the empty cabin neighbouring Blake's, Blake the only person in his cabin of four bunks.

There's no way I'm sleeping anywhere but next to him.

Preferably on top of him.

He takes my hands and pulls me to my feet, our rifles tucked tight to our backs on their slings. Unfortunately, the doorway behind the men leads to our cabins, unless we want to choose another door and risk getting lost in the labyrinthine corridors of the three-levelled vessel.

Dunbar's famous warships are babies in comparison to the *Queen Elizabeth*. No, not babies, *cells*.

Positively mitochondrial.

The four men range themselves to block our path as soon as we near the door, the ringleader standing slightly forward of the others. An uncomfortable reminder of a forest path, muscled men and Blake battered in the head by a rifle butt.

"Benson, Dolt, Quagmire, Russell," I say, nodding at each of them. "Don't you need your beauty sleep for another day of swabbing the decks?"

They have no insignia on their epaulettes, say they're just cadets, but it bugs me.

They're hiding something.

The positive attention was a relief, at first, the banter funny rather than annoying or ominous.

No women throwing acid in my face.

I answered their questions, joked with them, smiled. They seemed to take it as flirting rather than friendliness.

"Now, why do you have to be all disrespectful, Carmichael?" Russell drawls, glancing at his comrades behind him, his blue eyes sparkling. "We just came to wish you goodnight. Big day."

"How kind of you. Goodnight then."

"Yeah, 'night, Russell," Blake says.

None of them move.

Russell's gaze flicks to Blake for a nanosecond, a sneer on his thin mouth. "When are you going to get yourself a real man instead of this skinny goth-boy?"

Blake smiles pleasantly but says nothing, his hands loose at his sides.

He never responds to their mocking. His brother teased him for his black hair and slim build, so like his mother's. Both of them beautiful.

His confidence can't be shaken by some navy beefcake.

Russell's jaw bunches.

And Blake says I wind them up? What a hypocrite.

"The same day you do," I say.

Russell frowns. "What?"

"She's implying you're gay," Dolt says, his gaze travelling lazily up and down my body. The shortest of the four, his high cheekbones and almond eyes hint at something exotic in his ancestry.

Russell frowns harder but then his face smooths to a cocky grin. "Oh, baby, I'm definitely not gay. I'd be happy to prove it to you."

"Don't call me baby."

Cue jeering exclamations and nudges from the cronies.

"What would you prefer—sweetie, honeybunch, hot-piece-of-ass?"

"Get out of the way, Russell. Or I'll make you move."

He laughs but it fades quickly, replaced by derision as he

switches his attention to Blake. "You going to hide behind your woman and let her do the fighting?"

Blake treats him to a smirk—dark, knowing and sexy.

Not that Russell will think of it in those terms.

Or maybe he does. Maybe that's why he took an instant dislike to Blake.

"Wasn't aware we were fighting but she can take care of herself," Blake says.

Russell snorts, planting his hands on his hips and widening his stance. "Go on then, sweetheart. *Make* me move. This'll be good."

I peek at Blake. He shrugs.

Well, Russell dared me, so…

I step closer and Russell tenses.

"So twitchy. You sure you want this?"

"Oh, I want it, honey."

"Then why don't you—"

I swing my left arm out as if I'm going to slap him. He catches my wrist easily, a smug smile blooming on his slab of a face.

He sees me as a girl so he thinks I'll hit like a girl.

His mistake.

Girls in my world hit to wound.

I tug on my arm and fake a stumble. Russell's other hand comes up to grab me. My knee catches him square in the balls, hard enough for them to pop into his abdomen. His face flickers from red to white to grey to green. He collapses to the floor and cradles himself.

"You're right, that *was* good," I say. "'Night, Russell. Douchebags."

We escape while their mouths are hanging open and wait

until we're in Blake's cabin before we burst out laughing.

"They might make us pay for that later," Blake says, scrubbing tears from his cheeks.

"Maybe, or we never see them again. We leave in a few hours."

Blake pulls me into his arms and his hands slide around my waist. I slip my fingers up his chest to stroke along his collarbone.

"Then let's waste no more time"—he bends his head, a smirk on his lips—"baby."

28

Moonlight silvers the expanse of the *Queen Elizabeth*'s flight deck, glinting off the wingtips and rotor blades of the slumbering military vehicles. The two looming islands of the warship—one for the bridge, the other for flight control—interrupt a breath-taking sky crammed with stars.

Major-General Lamb, delivered by skiff to see us off, marches us towards the port edge of the deck where a small group waits, dressed in dark clothing and black wool caps, the air chilled so far out to sea. I fiddle with my rifle, checking and rechecking its position on the sling, the safety on. A light pack on my back—stamped on and ripped a few times to match our doctored weapons and clothes—carries spare ammo, a tiny sleeping bag, heat blocks, a change of clothes, a lighter and a water purifier. Blake's pack also has boil-in-the-bag food packets, the MOD label carefully removed, a water bottle, small first aid kit and some battered cans of fruit.

Enough to explain how we survived in no man's land but nothing to raise suspicion.

We have no idea how long an Alba gu Brath patrol will take to find us. Lamb is confident it'll happen quickly, maybe before it gets light, but that seems optimistic. I anticipate a fraught wait, hoping abominations won't find us first.

We near the huddled group and pale faces turn towards us. I slam to a halt.

"What the hell are they doing here?"

"Ah, good, you've met my operatives," Lamb says, apparently unperturbed by the growl in my voice.

Russell, Dolt, Quagmire and Benson glare at us with varying degrees of contempt, though Dolt still does his usual wandering-eye thing.

It seems he doesn't hate me enough not to ogle.

"I thought they were with the Royal Navy."

Lamb clears his throat. "A slight misdirection. They are part of my A-squadron."

"You agreed to us going alone."

"And so you shall, Miss Carmichael. My operatives will be dropped at a separate location to the west of Inverness whereas you will be dropped to the east. They will disable the nearest jammers. You will not see each other unless you meet within the encampment. I cannot in good faith leave the nation's—*the world's*—security in the hands of two untrained civilians. My men are built for this kind of mission."

He claps Russell on the shoulder. Russell puffs his chest and flashes me a smug smile.

I want to knee him in the balls again.

"Shame about the ones you lost," Blake says, quietly, earning himself a scowl from the gathered military men.

I stab my finger at Russell and his cronies. "If they jeopardise Blake and me in any way, so help me god, Lamb, I'll make you eat your fucking medals."

I hate to waste a good threat when it's unlikely I'll carry it out. If the goon squad blow our cover, I'll end up in the same place as the rest of Lamb's missing men.

In a ditch, Blake's body cooling beside me.

Dolt jerks forward. "How dare you threaten the Major-General. You show him the proper respect!"

"Stand down, Dolt," Lamb says, patting the air. "I've come to learn Miss Carmichael is not one for doing anything in the proper manner."

It's how I've lived so long.

"Yes, Sir. Sorry, Sir." Dolt settles himself like a soothed dog.

"Now, if you've finished arguing with me, Miss Carmichael, are you ready to board?"

"That depends. You have any more surprises?"

"I believe everything should occur according to your briefing from this moment on."

"Great," I mutter.

Lamb waves us towards the edge of the deck where a vertical chute disappears into the darkness down the side of the ship. Water slaps against the hull far, far below, invisible in the black. I swallow and ease away, not particularly comfortable with heights.

"Gentleman, would you show Miss Carmichael and Mr O'Riley how it's done?"

One after the other, Russell, Dolt, Quagmire and Benson drop into the chute, a whisper of canvas the only sound.

No splash, no agonised scream as they smash their body to pieces on some hard surface.

"What is it?" I say.

"We modelled it on the mass evacuation system used in large cruise-liners. The chute connects to a landing platform, which in turn connects you to your deployment vessel, the *Sea Shadow*."

Sea Shadow—how fancy. In the briefing, it was 'stealth ship'.

Blake slides his arm around my waist. "So which of us gets to go first?"

"Definitely you this time."

"Coward."

He kisses me, a slow exploration of lips despite the watchful eyes of Lamb. His thumb brushes my cheekbone then he salutes to Lamb and steps into the void. My heart constricts and my boots hurry to the edge.

"I'm fine, Anita." Blake's soft voice echoes up the chute. "You can come down."

It's scary how much he can read my mind.

No, not scary—wonderful.

"Good luck, Miss Carmichael," Lamb says as I prepare to jump, or fall. "We will await the signal."

I quirk my mouth. "Ours or theirs?"

"Either would suffice."

What a rousing pep-talk.

"Then may the best team win."

I hop off the edge, and wind rushes in my ears. The drop lasts a couple of seconds, my arms and legs pressed together. I bounce at the bottom and tumble to a stop at Blake's feet.

"Hey, baby," he says with a grin.

I wobble upright and we cross the gently undulating break-away platform to the twin-hull curve of the *Sea Shadow*. The dark coating absorbs the moonlight, reflecting nothing, smooth and unbroken by antennae or equipment.

The ship is designed to skim along the surface of the water like a pond skater, copied from a similar vessel built by the US Navy.

The door, flush with the side of the craft, hisses shut behind us, sealing us into a cramped compartment lit by a dull-red light. The goon squad are already strapped into seats fastened to the walls.

"Where's the captain?" I say, an archway opening into an empty bridge, the windows dark. Buttons and screens flash and blink on the blocky instrument panel.

Dolt sniffs. "It's automated. It's just you and us for the next few hours."

Brilliant.

Blake and I strap ourselves in to seats opposite the goon squad, the maximum distance possible from them without swimming alongside. A clunk signals the separation of the landing platform and a light vibration shivers through the ship.

"Next stop, Scotland," Blake whispers, taking my hand, his fingers cold in mine.

The nerves return in the silence of the boat, the urge to get off expanding like a scream in my throat.

Christ, it's really happening.

We're going home.

29

Scotland is the same as I left it—a scorched ruin of what it used to be. Not that I see much as the *Sea Shadow* slips into a quiet bay at 2am, the door whispering open to darkness and the slap of water.

"Welcome home, refugees," Russell sneers. "Bet you don't last five minutes."

"That's where you're wrong. This is our country, now. We lived this shit for ten years."

"Not in this part, you didn't."

I shrug. "More than you have."

Blake and I unstrap ourselves and head for the door, a warm, salty breeze swirling inside. The horizon to the west glows bronze against the night, a jutting headland hiding the encampment of Inverness. A strip of lapping sea separates us from the beach and the black hummock of land beyond. Blake lowers himself first, the boat bobbing gently, his boots splashing in water.

"Enjoy the rest of your short life, sweetheart," Russell says.

I curl my fingers around the edge of the door and treat him to a winning smile. "Try not to piss yourself when they capture you, asshole."

Cold water glugs into my boots and up to my ankles.

Blake and I slosh towards the shore, a faint rippling the only indication the *Sea Shadow* is on the move.

It's hard to pick out against the blackness of sea and sky.

I don't envy the goon squad for staying on the boat. They have to pass under the heavily guarded Kessock Bridge to reach their drop-point.

I swing my rifle on its sling and into my hands, scanning the beach. "This feels like a huge step backwards."

The beach, the chill of the sea, the heavy thump of my heart remind me of the night Blake and I attempted to steal one of Dunbar's warships, and failed.

"Can you believe it's been a month? I thought we'd come back one day when the war was over." The sweep of his rifle mirrors mine.

Sand slithers beneath my boots, coating the toes in what looks like snow under the shine of the moon. My eyes adjust quickly, my wet socks squelching with each step.

"This is a bit conspicuous if we're picked up immediately."

"We fancied a night-time paddle. Or waded through a river." Blake stops a clump of broom from swinging into my face on the edge of the narrow beach, holding it in place for me to pass through.

The thicket surrounds an old golf course, the grass over-grown, a lone, tattered flag wavering in the wind. Sand buries the remains of a road bordering rank agricultural fields that will deliver us to the factory picked out by Lamb.

We'll rest there until daylight, moving closer to the encampment in the hope we'll be spotted by a patrol.

But not too close.

The boundary fence starts beyond what used to be a retail park on the outskirts of Inverness.

The bobbing heads of oats brush against my thighs, out-competed by non-agricultural grasses and weeds. I place my feet carefully on the hardened, uneven dirt, the barrel of my rifle in constant motion, Blake watching our backs.

"You think they have giant snake abominations in this part of the country?"

I shiver despite the warmth of the night. "I'm trying not to think about abominations right now."

I widen my eyes, as if that will help, my imagination conjuring visions of dripping teeth and shining claws.

"I liked what came after the snake attack."

The warmth in Blake's voice banishes the unease. My boots crunch over the flecks of a rusted barbed wire fence and a dirt track into a field of nodding daisies.

Words can't get past the sudden obstruction in my throat, stoppered by the relief of having him with me.

Even in the midst of death and disaster, I want to hug him.

The field ends in a block of pine trees, the Christmassy smell of sap thick on the air. We skirt around to the remnants of a railway line and the pale, hulking buildings of the factory. The moonlight reflects off a pond beside a car park, one ancient, burned-out specimen left behind. Opposite the car park, a pile of wood slowly rots, tufts of grass and slick fungi growing between the trunks. Wide doors gape into deeper darkness, the sagging body of a curtain-sided truck sticking out, the material ripped and flapping on the frame.

"Too open inside the factory. Let's check out the office building." Blake waves his rifle and we lope across the car park.

Glass cracks under my boots, the sliding doors fractured and canted. The light of the moon fails to penetrate the blackness. I click on the torch mounted on my rifle barrel, the bright glow highlighting faded blue walls and piles of dust. A door straight ahead appears to lead into the factory buildings.

We check the other rooms on the ground floor—a board-room and a cluster of offices including a nurse's station. Blake nods at my tilted chin and I lead us up the stairs to the top level. More meeting rooms, toilets and an open-plan office space, the smeared windows looking out over the front door and the car park.

"Since we're not bothered about attracting attention, let's build a fire," I say. "It'd be nice to dry my boots."

"And, you know, I could eat."

I smooth my hand over my cramped stomach. "How can you think about eating?"

He slides his arms around me and tucks his chin on my shoulder, the moon bright through the glass and gilding the ratty furniture separated by partitions.

"I'd say we'll be okay but I don't know that and I try not to lie. I'm pretty confident you and I will still be alive, however this ends."

"What do you think she's like?"

"Dorothea Nadir? No idea. Maybe she'll be the leader who surprises us."

"It's not a good sign when she refers to herself as a warrior goddess."

"True." Blake nuzzles my ear. "You're the only warrior goddess in this country."

"You, my friend, are biased."

"And you never see yourself like others do. Like I do."

I turn in his arms, his face perfectly level with mine. His eyes are dark, the colour hidden in the night, his skin kissed by moonlight. My lips capture his, my fingers tangled in his hair, his hands tight on my hips, rubbing me against him.

I gasp and pull away. "I miss the pod. We didn't have to worry about being naked in no man's land and letting our guard down."

"Didn't stop us before. And considering we want Alba gu Brath to find us, melting their faces off would be counter-productive."

I slap his chest and ease out of his arms. "Let's get a fire going first and build a warning system. We want them to find us but we're not amateurs."

"Of course," he says, swiping my hand and kissing my knuckles. "We are the epitome of professionalism."

I gather pieces of wood from the plentiful supply outside, stacking it in his arms while he trails after me, the pile balanced against his chest. An explosion, softened by distance, crackles over the darkened landscape.

"What did they make here, anyway?" I say, eyeing a sliver of wood. "What's OSB mean?"

"Something-something-board?"

"Helpful."

I construct a pile of furniture at the bottom of the stairs and balance other pieces carefully on my way up, ready to topple if anyone breathes on them. Blake builds a fire on a broken concrete slab in the office room, forcing open stiffened windows for ventilation. Flickering orange light dances on the glass and cavorts on the roof, the smoke sucked into the night. A pot bubbles on the flames, bags of food floating within.

Turns out I *am* hungry.

We nudge our boots and socks close to the fire, our feet pale and delicate on the ribbed carpet. I take a second to appreciate the figure Blake makes in his t-shirt and combats, painted by the light of the flames.

"You're staring at me again," he says.

I cock my head. "I feel like we're missing something. Wait—I got it."

I spit on my hands and rub them over my boots. Blake smirks at me but stays still while I trace some mud across his cheekbone and pat the rest on his clothes.

"There. Now you seem like you've been out here for weeks. Reminds me of how you looked when we first met."

Torn navy t-shirt and combats, dirt streaking his skin, his eyes shadowed by grief and exhaustion.

No hint of that now, only a tenderness that tightens my stomach.

He suffered in no man's land but didn't hesitate to follow me back.

I hug him hard and bury my face in his neck. He strokes my hair.

"You okay?"

"Please don't die," I whisper to the steady beat of his pulse.

30

Blake shakes me awake to a meagre fire and the first blush of dawn through the windows.

"Someone's here."

I scrub gritty eyes and climb out of his lap. "How long was I asleep?"

"Just under three hours. Listen."

Faint scraping, a rattle and a hushed curse.

Heavy, heavy silence.

We wriggle into our dry socks and moist boots and crouch in the hallway, out of sight of the person trying to negotiate my obstacle course on the stairs. A conversation of hissing whispers follows. I glance at Blake, his fingers tight on his rifle, his shoulder pressed to the wall opposite me.

"We know yer up there." The man's deep voice floats to us, his Scottish accent thicker than mine and Blake's put together. "Ye dinnae need to hide, we're no' here to hurt ye."

I cock my eyebrow at Blake. He nods.

Hearing a woman may change their response. Maybe they'll assume I'm alone and hesitate before they attack. It depends on whether they're as sex-obsessed as every other male soldier I've encountered.

An object clatters.

"For god's sake, Dunn!"

"You gowk—"

"What if you're lying?" I say, and the angry muttering ceases. "The second I show my face, you'll shoot me."

"I understand yer concern, ma'am, but yer obviously no' from around here. We're Alba gu Brath."

"You saying you don't shoot people?"

"Well, no. This is a war zone. But we dinnae shoot anyone genuinely seeking refuge."

"So you're just doing your civic duty rounding up the strays?"

Blake quirks his mouth.

He looks tired, though there'll be no sleep for him any time soon since he took first watch. The three hours I slept feel worse than none at all.

"The more people on our side, the stronger we are. Anyone we pick up is given a fair chance tae prove they want to be one of us."

Then what happened to Lamb's men?

"And how do they do that?" I say. "You shove them out on a suicide mission and see who survives?"

"Nothing so extreme. We have a probationary period. And our leader is pretty good at reading people."

Blake and I share a look.

Well, she is a warrior goddess. Telepathy isn't too much of a stretch.

I shift, and grit crunches under my boots on the cracked linoleum. "What if I don't want to come with you?"

"We leave and wish ye good luck."

My eyebrows lift.

Most soldiers force you to do what they want or kill you if

you won't.

Live and let live is not anyone's motto.

"Consider this though, ma'am—if ye come with us, you'll be safe inside Inverness. We have plenty of food, hot water and comfy beds. I dinnae know how long you've been in no man's land but you'll likely die out here."

Shows what he knows. Blake survived two months with nothing. My two weeks were less impressive given my equipment, but still…

Oh, and we have the might of the British Army poised to assist.

"How many of you are there?" I say.

"In Inverness or doon here? Nearing a million at last count. Only six of us in my squad."

A million? How the hell do they fit in a town built for one tenth of that? And why have Saorsa or Soldiers of the Lost not taken advantage of their open-gate policy to send attackers in?

Alba gu Brath would be less accommodating if their strays kept blowing shit up.

"Sorry to rush ye, ma'am, but we need an answer. We dinnae like being outside the fence. This land is not ours anymore, but it will be again."

How poetic.

"I'll admit, it's tough out here. Some security would be a nice change, though trusting people has never done me any good before."

Blake gives me an affronted face. I grin, and flap my hand.

Not him. He's the exception to everything.

"Then in a show of good faith, allow me to send one of my men up to ye, unarmed. If you dinnae believe me, use him as a shield." Bodies shuffle in the entranceway below. "Dunn, give me yer rifle and get up there."

"Is this because I knocked over the box? Come on, man—"

"*Dunn.*"

A heavy sigh.

"Okay, ma'am, he's coming up. Please dinnae kill him but if ye accidentally shoot him in the foot, I'm prepared to let it slide."

"Har-de-har, you asshole," Dunn says.

The shriek of metal and crunch of wood muffle his voice. I change position to stand behind Blake, training my rifle on the top few steps visible over the solid banister.

Unless Dunn walks up the stairs backwards, he won't see me.

"Speaking of good faith, I'm not alone up here," I say, raising my voice over the racket of Dunn fighting through the barriers. "There's two of us."

"Yer friend has been very quiet."

Dunn's muttered curses provide a background chorus.

"We figured you might respond more amicably to me."

"I like to think of myself as an equal opportunities soldier."

I laugh. "You're different, I'll give you that. What's your name?"

"MacKelter, ma'am."

"I'm Anita and my *friend*"—Blake smirks at me over his shoulder—"is Blake."

Dunn's hands appear first, held high above a shaggy blond head and a figure that's all limbs. He cranes his neck, his back to me, stubble shadowing his jaw. Honey-brown eyes meet mine and he trips over the last step, sprawling in a heap of elbows and knees.

"She has a gun, Mac!"

"This is Scotland, of course she has a gun. Now, get off yer arse."

Dunn scrambles to his feet and thrusts his hands into the air, fidgeting on the top step, his eyes flicking from me towards the bottom of the stairs. Blake remains out of sight behind the banister.

"Don't move, Dunn," I say. "I'm coming closer."

His throat bobs. I signal for Blake to stay put and sidle over to Dunn, my rifle steady. Circling behind him, I press the barrel lightly to his back.

"I'm going to search you."

At his rapid nod, I pat him down, his body all bone and edges. No weapons. I peek past the sharp jut of his shoulder to the five faces staring up at me from the gloom of the lower level.

"Hullo, Anita," a huge man in the middle says, his white teeth flashing in a grin through a thick, ginger beard. "Is yer friend still too shy?"

"Oh, he's not shy, MacKelter. I just don't trust you yet."

"An honest woman. Such a rare breed."

A quiet snort from Blake's hiding place. I smother a smile.

SA80s hang loose in their slings, none pointed my way by the men at MacKelter's back. They seem relaxed but watchful, their eyes shining in the shadows. They're all wearing dark green combats and shirts, the insignia of a mountain range embroidered over the breast pocket, the silhouette of a stag on the highest peak.

"So what happens now? I'm afraid I'm unfamiliar with the protocol of collecting strays."

MacKelter chuckles. "Aye, I guess ye are. Just how far have

ye travelled?"

"I'm from Calders and Blake is from Livingston. So pretty far."

"The People's Republic and Nationless? I'm surprised ye didn't kill each other."

"We tried. Well, he tried."

"Anita," Blake says from behind the banister, "that's not exactly a glowing example of my character."

"I'm trying not to lie these days. And I deserved it."

He sighs.

I can't see him but he's definitely shaking his head at me.

"She must have done something pretty special to win ye over."

"She makes it very hard to hate her."

"I can imagine."

The five men give me an appreciative glance, or the sliver of me visible past Dunn's quivering shoulder. Most of it is blonde hair.

"You'd better not be checking out my woman," Blake says.

"Wouldnae dream of it." MacKelter's grin splits his beard and crinkles his eyes. "However, I would like—"

"*Mac*," Dunn whines, jiggling on the top step, "how long do I have to stand here with her gun in my spine?"

The men laugh and the back of Dunn's neck reddens.

MacKelter bows at the waist. "Begging yer pardon, Dunn. To answer yer question, Anita—let Dunn come down here before he wets himself then, if you and Blake decide yer comfortable with it, join us and let us take yer weapons. We have two jeeps outside to return us to Inverness."

"Blake?"

He stands from behind the banister. My heart leaps as if I

haven't seen him for days rather than minutes, separated by miles instead of a hunk of wall.

How did the women of Nationless get anything done with him wandering around?

"I would like to lie down on one of those comfy beds he mentioned." His light voice belies the tension in his face, his gaze intent on mine.

Will Alba gu Brath shoot us as soon as we're unarmed or will they throw us in a cell and mock our naiveté?

We have no choice. We need to get inside Inverness.

The safety of the free world depends on us.

31

Dunn scurries down the stairs to jeers from his comrades, scattering obstacles he somehow missed on his ascent. Blake joins me on the top step, our guns aimed at the floor. Our two groups regard each other for a beat of silence, the building creaking around us as the rising sun heats the exterior and chases the gloom from the entranceway.

"Blake," MacKelter says on a nod. "I see there's no point even trying to compete. Morrighan is going to love the pair of ye."

I manage not to grab Blake's hand for reassurance. "That sounds ominous."

"Wisnae meant to. Our leader is simply a collector—no, an appreciator—of, ah, fine things."

The assembled men share a look.

"My leader was the same," I say. "Pity he tried to hump all the fine things."

Blake turns his laugh into a cough but MacKelter guffaws and slaps his knee.

"I like you, Anita. Seems ye have some interesting stories to tell. You'll be popular at our gatherings, that's for sure."

"Gatherings?"

"We get together every month or so and talk about the old

days. Swap stories, sing. It's always nice to have newcomers when you've heard the same tale fifty times." His gaze shifts to Blake. "You'll be a hit with the lassies, no doubt about it. And probably a few of the lads."

Screw it.

I take Blake's hand and he squeezes my fingers.

"As long as they keep it friendly. I'm a one-woman guy."

"I can see why."

I suddenly feel very exposed despite my weapons and the heat of Blake at my side.

Shit. Am I blushing?

I duck my head at Blake. "Ready?"

He nods but skims a finger along my definitely pink-tinged cheek. "You not used to people complimenting you yet?"

"Most of the men I knew thought grabbing my ass was a compliment."

"Let's hope that doesn't happen here. They might chuck me out if I start breaking fingers."

I force myself to move or I'll linger on the top step all day, afraid of what comes next. Blake matches my pace down the stairs. The men ease back to offer us a semi-circle of space at the bottom, though the mountain of MacKelter makes it seem small.

"Thank you for trusting us." He offers a giant paw of a hand and we shake it. Gentle, hazel eyes flick between us, framed by the bushiness of his beard and brows. "If you wouldnae mind passing yer rifles to Dunn, we can get the awkward part over."

Blake relinquishes his first. I hesitate and frown at Dunn, my knuckles white around my weapon.

"Just remember I didn't hurt you."

His eyes widen. "I'm not going to hurt you, either."

Heard that before.

Two other men search Blake and me at the same time, claiming our knives and handguns. I flash a longing look at my Glock as the soldier fastens the holster around his waist, digging my nails into my palms to stop from lunging for it.

I hate being unarmed. It's the one good thing about returning to Scotland.

"It's amazing how much we depend on them now, eh?" MacKelter says with a deep chuckle. "To think we used to be a country withoot guns."

Have I forgotten how to control my expression in the few weeks I've spent in the normal world?

I need to be more careful.

The men sift through our packs, taking my spare ammo, before they hand them back. I cock an eyebrow and shrug mine on.

"We have our own supplies, which ye will of course be able to purchase, but there's no reason ye can't keep yours." MacKelter sweeps his arm towards the front door. "If you'll follow us out to the jeeps."

His men range ahead, their rifles raised, two guarding the entrance while two slink outside to cover the car park. Dunn hangs back, our SA80s clattering together on his shoulder.

"Purchase?" I say to MacKelter walking beside me.

The ground should shake under his tread.

"We have a credit system. Credits are earned through particular tasks and redeemed for buying the essentials or little perks, once you've saved enough. Goods can also be traded. We have a bustling market."

"But what if it takes us a while to earn credits?"

MacKelter pauses at the canted doors, two jeeps visible out the smudged glass. His men group around them, their guns scanning the rotten piles of wood and the gaping doorways into the rest of the factory.

"You'll receive a welcome package to last ye about a week but it's quite easy to earn credits. It's really just a way to encourage people to keep busy. Yer even awarded credits for participating in battles, more if ye volunteer."

"You getting credits for this?"

"Yes, ma'am." He motions us outside. "Hoping to buy myself some new books."

"You read?"

He winks at me. "Are ye trying to insult a man's intelligence?"

"She has no filter," Blake says, his voice warm. "Her mouth is always getting her into trouble."

I smirk at him. "Let me rephrase—*what* do you read?"

Dunn tosses our rifles into the boot of the lead jeep and slides behind the wheel. The other four men jump into the rear vehicle, the bodywork painted in camouflage colours with a cage protecting the windscreen.

MacKelter holds the door open into the back seats of Dunn's jeep. "Epic fantasy. Anything with knights and wizards. I like a bit of blood and magic."

"Clearly."

Blake sighs. "Anita…"

"What? This is how I make friends."

We grin at each other and enter an immaculate interior of buttery leather seats. The dashboard contains the usual controls plus an array of switches, levers and dials. MacKelter drags himself inside and the vehicle dips alarmingly. He pulls a wad of black material from the glovebox and waves it between the seats.

"You'll need to put these on for yer own safety. I take it yer familiar with laser-cameras?"

We accept his offering, which separates into two hoods, the fabric silky beneath my fingertips. I glance at Blake. He shrugs one shoulder. I take a breath and slip my hood on, the world smothered in darkness, no hint of light through the material. My flapping hand finds Blake's and he smooths his thumb across my palm.

It's a bit more professional than climbing into his lap.

"How does it work?" I say, my hot breath buffeting my face. "Is the hood enough to confuse them?"

"The material itself isnae enough. The lasers still lock onto the movement of the body but the hoods have a code embedded in the fibres. It's recognised by the lasers and tells them not to activate. Came from the same traders we bought the cameras aff of."

The seat vibrates under my butt, the roar of the engine muffled through thick armour plating. Nothing happens for a few minutes and I open my mouth to ask if something's wrong. The jeep lurches, throwing me against Blake.

"It's pretty rough from here on out," MacKelter says over my thundering heartbeat. "But it'll only be for fifteen minutes."

I use the jostling as an excuse to wriggle into Blake's lap.

Fuck professionalism, I want a cuddle.

His arms circle me and he nuzzles my cheek through the material of our hoods.

I survived most of the war by avoiding intimacy. Now, I barely manage two seconds before I crave Blake's touch, the feel of his body against mine. Under mine. Or on top.

Shit. Must stop that.

"You're thinking naughty things about me again, aren't you?" he whispers in my ear.

"I have no idea what you're talking about."

"Then why are you rubbing yourself against me?"

I freeze. "Bugger."

His quiet chuckle tightens places low in my body.

The man is a danger to my reputation in polite company. Though what do I know? Maybe MacKelter and Dunn would enjoy a live sex show.

"We can do that later."

For an instant, I think he's read my mind and then it dawns. Oh. Holy. Fuck.

Heat washes through me. I swallow to keep my tongue where it belongs instead of panting into my hood.

Jesus. Sweet Jesus. How did we get on this topic in the back of an enemy jeep carrying us into what may be the most impenetrable stronghold of all the factions?

Blake hugs me tighter and a purr rumbles in his chest. "My wonderful hussy."

"We're coming to a halt soon," MacKelter says. "Don't remove yer hoods."

I struggle to remind myself I'm a soldier and an intelligent human being. "Are we there already?"

"Not quite but I'll need ye to step out of the jeep in a moment."

Doors thunk. A blast of warm air caresses my face, bringing sunshine and a hint of the sea, gulls squawking in the distance.

"Give me yer hand, Anita, and I'll help ye out."

A large, dry palm engulfs my hand as I attempt to slide off Blake's lap with some kind of dignity. My boots hit springy ground.

Grass?

"Stand still for a minute," MacKelter says, a steadying paw on my shoulder.

"Blake?"

"I'm here."

Something whirrs and clicks in front of me, smelling of metal and oil.

"What is that?" I breathe.

"It's best ye don't know."

Not comforting.

The drone fades and MacKelter herds us back into the vehicle. The journey changes from bone-jarring to a gentle rocking and the jeep eases to another stop. Voices call from outside. I sit up straighter, Blake's fingers gripping my leg. A loud rumble shudders through the car. The engine revs. We jerk forward and halt again. The familiar thunder and clang of a gate sounds behind us.

Welcome to Inverness.

32

I'm not one to kneel for anybody but MacKelter asks nicely and it's better than a rifle butt to the back of the leg.

Not that we've encountered any such violence.

Yet.

He removes the hood, managing not to tug on my hair, and I squint in the sudden brightness. Blake kneels next to me, blinking at the familiar surroundings of the room from Bursey's video.

A slab of stone gleams on a plinth with a fan of spikes for a backrest, Saltires gently rippling in a draft. The bronzed Egyptian queen of Inverness reclines on her throne in a flowing dress of white split to the thigh on both sides beneath a belt of gold.

"Don't you two make a breath-taking pair," she says, her voice holding a trace of the exotic under the Scottish burr.

She glides down the short steps of the plinth on bare feet. Feathered earrings brush the curve of her shoulders, a gold band twined around her bicep. Her black eyes linger on me and I fight an unpleasant flashback to Wick.

Her eyes are curious—human—not pitiless and empty. No need to panic.

Oh god, what am I doing here? I should have argued.

Refused. Prison in the normal world would be more civil than this one. Blake could've visited. He would've been safe.

Until the Second Nuclear War vapourised us both.

"Scan them, please, MacKelter."

"Of course, ma'am."

Blake's gaze locks on mine. Something touches the back of my head and I flinch. A beep freezes my heart. I know what happens next—a bang and static—but MacKelter moves to Blake. I sway on my knees as he heaves a thick, gun-like contraption in his hands, the muscles in his arms bunching, and presses it to the base of Blake's skull. He frowns at some kind of screen mounted above the handle. Another beep.

"Both clean, ma'am."

She claps her hands. "Excellent! It would be a pity, otherwise."

"What was that?" I say, my voice quavering only a little.

"That's my portable MRI," Dorothea says with a smile. "It weighs more than me. MacKelter here is one of the few strong enough to lift it."

She pads behind us to the bear of a man and brushes her fingers across his chest. The top of her head comes to his collarbone, her slim frame dwarfed by his. His face softens and adoration fills his eyes. The rest of his men stand to attention in a line behind him, their rifles ready.

"But what's it for?"

"I use it to scan all my strays. The recent ones have been from the outside world. The idiots don't seem to realise their implants give them away."

Ice slithers through my veins.

The neuralnet they were so desperate to attach to our brains. The downfall of every person Lamb sent out.

"The outside world?" I manage to say. "You mean they're okay?"

If we were real strays, we wouldn't know about them or their shiny neuralnet.

Dorothea quits petting MacKelter and skips around to us. "Okay by most definitions, though fewer in number. They had their own war, would you believe, but seem recovered enough to send spies into my territory. Keeps me amused if nothing else. Now, please, get off your knees. This will be the only time you have to kneel in front of me. Unless you want to. Some things work better on your knees."

Her men chuckle. Blake and I stand while I struggle to process everything she said.

Did she break through Buxton's jammers? Christ, can she access the neuralnet?

No. She would've killed us already, knowing exactly who we are.

Wait. Did she just make a joke about oral sex? And why was she looking at me when she said it?

She steps in front of me in a waft of patchouli, her head tilted up to meet my gaze. Her dress barely covers the swell of her breasts, a tight, golden ribbon performing better than a push-up bra.

"And what can I call you?"

"Anita," I say, no quaver this time.

"A lovely name." Her eyes drop to somewhere far lower than my face. "Truly lovely."

Fucking hell.

Blake seems to be having trouble controlling his expression. Dorothea turns away and I scowl at him over her head.

"What about your gorgeous companion? I take it he is yours,

yes?"

"Yes, he's mine." Whoops. Must not growl at the leader. "His name is Blake."

"Is he the sexy, silent type?"

She reaches out a hand but appears to think twice about touching him.

The snarl on my lips probably warned her off.

Blake clears his throat. "I can talk."

"So just the sexy type." She grins and waves her hand. "I'm sorry, I'm teasing. Lord, she is quite protective of you, isn't she?"

"Yeah, she is." Blake's face does the whole softening thing, and my knees wobble.

"Well, I'm Dorothea but everyone calls me Morrighan." She cocks a perfect dark brow at Blake.

"Sure, Morrighan," he says.

The coward.

She turns to me.

Crap. Is capitulating to her ridiculous name a sign of weakness? Or will she respect me for refusing?

I raise my chin. "I don't think so."

Silence settles over the throne room, heavy enough to crack the shining marble floor and fracture the pillars supporting the arch of the roof. Dorothea's black gaze drills into me.

My mind bombards me with details from my nightmare—the knife slicing deep, my kidney splatting on the floor, her petite hands caressing my liver.

Call her a stupid warrior goddess before you get Blake killed, you stubborn bitch!

A slow smile spreads across Dorothea's face and sparks in her eyes. "I love a woman with balls."

I ease out a breath instead of letting it rush free in a whoosh. Would ruin my macho image.

Dorothea struts back to her throne and settles in a swirl of skirts, flashing tanned legs.

She beckons to us. "Please, both of you, join me up here now that the formalities are over."

We walk towards the plinth, Blake's hand in mine without me having to think about it. He flashes a tender smile that soothes my clenched stomach. Dorothea's gaze fixes on our linked hands, her dark eyes difficult to read.

The possibility of her respecting me less isn't enough to make me let go.

I place myself next to her throne, Blake on the outside, and slide a little further from the face-gouging spikes.

"They're quite dramatic, aren't they?" she says, craning her neck to look at me. "It's all about presence. You act like a badass and people soon believe it."

"You telling me you're usually warm and snuggly"—say it, you coward—"Dorothea?"

She laughs and it lights up her whole face like a candle beneath her skin. "Only with the right people, Anita."

And I thought my name sounded exotic on Blake's lips.

"Ma'am, sorry to interrupt but Norris's squad is outside."

"Ah, yes, thank you, MacKelter. I was expecting them. Seems like it's a morning for strays."

Blake squeezes my fingers and I jump but stare straight ahead, a pleasant expression frozen on my cheeks. The elaborately carved double doors at the other end of the room swing open. Another squad of six in camouflage uniforms troops in, circled around a group of men in dark clothes. The soldiers herd them into a line in front of the plinth and tug their hoods off.

Russell sneers towards the throne.

33

The bastards couldn't hide out for a day to make it less suspicious? Even minus the implants, they look like they don't belong. They move wrong, dress wrong—

Shit. The implants.

Dorothea floats down the steps for round two of the stray admittance procedure. Blake tugs on my arm as I strain forward but it's impossible to signal any of the goon squad. Too many of Dorothea's people are facing me.

What could they do if I somehow communicated how much trouble they're in? They're unarmed, outnumbered and surrounded by gun-toting soldiers.

We'll have to watch them die to maintain our cover.

Blake gives a tiny shake of his head. I settle my shoulder against his, my muscles tense with the effort of keeping my face blank. His arm comes around my waist for a second to hug me tight.

"On your knees, please, boys," Dorothea says, planting herself near Russell at one end of the line.

Dolt checks her out and seems to like what he sees but none of the other men move, their features twisted into various expressions of superiority. MacKelter looms over Benson at the opposite end, the portable MRI at his side, his broad figure reducing Lamb's muscular men to children.

"She asked ye nicely," he says. "I won't do the same."

The goon squad obey the growling man-bear so perhaps they aren't completely stupid.

"And where did we find these fine gentlemen?"

"We met them walking towards us on the road through Bunchrew, ma'am," says a bearded man with dark hair.

"We heard you offer shelter," Quagmire says, his hands clasped behind his bald head, his black knit jumper stretched across his chest. "We've been wandering in the wilds too long."

Dorothea taps her chin. "Heard from whom?"

"We were Guardians of Scotland. Practically neighbours."

They've done their homework but not well. Guardians of Scotland were weak as a political party and weaker as a faction.

They were the first to fall.

"Ah, yes, the Guardians. How they liked to try and sneak in their abominations. Did you know their creatures had skin that absorbed carbon dioxide? Like plants with teeth. I guess it suited their original party manifesto. You have been wandering long." Her black eyes sweep the kneeling men. "Unbelievably long."

The idiots. No one survives seven years in no man's land.

"We were lucky, ma'am," Benson says, sharing a glance with his comrades. "We found a workable farm in the west, rounded up some livestock gone feral. It wasn't much of a life but it was enough to sustain us for a while."

"Then I imagine you are quite desperate for some security and social interaction."

"Very much so, ma'am."

Benson has never been this polite to me. I guess he thinks

Dorothea's hulking guards are more of a threat.

Dorothea nods at MacKelter. He presses the bulky MRI to the back of Benson's skull. My stomach falls to my knees. At the beep, MacKelter raises his eyes to Dorothea and shakes his head. He lowers the MRI and slips a black gun from his belt, the silver barrel wider than the body.

A bolt gun?

Blake's hand grips mine, hard enough to mottle the skin. MacKelter touches the contraption to Benson's head and pulls the trigger. A loud bang and a hiss. Benson flops face down on the marble, a neat, round hole dribbling red from the back of his skull. His comrades yell and leap to their feet. A scrum of camouflaged men tackle Quagmire and Dolt, slamming them to the floor. Russell lunges for Dorothea, wrapping his arm around her throat and keeping her body between him and her guards.

"Come any closer and I snap her goddamn neck!" He backs towards the far corner of the plinth.

MacKelter's face darkens to an unhealthy purple, a terrifying scowl furrowing his brow. The rest of the soldiers not pinning Quagmire and Dolt aim their rifles at Russell, their knuckles bleached white. Russell continues to retreat, Dorothea passive in his arms. He cranes his head and meets my gaze. A slow smile worse than his usual sneer stretches his lips.

He won't jeopardise the whole mission just to be a dick.

Right?

He's supposed to be a professional, a highly trained covert agent. He should be able to rise above the pettiness as long as the job gets done.

Russell opens his mouth. Blake stiffens, one squeeze away from breaking my fingers.

"Now who's piss—"

Dorothea claws at Russell's face and yanks on the arm around her throat. She breaks his hold, twirls out from his body and, still gripping his arm, forces him to bend. Her lovely bronze knee crunches into his nose. She twists his hand almost up to his shoulder blade and drives him to the ground.

Maybe she is a warrior goddess.

MacKelter bounds to her side and drops to his knees. He thrusts the bolt gun into Russell's cheek so hard it bunches his skin. Russell's dazed eyes blink at him, his blood staining the marble.

Christ, is MacKelter going to pepper him full of holes before he places the killing blow? Better to silence him quickly so the asshole can't scream our names as he dies, like the little fucking snitch he is.

Dorothea's slim hand covers MacKelter's shaking paw. "Keep it quick and clean, we're not animals."

The bolt gun swings to Russell's temple.

Russell's jaw works. "Wait! I have valuable—"

Bang.

Russell's body slackens, a bead of red running from the hole in his temple to pool in the corner of his eye. MacKelter helps Dorothea to her feet and they cross the room to the pinioned Quagmire and Dolt, who watch their approach but don't struggle.

"I'm sorry, boys," she says. "Only those genuinely seeking shelter are allowed. Your leader should really give it up."

My heart thuds at each passing second.

When did I last take a breath?

Dolt glares at Dorothea as MacKelter presses the bolt gun

to the top of his head and pulls the trigger. My eyes jerk to Quagmire, my muscles too stiff to function.

Please don't be a dick. Be a soldier.

He gives a minuscule twitch of his shoulder. I can't decide whether to faint or throw up. He stares at me while MacKelter lines up his shot on his bald pate.

Another hissing bang ends the last of Lamb's men.

34

"Darn it. The idiot got blood on my dress." Dorothea swipes at the offending red splotches and strides to the plinth where Blake and I are pretty much propping each other up.

Big tough soldiers disarmed by lack of sleep, too much adrenaline and the threat of mouthy bastards blowing our cover. I want to scamper back to the Townhouse to hide in the king-size bed on layers of recycled cotton. I'm not a spy, just an evicted refugee dragging the person I love into danger and leaving a swathe of bodies wherever I go.

Though I guess I have some experience of reconnaissance in Embra and Fellhill.

Neither ended well.

"I'm sorry you had to witness that," Dorothea says, pausing at the bottom of the steps, her dark eyes on me. "It's an unpleasant business better to get over quickly. I have frequency jammers all through this building but I never know how much slips through on their brain doo-dads."

Not a great deal going by Bursey's one and only video clip.

Pairs of soldiers haul the remains of Lamb's men out of the throne room, mopping up the blood and liquefied grey matter with smooth, sure strokes.

A choreographed dance they've performed many times

before.

I jerk my gaze away. "It's not like we're new to violence."

"No, I suppose not, though one's encampment should be a place where you feel safe."

"Can't say it worked out like that for me in the long run. Or Blake."

He squeezes my hand. "Yeah, more terrified than safe."

"I imagine you have some fascinating stories to tell."

She repeats her full-body scan while I force myself not to hide behind Blake.

Seriously, I prefer women hitting on him. This has never happened to me.

The rest of the men troop out of the room, leaving MacKelter and a sparkling marble floor. Dorothea sweeps her arm towards the door, her gold band flashing in a beam of sunlight through a small, glass dome in the centre of the ceiling.

"But stories can wait. You look exhausted. Please, let me show you where you can rest. Completely safe, of course."

I stumble instead of floating gracefully down the stairs.

In Dorothea's dress, I would've been on my ass more than my feet.

I have to respect a woman who can pull that off and drop a man four times her body weight.

She smirks as I sidle out of reach and head for MacKelter.

"Where would ye like me to escort them, ma'am?" he says. "Barracks J through N have space."

"I think our new arrivals might appreciate some privacy and I have plenty of spare rooms here. It is a castle after all." She skips ahead through the door, peeking at me under her lashes. "Once you're rested, you can join me for dinner."

Please god, let the invitation include Blake.

Screw it, I'm taking him anyway.

"Thank you, Dorothea," I manage to say without stuttering. "That's very kind."

"Well, you are my first proper guests in a long while. The attention from the outside world is flattering but killing them grates on the nerves."

From strays to guests. How quickly we climb the hierarchy.

The throne room exits into a hall only slightly less grand, complete with marble pillars and a domed roof. Two soldiers guard a metal double door opposite us, the air heavy with the scent of patchouli and incense. MacKelter and Dorothea lead us up a staircase that splits into two on the first landing. We choose the left fork to a corridor of plush carpet runners and golden walls, yellow sconces lighting the paintings of stern-faced kings and one woman I recognise—Mary, Queen of Scots. I stop at an alcove containing a narrow plinth. Blake's fingers flutter across my shoulder blades.

"Are they—"

Dorothea smiles. "The Honours of Scotland? Yes, they are."

A jewelled crown perches on a tasselled pillow of red and gold, flanked by a sword and a sceptre.

"How the hell did you get them out of Edinburgh Castle?"

"There was a lot of looting in the early days but I'm a determined woman. I also have the Stone of Destiny in my bedroom. Ancient symbol though it may be, it's a little drab. You're welcome to see it any time you like."

Must not go anywhere near Dorothea's bedroom.

Her eyes glitter in the lights and I get the distinct impression she's enjoying my discomfort.

I edge closer to Blake. "Do you have any other Scottish artifacts in your collection?"

"Oh, no, these are the ones I wanted. They're for the crowning of monarchs. Handy, since I plan on being the next queen of Scotland."

I have to admire her ambition.

"I've shocked you. Have you never desired to lead, Anita?"

We continue along the corridor, our steps muffled on the thick runner. It separates at a T-junction and Dorothea turns right, the paintings replaced by wooden doors.

"There was one faction," I say. "But they no longer exist."

Blake's hand strokes my back for a second of comfort.

"Blake was the aerial team leader back in his faction," I add. He flashes me a grin.

The poor guy must be getting used to being ignored. I have no idea how people manage it.

"I think you have the perfect qualities for a leader," Dorothea says, yanking my adoring gaze from Blake. "You're wearing two pairs of dog-tags—not many are accepted into another faction where you're from. You survived a perilous journey through no man's land and charmed MacKelter. You're strong, stubborn. Resilient. A woman is at her most powerful when she learns to stand alone."

"Maybe." I take Blake's hand. "Or maybe she's strongest when she has someone who helps her stand."

Dorothea laughs. "Especially if that someone is as delectable as Blake. He is quite distracting."

The growly thing happens in my chest again but I swallow it.

She can see he's gorgeous, she has eyeballs, as Blake once said, though her interest seems to end there, like studying a beautiful work of art. You look at it for a while but you don't want to take it home and make it moan your name.

Dorothea halts at a door and her fingertips trace a carving in the wood. "Welcome to my faction wing. Each door is decorated to honour a different one. I thought you might feel most comfortable in this room."

Two crossed Glocks over a Saltire are etched into the centre of the wood—the insignia of The People's Republic. Behind me, a rampant unicorn marks the door as Soldiers of the Lost.

"I have the symbol of Alba gu Brath carved on the entrance to my bedroom, of course," she says, stroking the mountain range stitched onto MacKelter's shirt, her gaze on me. "It's on the top floor. The whole ceiling is made of glass. The stars are truly wonderful. One night, perhaps you'll watch them with me."

How can I be clearer? Maybe I should mount Blake in front of her. She'll understand.

Or ask to join in.

Yikes.

"Um, I'm not a huge fan of the stars but thanks for, ah, thinking of me." I nudge Blake towards the door.

Dorothea grins. "Anita, you make it very easy to tease you. Rest up. I'll see you both at dinner."

MacKelter nods at us and trails his leader down the corridor. Blake twists the engraved handle and I tumble into the room. He shuts the door and I sag against the wood.

"Jesus. Jesus Christ. She is flirting with me, right?"

"Massively. And there was me thinking it was the men I'd have to protect you from. You really make my job harder."

I shake my head at his smirk. "I'm sure the tables will turn when we mingle with the rest of the encampment."

I shove away from the door to explore our bedroom.

It's temporary but who knows for how long.

I drop my pack at the foot of a four-poster bed of mahogany, gossamer curtains hanging at each corner and matching the creamy silk sheets and pillowcases. Two dark cabinets flank the bed, the edges carved to complement the four twisting posts. A thick blue and gold rug covers the polished wooden floor, the same colour as the walls. I cross to the multi-paned window and look out onto an inner courtyard with a fountain, benches and lush green grass. I crook my finger at Blake and he follows me into a marble bathroom. I twist the handles of the walk-in shower, all fogged glass and gilt edging, and wait for the hiss of the water to build.

I step in close and my lips brush his ear. "We can't talk openly here. Just to be safe."

He nods, his nose tickling my throat. His fingers grip my hips and pull me into him. My breath catches, the longing for him enough to banish the last of the horror from the execution of the goon squad.

"Well, since you turned the shower on, it seems a shame to waste it."

He pulls my top off in one smooth movement and tosses it to the floor. I cajole my brain into forming words but his top follows suit and I gape at him for a little while.

He's too damn beautiful for his own good.

And mine.

He smirks and strokes a finger down my hot cheek. "God, I love the way you look at me."

Am I drooling? Probably. Shit.

"What if she's listening?"

"Then she is about to get jealous."

He teases me from my clothes and I wriggle under his touch, always so eager. He guides me into the heat of the shower and kisses me under the pounding water until I drown in the taste of him. He eases away, smirking at my disappointed noise.

"I haven't forgotten what you said in the jeep."

All air and sense rush from my body, his wicked grin electrifying my pulse. He spins me around and moulds himself to my back, his skin hot and slick and glorious against mine. He lifts my arms and places my palms on the tiled wall.

"You might want to brace yourself, baby," he says.

35

The city of Inverness has grown since I last saw it over a decade ago, when my fellow countrymen were normal people rather than savages.

MacKelter ferries us from the castle in his jeep past row upon row of regimented barracks blocks interspersed by larger buildings.

"You've removed all the residential streets," I say, gazing out the window at what could be a proper military base.

"Most of them, yes," Dorothea says, twisting in the passenger seat to look at Blake and me. "My faction grew extremely fast and houses take up too much space. I saved the nicer properties along the river and in Milton of Leys. My senior personnel prefer them. A bonus for all their hard work."

It didn't need much to convince Dorothea to give us a tour of her fair city. One subtle comment at dinner the night before and she offered to show me around herself. She'd monopolised my attention the entire evening, sitting at the head of the table and placing me next to her, Blake on my right opposite MacKelter and Norris. She asked about our journey to her territory and even what I did before the war. I stuck to the truth as much as possible but fabricated our month-long trip north on the remains of the A9 trunk road.

Blake attempted to join in but soon gave up and chatted to the other two men, his hand on my leg under the table. He regaled them with his stint in no man's land before he met me, comparing our three-course meal served by people in pristine white to eating butterflies and wood sorrel. MacKelter and Norris seemed particularly interested in the details of our first encounter, their laughter sparking an ache in my chest.

Blake could have friends here.

We were so isolated, ten days of just him and me then in the outside world but not really a part of it.

Is he lonely without other guys to talk to? I'd happily spend the rest of my life in only his company but I'm a distrustful bitch. Maybe he needs more.

Though any friendships will disintegrate when we invite the British Army down on their heads.

Perhaps Dorothea is innocent. No nukes, no plans for world domination. We don't have an exit strategy for that scenario. What the hell will we do, stay in Inverness forever? Imprisoned again by the goddamn Faction War.

Unless we get everyone to stop fighting.

Dorothea squeezed my hand and distracted me from a possible panic attack, a flash of annoyance quickly hidden on her face. The rest of the dinner passed in a smooth blur of clinking crockery and relaxed conversation. No work talk or shouts of, "Impostor!"

I forgot we were in Scotland. It was so civilised.

MacKelter turns the jeep south along the Essich Road past arable fields and more barracks. He stops the vehicle on a rise before the road dips through once open moorland, the glistening glass of aeroponic farms replacing the purple bloom of heather.

All of the encampment's vegetables grow in suspended layers, their roots misted by nutrient-rich water.

"You get the best view from up here," Dorothea says, unbuckling her seat belt and sliding out.

She strides to a gate leading into a field of sheep, her loose red trousers split to the knee and swaying more like a skirt. Her black silk top flashes the curve of each shoulder through peek-a-boo panels. I feel drab in my dark green combats and t-shirt, the same outfit I wore to dinner. Dorothea plants one polished combat boot on a rail of the gate and boosts herself up, the sheep barrelling to the far end of the field. MacKelter moves to her side and she braces a hand on his shoulder. She flings her other arm out towards the sprawl of Inverness below us.

"Look, Simba. Everything the light touches is my kingdom."

I tilt my head. "I feel like you're quoting something."

"Come now, Anita. As a lover of old movies, I thought you would get the reference." A light breeze flops her hair across her forehead and she brushes it away.

"I think we have slightly different tastes."

"She prefers action and swearing to animation," Blake says, the grin clear in his voice.

I cock an eyebrow at him. "You know the movie?"

"*The Lion King*. A classic."

"I thought you only liked superheroes and CGI."

He steps in close behind me, the heat of him against my back for the space of two swollen heartbeats. "I like *many* different things."

I grab the top bar of the gate instead of pooling at his feet, pretending to survey Dorothea's kingdom—queendom?—while a flashback plays havoc with my nervous system.

He carried me to the bed after our shower, my legs too wobbly to function. I passed out immediately, curled in his arms, wrecked by the most intense orgasm—or freaking *five*—I'd ever experienced.

If Dorothea was listening, she got one heck of a soundtrack. Blake's name featured heavily. I forgot my own.

He kisses the side of my neck and leans his hip on the gate, smirking at my shiver. "You're all flushed."

"It's a hot day."

His face softens. "I've heard that before."

Yup, right around the time I first saw him without a t-shirt on and lost 99% of my brain cells.

Dorothea clears her throat. "Anyway, my point is you can see the extent of my stronghold all the way from here to north of the Kessock Bridge. We're not at the southern boundary, either. This road continues to some lochs I use for freshwater. I have other encampments, of course—Beauly, Dingwall, Invergordon, Dornoch—but they're mostly for surveillance. Most of my people want to stay in Inverness."

No wonder.

"You must have one of the longest boundary fences of any encampment," I say, painfully casual. "How do you have enough power for all the particle beams? And the laser-cameras?"

She hops down from her perch, and beams at me. "All in good time, Anita! The tour is just getting started. Come, I want to show you my favourite place."

MacKelter returns us to the heart of the city, passing the castle on its hill. Other jeeps use the immaculate roads—no muddy ruts for Inverness—but not enough to cause any traffic despite the number of inhabitants. MacKelter parks on an old pedestrian street where a stream of people disappears through a garlanded archway. A bubble of excitement swells at Dorothea's exit from the vehicle and her minions rush over. I manage not to launch myself back inside the jeep but I grab Blake's hand.

I hate crowds. It doesn't take much to incite them into stomping you to death.

Blake squeezes my fingers. "Listen to them, they're happy."

"Morrighan! I love your outfit—"

"I'm so glad you're here! I just made another batch of lipstick—"

"Are these our new strays—"

"I cannot wait until the Gathering tomorrow—"

She smiles, waves, shakes hands and answers all their questions.

Not a single person shies away from her.

It says a lot about a leader when people aren't scared shitless in their presence.

Maybe Dorothea won't turn out to be a psychopath like the rest.

The crowd disperses, casting curious glances towards me and Blake but too polite to bombard us with questions. Or Dorothea warned them off.

No doubt our first Gathering will be mobbed.

She guides us beneath the archway into a huge, open space set out like a Turkish bazaar. Stalls topped by colourful sheets form a maze of bustling corridors, the scent of ginger and cumin heady in the humid air. Two things I haven't smelled for years but recognise immediately.

"Welcome to the Market," Dorothea says, grinning wide. "I

razed the whole area right up to the railway station to build this place. It's formed a wonderful community hub where you can buy, sell or trade anything. We use a credit system but I'll explain that later. You should have a couple of days to acclimatise before you decide what role you want to play."

She skips down one of the corridors and I trail after her, staring at the assortment of objects for sale. Clothes, fruit, cosmetics, books, even knick knacks built for no other purpose than decoration.

"Are those real spices?" Blake says, steering me over to a stall where ceramic bowls contain powders of red and yellow hues.

"Ah, yes! We have quite a busy little spice enterprise. Only the lower-growing species but they do well in heated buildings and on sunny ledges. No cinnamon, alas. We have a dining hall for each sector in the encampment but I find people are happier if they can also buy their own food to cook on portable stoves at their leisure. Or have snacks for eating in bed."

"God, it's been ages since I made a curry."

I cock an eyebrow. "You cook?"

Blake shares a look with MacKelter, who coughs into his fist and feigns interest in a bowl of turmeric.

"Yes, woman, I cook." Blake smirks, tugging me into him, his hands on my waist. "I'd love to cook for you."

His eyes are even more beautiful close up. Cobalt and violet and filled with a tenderness that sends tingles to my stomach.

It surprises me how long I managed to resist him. Okay, it was only four days and mostly because he hated me. As soon as he changed his mind, I practically ripped off my clothes. It was quite embarrassing since I'd vowed never to fall for anyone again when I left Fellhill.

Blake's soft smile spreads the tingles outward. He kisses me and the hubbub of the Market fades, the bite of the spices mixing with the sunshine and earth scent that is all Blake. He smells like a forest after rain. Like life and rainbows and—

Fucking hell, will you shut up!

I fist my hand in his hair and arch into him, a moan shivering in my throat. What we did yesterday was—amazing, world-shattering, unbelievable—great but I want to see his face. To watch his eyes darken when he loses control.

Someone whistles.

I gasp and break the kiss. "Shit. Dammit. How do you do that?"

"I have no idea." He laughs, somewhat breathless. "No one else ever reacted this way."

"I find that hard to believe."

He strokes my raised chin. "I love you."

Then I remember Dorothea, MacKelter and a third of Inverness are probably watching us. My flushed cheeks flare bright enough to power a field of solar panels. MacKelter isn't looking our way but he seems to find a bowl of paprika weirdly hilarious. Dorothea's black eyes are blank, almost alien.

"Sorry, Dorothea," I say, licking my lips and easing away from Blake. "You were showing us the Market?"

Her face brightens and she claps her hands. "Yes! We haven't reached the best bit yet!"

She races off down the corridor, people making way. MacKelter gives us a serious nod, his hazel eyes sparkling, and follows in her wake.

"Smooth," Blake whispers as we hurry to keep pace.

"Shut up." I march a few steps—a professional, intelligent

soldier, nothing to see here—but can't stop from peeking at him under my lashes. "I love you, too."

"Damn right you do."

We catch up to Dorothea in a swirling throng of people and stalls. Bolts of fabric and clothes of all kinds drape every surface, fluttering in the warm breeze from the sea. I run my fingers down smooth, cold silk.

"That would look lovely on you."

Emerald-green eyes assess me from behind the table of the stall, a mop of brown hair framing an ethereal face.

"Pink's not really my colour," I say.

And the dress would barely cover my ass.

"You'd look lovely in any colour," the man says, a quick grin flashing perfect teeth, "even dog-crap brown."

"Um, thanks?" I sidle away at his chuckle, joining Dorothea and Blake at a different stall.

She holds a spill of forest-green velvet up to my chest. "This will do perfectly, I think."

"For what?" I say, managing not to gulp.

"For the Gathering tomorrow. We all get dressed up and make an event of it, even the men. Blake, why don't you pick out something for yourself, and maybe some normal clothes? It'll come out of my credits." She quirks her mouth, her fingers hot against my collarbone. "I get more than I can spend for being the queen bee."

I take the dress from her grip and keep it at arm's length, the hem of the material brushing the concrete. "It's a beautiful dress but it's backless."

Dorothea tilts her head.

"I don't wear backless," I say.

"Why?"

"I have scars."

"Ah." She plucks the hanger from my fingers and returns the dress to the stall. "Tell me, which abusive faction was it?"

"Nationless."

"Blake's very own." She glances at where he's drifted off with MacKelter to browse for an outfit. "I know of the infamous Wick but who doesn't? And you were a prisoner of his?"

I nod, not trusting myself to speak.

His damn name still causes goosebumps and a sick clenching in my gut.

"Then you are far stronger than I thought. Whatever he did, it haunts you, I see that, but you are not defeated. I need more women like you, Anita."

"I appreciate that, Dorothea, but I'd rather not talk about it."

"Of course." She strides to the next stall. "Any other scars you do not wish to reveal?"

I tap a finger to my left shoulder and draw a line down my stomach.

She shakes her head. "Fascinating."

She turns away before I can respond and chats to the owner of the stall, his weathered face beaming at her, his skin a darker bronze. It gives me time to compose myself. Blake appears at my side, a paper- and string-wrapped package tucked under his arm. I lean into him, grateful for his warmth.

"You okay?"

"Yeah. You finished your shopping already?"

"Hey, I'm a man. It takes me two seconds."

Dorothea hands me a bright red bundle, her gaze flicking to Blake. "I believe this will be our winner, given your stipulations: A-line, split to the thigh, V-neck. Sleeveless but the straps are thick enough to cover your shoulder, and it's high-backed."

The dress unfurls to my feet, beautifully soft and light. I measure it against my chest.

Christ, the V-neck seems deep enough to reach my belly button.

"Oh, yes, this is the one!" Dorothea gathers the material and returns it to the seller. "Parcel this up for me, please, Max, plus the silver heels and have them delivered to the castle. This too."

Blake relinquishes his package and it disappears into the back of the stall, Max bowing at Dorothea. She threads her arm through mine and drags me further into the maze of the Market.

"Let's find you some comfortable clothes. Something branded with my wonderful insignia and a little more flattering."

I cast a pleading glance at Blake but he just grins and falls into step behind us.

Shopping. Now, *this* is torture.

36

Dorothea has created a star.

I stare at it through the thickened glass of the observation window in a blast-proof room several hundred metres below the Moray Firth. Its bright yellow blaze leaves flickering afterimages but I can't look away. It glows on its frame of metal, breath-taking in its vacuum bubble.

"How the fu—how the hell did you manage that?" I hold up a finger before she opens her mouth. "And, follow up question, is it going to explode and vaporise us all?"

She shares a laugh with MacKelter while Blake and I edge a little further from the shining ball of death.

"No, Anita. I have safety mechanisms in place. Any abnormal readings or uncontrolled reactions will flood the core and end the process."

"And what exactly is the process?"

"Nuclear fusion on a slightly smaller scale than true stellar nucleosynthesis."

"Right. I feel safer already."

"You should. She is the heart of Inverness. I'm the brain, of course."

"She?"

Dorothea places her hand on the glass, the light of the star dancing in the black depths of her eyes. "I named her Bellatrix, which means female warrior in Latin. Her predecessor was Libertas. I'm sure I don't have to explain what that means. She protects my encampment by producing the massive amount of energy needed to power my boundary fences, laser-cameras and numerous other defences. The technology was a godsend from Mauritania."

My skin prickles as if heat is leaking from the star through the armour-plated walls, though the observation room feels cool. The weight of earth and water above us shrinks the small space to the size of a coffin.

"How long does she produce energy?" Blake says, glancing between MacKelter and Dorothea.

"Each star lasts about four years before it goes supernova in a beautiful burst of power. And then I restart the process to create a new star."

I back up a few more steps and tug Blake with me. "I think I've seen enough of the exploding death star."

"Oh, Anita, you're being silly. She is perfectly contained."

"Even so, I prefer above ground."

At a nod from Dorothea, MacKelter yanks the lever of the blast door and swings it open, the metal thicker than his body. A long corridor stretches to the next door, dark despite the lights when compared to the mini-sun burning away in the core. I force myself not to run but ease out a breath at the clang behind us. Our boots ring on polished metal, the roof low enough to touch. My throat tightens to match my clenched stomach.

Blake slips his hand in mine. "I'm not a fan of the underground, either. Reminds me of our bunker in Nationless and my buried comrades. I wonder if they're still alive."

I shiver.

They were buried because of me. I destroyed their encampment and forced them to hide in a bunker.

Revolutionary Front turned it into a tomb.

"Sorry," Blake whispers. "I think about them sometimes."

"I know. I do, too."

He mentioned their plight to Lamb before we left for the *Queen Elizabeth*. Lamb said he'd see what he could do.

Blake smiles at me and raises his voice. "So, Morrighan, how do you create a star?"

MacKelter marches ahead to the next blast door, one built every hundred metres on the kilometre trek to the elevator. My clammy skin aches for the soft, sea breeze and real sunshine, not an impostor's glow.

"From a compressed hydrogen fuel pellet. Lasers start the fusion and the fuel becomes plasma. It takes a considerable amount of energy but it always releases more than I put in, especially as the reaction becomes self-sustaining. Plus the death of the predecessor powers the birth of the next. Kind of like a phoenix. Another star rises from the ashes."

Everyone in Inverness is a bloody poet.

"Does the star also power the rest of the encampment—the lights, the appliances?"

I focus on Blake's voice, on the pulse in his thumb, the confident way he moves, and my panic ebbs.

"No, there's very little surplus. My defences are greedy. The rest of the encampment is fed by the usual means—wind, wave, solar."

"What happens between one star dying and creating the next? Are you defenceless for however long that takes?"

She chuckles and ducks through another blast door.

The third, fourth? How many damn doors do we have to go?

"My, you two are full of questions! I don't blame you, considering the factions you came from but please be assured— Alba gu Brath is far superior. It's laughable, really." She walks backwards, her face in shadow. "But to answer, no, not defenceless. I always have another fuel pellet ready to go in my second core. There's a space of maybe ten minutes where I reroute the renewable energy to maintain the fence but the transition is fairly smooth."

She twirls around at the next door, the hinges creaking as it swings open. Blake and I step through, my foot catching on the metal rim. I stumble and he catches me. Dorothea glances over her shoulder.

I clear my throat and flash her a serene smile. "I take it it's the heat you use to make your electricity?"

"Exactly, yes. The heat produces steam to drive the turbines of my electric generators. You should see them, they're huge. In fact, that's what's in all the hangars up top. I have about a hundred."

Jesus. A hundred generators. A star in a nuclear core that could explode at any moment.

How the fuck are we supposed to work with that?

The last blast door opens into a square space housing the elevator to the surface world. Dorothea takes her sweet time pressing the button, in my opinion. I lean into Blake and try not to fidget. He kisses my temple while no one is looking.

The trip up lasts an age, no numbers ticking off the floors to distract me. I drag Blake out as soon as the doors slide wide enough and gulp the glorious air of the lobby. Two guards watch our exit, one at the front entrance and one at the doors to the second lift, which only goes up.

"That pretty much concludes our tour," Dorothea says, striding for the glass of the double front doors and nodding to the slab-faced guard. "Why don't we walk back to the castle and you can have this evening and tomorrow to explore without me?"

The warmth of the sun banishes the last of the chill. Dorothea's control centre looms at our backs, a black mono-lith in a bustling industrial area close to the Kessock Bridge. She guides us on a route to the bank of the River Ness, the factories and hangar structures replaced by barracks and the green of a park circled by trees. A group of children chases each other across the grass and their screams shiver down my spine.

"You have kids here," I say, unable to keep the horror out of my voice.

Dorothea frowns. "Why are you—Oh! Lord, no! They are *not* child soldiers. Bearing children is one of the many roles you can choose from, and the credits are good."

I suppress a shudder and rub the contraceptive implant in my arm for comfort.

"Do you not wish to have children, Anita?" she says with a small smile.

"Hell no."

"But you would make beautiful babies."

"Beautiful or not it's never going to happen." My shudder externalises despite my best efforts.

Her smile widens. "I'm glad. Miracle of life it may be, but having children tends to limit one's power and blunt one's focus."

Man, she is obsessed with power. I guess a leader has to be

to some extent. I have no desire for true power.

All I want is a life with Blake.

"And you, Blake?" Dorothea says, cocking her head. "Do your plans align with Anita's?"

"Yeah, I'm not into kids, either."

"Well, the children of Inverness are not rabid little monsters. Once they turn eighteen, they can enter my army if they choose to. Everyone receives training from fourteen to eighteen but they are not conscripted."

We stroll down a tree-lined avenue following the river, my thoughts on feral children with bloody grins.

I've never been interested in reproduction even when kids weren't trying to gut me and flail around in my entrails.

The river curves towards the castle, a steady flow of people greeting Dorothea on the path. Across the water, a high wall rises behind a row of low buildings, possibly classrooms.

"What's that?"

Dorothea turns in the direction of my pointing finger. She winks and continues down the street.

"A woman must keep some secrets, Anita."

Blake's eyes meet mine.

Oh, god. I bet it's fucking nukes.

37

The wall appears to contain the stones of all the buildings demolished to make space for Dorothea's barracks. Pink granite, grey basalt and limestone are cemented next to modern clay bricks, creating a colourful tapestry taller than a house. Shards of glass embedded in the top edge glow in the setting sun like bloody fangs.

What secrets does it protect? Maybe it's Dorothea's private sanctuary where she bathes in a tranquillity pool and lies in the sun.

Sure, and Russell wasn't a low-life rat.

Blake and I avoid the black-barred gate guarded by two sentries and slip around the corner.

Just a couple out for a lovely evening stroll to avoid the crowds.

A path follows the wall to a small marina on the Caledonian Canal, yachts and fishing boats moored next to bulkier military vessels with turrets. A tangle of bushes separates us from the wall, the creamy scent of elderflowers thick in the summery air.

"It curves away from us here," I say.

Blake glances both ways down the path and jerks his head. "Come on."

We crunch into the bushes, the sting of nettles sharp through my combats. The wall skirts a pond where a grey heron eyes us from the reeds, stalking away on its long legs. The Beauly Firth sparkles beyond a sea wall and the shimmering of the particle beam boundary fence. Our mystery wall straightens at a railway line, the metal rails intact and shiny.

"Looks used," I say in a hushed voice, the rustle of leaves and the slap of water the only other sounds.

"Maybe they kept it to move things around the encampment."

"Let's get past it before a train catches us snooping."

"We're not snooping. We're fascinated by the pretty stone structure."

I snort and fight through a thick clump of elder. The railway line runs parallel to the wall back towards the River Ness and the final corner before we return to the gate into the secret compound. A few streets of residential houses fill the land to the north, the rest replaced by barracks right down to the riverbank.

"Only one way in," Blake says with a sigh. "Typical. The only building tall enough to see inside is her control tower."

"I doubt she'll take us to the top levels of that any time soon. What the hell are we going to do? Perhaps I should tell her I want to work with nukes. 'Hey, Dorothea, you got any nukes lying around?'"

"I do admire your subtlety."

"And say, by some slim chance, we find these nukes, how do we know if she's planning to use them on the rest of the world? They could just be for her own defence. Calders may not have had nukes but we had missiles."

He shrugs. "Any nukes at this stage are enough to concern

Bursey and Lamb."

We approach the last corner, the railway line continuing over a bridge. I slither down the embankment onto the road.

"Head north and turn towards the river. Less obvious than—"

"What are you doing?"

I jump at the gruff voice. A sentry in black stands at the corner, cradling his SA80 rifle, a wool cap pulled low despite the warmth of the evening.

"Shit, you scared me," I say in a breathless voice only half-faked.

His face remains impassive.

Maybe I should bat my eyelashes and stick out my breasts.

"Why are you this close to the wall?" he says.

Blake steps beside me and takes my hand. I glance between him and the sprawl of stone, my mind spinning furiously.

Will it be MacKelter who silences us with his bolt gun?

"I'm sorry, are we not supposed to be this close? There are some wonderful plant species growing between the bricks. Look!" I gesture and nearly yank Blake's arm out of its socket. "Maidenhair fern and—and ivy-leaved wallflower! They're really quite beautiful."

The guard frowns at the wall. "That fuzzy green stuff?"

"Well, it flowers late in the season. Deep blue. You should watch out for it." I edge away. "Sorry to disturb you. We won't come this close again."

The man drags his gaze from the unremarkable clump of moss. "No harm done. Are you new here?"

Our heads bob.

"Okay then. You should probably get back to your barracks."

"Of course, thanks. It's getting a bit dark, anyway." After

a few steps, I force myself to turn. "But watch out for the flowers in a month or two. You won't be disappointed."

Hopefully, Blake and I will be long gone, Inverness under control of the British Army.

"Sure, ma'am," the sentry says, returning to his post.

We scuttle out of sight, only slowing our pace at the bank of the River Ness. The water rolls towards the Moray Firth and through a thick grate, the boundary fence running above. Spikes and mines embedded in the channel prevent anyone from sailing through.

And the laser-cameras.

Blake releases a breath. "Blue flowers, really?"

"I've no fucking idea. Think I made the last one up. There was maidenhair fern, though."

We head for the castle on the hill, our steps unhurried, solar-powered streetlights popping on.

"I bow to your superior botanical knowledge. I recognise the ones you can eat, not the ones that are pretty."

I smirk at him. "Are you saying I'm better than you at plants?"

"No. You must have hallucinated."

"That's my line."

He tugs me into his side and slings his arm across my shoulder blades. My hand snakes around his lower back without any command from my brain, my fingers curled on his hip. His slim waist distracts me for a second before my thoughts return to the wall.

"I think it's safe to say she's hiding something but we need to know more about her motives before we rat her out."

"You like her."

I open and close my mouth. "She's quirky. Intelligent.

Doesn't appear psychotic. And she's built something impressive. I don't want to ruin that just to appease the fear of Bursey and Lamb. Maybe Dorothea running Scotland wouldn't be a bad thing, as long as there's finally peace."

"Should we tell her the truth about the start of the war?"

"Definitely. But first I want to know if she's planning world domination like most leaders I've met. If she's only focused on this country, maybe we can get her to stop."

A group of girls passes us on the path in the darkening light, slender legs and bellies showcased in mini-skirts and cropped tops. Perfect creamy skin unmarred by war. They stare at Blake and toss their shiny hair.

He tips his chin and fires off a salute. "Ladies."

They giggle behind their hands and skip away. Blake tracks them until they turn a corner out of sight.

"Do you think they heard us?"

I shake my head. "They were too busy drooling. It's weird seeing so many young people."

"Because you're so ancient."

"Some days, I feel it."

We cross the bridge to the east side of the river, dawdling as we near the castle. The streets are quiet, the stars winking on despite the light pollution.

"Let's say Morrighan's not planning world domination," Blake says. "What if she doesn't believe us about the debating chamber assassinations or she doesn't care? The war could drag on for another ten years."

"I doubt she releases her strays once they're inside. Maybe we could volunteer for a mission and sneak away. We escaped this country once, we can do it again."

Blake pulls me into an alcove and cups my face. "Another

journey through no man's land with you? Count me in."

He kisses me and I laugh against his mouth. He nibbles my lips, his fingers sliding into my hair. My bones start to melt.

"God," I groan, "now I want her to be a power-hungry psychopath. It'd be simpler to call in the troops and have them take our butts home."

Blake's other hand smooths down my back and presses me into him.

A reminder of the first time he touched me like this, his skin hot on mine, his mouth on my throat…

Shit. What were we talking about?

"Blake," I say, ridiculously breathless.

His lips move to my neck and the throb of my pulse. "Yes?"

"If she is a psychopath, how are we going to interrupt the defences to let the Army in? Lamb didn't account for a freaking miniature star. I was hoping for one of those big power switches you see in the movies."

Blake's chuckle vibrates against my skin and pulls a gasp from my throat. His hands trap me, the scent of him drowning my senses.

"You're not helping."

"Sure I am," he says, trailing kisses to my jaw. "Just give it a minute."

His hand slips under the hem of my t-shirt, his fingers tracing my scars. The delicate touch tingles to my belly, and lower. Always lower.

Christ, I want to get him naked so badly.

He buries his nose in my hair and purrs in my ear. "Plus, you're not getting any until you come up with a plan."

"That's blackmail!"

"I prefer to call it an incentive."

I wriggle in his merciless grip, his hand continuing its teasing caress and scrambling my brain.

How can he expect me to think of anything but him? The way he touches me, looks at me. I could watch him breathe for hours and be content. All I want is him.

And the longer he stays in this country, the more likely he'll get hurt, or die.

I have to keep him safe, no matter what.

"We're not going underground to that explosion waiting to happen," I blurt, and his lips curve against the edge of my jaw. "There are too many generators to destroy."

"So what does that leave us?"

He sucks on my earlobe, and my knees buckle. He tightens his hold, flashing me a wicked grin that does not improve my mental capacity.

The play of darkness and light in the confines of the alcove enhance the beauty of his face. Black hair, dark eyes, shadows in his cheekbones and the Cupid's bow of his perfect mouth.

"Anita?"

"Huh?"

"God, woman, you are killing my self-control," he growls.

A dazed blink finds me against the wall, my legs around his waist, his mouth desperate on mine. His hands are everywhere except the place I ache for him. He thrusts his hips between my legs and we both moan.

"The goddamn control tower," I pant. "We get into the control tower and mess shit up."

"Thank you, Jesus. Come on." He shoves away from the wall and lowers my boots to the ground.

Cue more doe-like blinking.

He smirks and scatters the rest of my brain cells. "If I take

250

you here, you'll wake up half of Inverness."

I have no memory of reaching our room. Who knows what the guards see when we burst through the doors of the castle.

My eyes are all for Blake.

The one person I live for.

And the only one I'd die for.

38

"Anita. My. I understand your preference for combats and t-shirts. If you dressed like this in any other faction, no man would be able to keep his hands off you." Dorothea's gaze drops from the plunging neckline to the split at my thigh. "Women either."

I smooth my hands over the silky material.

Dresses and finery are too new to feel comfortable, or normal, despite Felice's best efforts. Though I liked the dress at Bursey's gala dinner.

Or Blake's reaction to it, anyway.

How will he respond to this one? It covers more but flashes a lot of cleavage and clings to my body, the cloth parting to reveal my leg every time I move.

Plus, it's definitely not made of recycled bin bags.

"You don't look too shabby yourself, Dorothea."

She twirls at the foot of her queen-size (what else?) bed and laughs, the sunset through the glass roof dipping the furniture in orange and gold.

"This old thing? How sweet of you to say. Come. Sit over here and I'll do your hair."

She skips across the plush carpeting of the huge room to a padded stool in front of a dressing table and mirror, tiny bulbs embedded in the frame glowing like fairy lights. Her black silk dress ripples, the long skirt covered in a floaty layer of chiffon. Thin straps criss-cross her perfectly smooth bronze back. I totter on my silver heels, thin bands winding up my calves, and try not to trip on the hem of my dress.

"Oh, Anita! We must get you used to heels again. A woman with your figure has to strut, glide, not tip-toe. And"—she reaches out, one fingertip lightly tapping my dog-tags hanging beneath Lamb's purple pendant—"these ruin the effect of the outfit. You don't have to wear the ugly things anymore. I don't need to label my people that way. Take them off and I'll get rid of them for you."

My hand curls around the embossed metal. "That's all right, I'm used to wearing them."

"But they do not suit the dress. Tell me, do The People's Republic and Soldiers of the Lost still mean that much to you?"

"They're part of who I am."

"Such loyalty. Very well, keep your trinkets just, please, remove them for tonight at least."

I glance down at the beaded chains disappearing into my fist.

She's right, they look odd with the gaping neckline of the dress.

I slip both pairs over my head and drop Soldiers of the Lost onto the polished surface of the dressing table. I knot the second pair around my left wrist.

"That still doesn't—"

"This pair stays on me. Always. I don't care what I'm wearing."

Dorothea tilts her head, her black eyes unreadable.

253

I raise my chin. "One tag is Blake's."

Something slips through her dark gaze but she blinks and it's gone. Her face relaxes into a smile.

"You swapped dog-tags? Well, that's practically marriage in our world. You've known him for a month, isn't that right?"

I stop myself from crossing my arms but my fingers stroke his name at my wrist. "A month and a half."

"Such a short time to feel so strongly."

I shrug. "I love him. I loved him from the moment I met him. After everything I've been through, I thought trusting someone would be the last thing I needed. Turns out, he's all I need."

Talk of Blake makes me aware of his absence. I lower myself onto the stool instead of rubbing the acres of exposed skin over my heart.

Dorothea meets my eyes in the mirror. "Well then, let's get you back to him. I must admit, I'm quite intrigued to see his response to you in this dress. Once I'm finished with your hair and make-up, you'll go from stunning to a goddess. You'll certainly turn a lot of heads tonight."

I smother a groan.

Hair *and* make-up? Why are women so obsessed with slapping powder and putty on their faces in the hope men will drool over them? I don't care about turning heads.

I've earned the attention of the one man who matters.

Doing my hair turns into half an hour of brushing, curling and pinning while I fidget and dig my nails into the edge of the stool. Dorothea delivers on her promise, teasing my locks into a half-up, half-down style that frames my face and spirals over my shoulders. She twirls her finger in the air and I spin to face her. She tilts my head up, her skin warm on mine, her sudden intensity shrinking the large room into an intimate space.

It's weird to have a woman look at me sexually. I'm all for lesbians but it sure as hell doesn't help my nerves.

Dorothea flips on the sconces lining the walls, banishing the gathering dark. She unzips a caramel-coloured pouch and places tubes and pots on the dressing table, petting each one.

"How do you have make-up?" I wrinkle my nose. "Surely it can't have kept this long?"

She better not try to smear rancid goop on me.

"A warrior must have her battle paint, Anita. And it's surprisingly easy to make from a few, simple ingredients." She unscrews a thin bottle and holds the glistening black tip of the wand for my inspection. "Charcoal and vegetable oil."

Bending slightly, she cups my cheekbone and traces a tickling swirl around each eye. I struggle not to blink or gaze into her face. The scent of patchouli coats my tongue and brands my sinuses.

A small screw-topped pot appears in her delicate hand. "Butter, hazelnut powder and fine flour. Close your eyes."

She brushes the mixture across each lid.

How quickly that soft pressure could increase and jam her finger knuckle-deep in my socket.

But there's no such violence here, just two women wearing pretty dresses in the middle of a war zone. Ready for a night of frivolity. No guns or blood or screaming.

Dorothea will adapt to England better than I did.

Mascara teases my lashes—charcoal, butter and lavender oil—and, finally, lipstick.

"Beetroot powder and peppermint oil," she says, her eyes on my mouth. "The taste is quite divine. And everyone will want a taste."

Everyone can kiss a different part of my anatomy.

Unless they want a punch in the jaw.

She steps away and tilts her head, one fingertip rubbing her chin. A slow smile stretches her pink-tinted lips.

"Oh, yes," she breathes. "Just as I thought. An absolute goddess."

I clear my throat and drop my gaze, a blush heating my cheeks.

Her laugh tinkles high and bright. "And wonderfully shy! A disarming combination. But look for yourself if you don't believe me."

I swivel towards my reflection. A smoky-eyed sylph blinks back at me, all perfect hair and glistening lips. The woman in the mirror is confident, sexy. *Alluring.*

Dorothea has done as good a job as Xia.

Are the make-up ingredients the same as those in the environmentally conscious New London?

"I look amazing," I say.

"Yes, you do, Anita. Even without the make-up and glad rags, you have a natural beauty most women would kill for. Luckily, I'm not most women." Dorothea leans over my shoulder and slicks on another layer of lipstick, pouting at herself in the mirror. "I do want something from you, though."

Oh, god. No fucking way am I kissing her or touching her or taking off my clothes.

Saving the world isn't worth that much.

"I want you to be one of my advisers. I need more women like you on my team—strong, smart, loyal. You've survived more than any soldier in my encampment. Your insight would be invaluable."

I stop myself from blurting, "Holy sweet Jesus, yes! I'll advise you. *Show me the missiles!*"

"You've only known me a few days," I say instead. "Won't that annoy your other advisers?"

She flaps her hand. "I'm good at reading people. I'll introduce you tomorrow. I'm sure they'll be interested to hear about your time in other factions. I'm intrigued to learn what Soldiers of the Lost are doing with themselves these days."

Recreating the armour of the dragon and building an indestructible army?

My shoulders prickle.

Buxton is pragmatic. He has a team of dedicated suck-ups. How long before he tries his hand at dominating the country? Maybe he's already on the move.

The quicker Blake and I get out of Scotland, the better.

"I'd be honoured to be one of your advisers, Dorothea," I say.

"Excellent! But that can wait until tomorrow. Tonight is not for strategy and war talk. Tonight is for fun and dancing."

Dancing? No one said there'd be fucking *dancing*.

39

Another staircase, another grand entrance.

I wait out of sight for a beat while Dorothea sweeps down the steps into the marble foyer to a chorus of male appreciation. I pause at the top, one hand on the cool stone banister. Dorothea's men flock to her, dwarfed by MacKelter, who has squeezed his large frame into a charcoal tuxedo. Dorothea stops in front of Blake and he tips his head to listen to her but his gaze zips to mine, raising goosebumps and tingling in my chest.

His suit looks black until he angles his body towards me and the lights in the entrance catch a sheen of blue. The subtle shift brings out the colour of his eyes.

I hesitate another dozen heartbeats, not to soak up the attention but just so my wobbling knees won't pitch me down the stairs.

The guy floors me.

My descent is more mincing than sweeping but Blake meets me at the bottom, the heat in his gaze raising a flush on my cheeks.

"Baby, you look…"

"Like a girl?"

He smiles, slow and wicked. "Like a fucking amazing girl."

He captures my hand and places a delicate kiss on the inside of my wrist, nuzzling the beaded chain of my dog-tags. My pulse bounds under the press of his mouth.

"You didn't want to take them off?"

I blink at him. "What?"

His smile widens into a grin and he turns my wrist, his thumb stroking embossed metal. I cajole my tongue into forming complete sentences like an intelligent human being.

"I'm never taking them off. Not this pair."

He keeps a hold of my hand and eases me down the last stair, the heels giving me a couple of extra inches.

"Why?"

"Because your name is next to mine."

"You like having my name on you?" He continues to reel me in, closing the space between us, the warmth and smell of him making me woozy.

"Hell, I'd brand your name on me."

Possession flashes in his eyes and stirs an ache deep inside me.

"Mine," he whispers, so close, his breath brushes my lips.

"We really should get going."

I jump at Dorothea's voice, saved from toppling on my ass by Blake throwing an arm around my waist and tugging me against him.

The feel of his slim, hard body doesn't help my ability to behave like a lady in polite company.

"We're already fashionably late." Dorothea stands at the imposing metal doors, MacKelter and Norris poised to throw them open to the night.

I steady my hands on Blake's shoulders and slide backwards a step. His fingers stroke along my waist and round to my hip, letting me go but leaving a burning line in their wake.

"You're wearing underwear," he says.

"Don't sound too disappointed." I lean in, my mouth at his ear. "There's very little material."

The low groan in his throat almost undoes me. I stumble for the door before I embarrass myself. He catches up easily in his fancy polished shoes and takes my hand, my heels loud on the marble floor. Dorothea and her retinue troop ahead of us, two guards remaining behind to watch the empty castle.

"Woman, one of these days, I'm going to put you over my knee."

I trip on the hem of my dress. Blake's grip keeps me upright, his satisfied chuckle rekindling my blush.

"Stop it."

"But it makes you all flushed and squirmy." He squeezes my fingers. "And so would that."

I scramble into the back of a black Range Rover parked in the turning circle, assisted by Blake's playful pat on the butt, and sprawl on the seat instead of settling gracefully beside Dorothea. She cocks an eyebrow at me. I shoot Blake a glare as he shuts the door behind him.

"I can just as easily put you over *my* knee," I hiss.

The thought of him stretched across my lap, watching me with hungry eyes, does nothing to slow my pulse or soothe the arousal tightening my stomach. I wriggle in the seat.

He smirks. "Picturing me naked backfired, didn't it?"

"Goddammit," I sigh.

He cups my face and his thumb skims my bottom lip. "I love you."

And just like that, I need to kiss him more than I need to breathe or think or speak.

"Are you all right, Anita?" Dorothea says. "You seem restless."

I swallow a snarl and coax my mouth into a smile. "I'm fine."

"If she stops us kissing one more time, I'm calling her Dorothea," Blake grumbles into my collarbone.

MacKelter drives us into the outskirts, the streets devoid of life.

Surely everyone in the encampment can't go to the Gathering? What kind of building is big enough to house a million?

And I was nervous standing in front of a few hundred at Felice's press conference.

A construction of steel and glass arcs out of the skyline, ringed by trees. Our vehicle speeds closer, passing wooden pavilions containing pillow-heaped daybeds, their gauzy curtains fluttering in the breeze off the sea.

"For anyone wanting a bit of privacy," Dorothea says. "People tend to dip in and out when the mood takes them. You should walk through the park at night, it's quite lovely. Though perhaps not this evening, unless you want to join in."

"Join in?"

Dorothea laughs, her hand darting out to squeeze my knee. "Why, an orgy of course, Anita."

"An orgy?"

I really must stop repeating her words.

"A product of the high spirits and alcohol. It tends to lower one's inhibitions. You should try it, it's quite freeing."

"I, ah, think I'm good, thanks."

"But until you experience the true beauty of it, how do you know? Hands and mouths everywhere. No idea where your body begins and the others end. It's wonderful."

I take Blake's hand. "One guy is enough for me."

Hell, most of the time I have no idea where I end and he begins. Who needs anyone else?

"Then there will be a few crestfallen people tonight, I imagine."

"Guess they'll have to get over it."

The jeep parks beneath an archway of filigreed metal leading into a smooth concrete tunnel lit by glow strips. Dorothea hops out, steady on her heels while I wobble onto mine despite Blake's help. She strides ahead, her hips swaying, and leads us into the tunnel. A low rumble vibrates in the walls. The noise builds to a roar of voices as the tunnel opens into a wide, bright space.

Dorothea flings out her arms and grins at us over her shoulder. "Welcome to the Gathering."

40

We walk into the largest stadium in the world where everyone is screaming your name.

Except it's not my name.

"Morr-i-ghan! Morr-i-ghan!" The chant rises from the packed, tiered seats circling the central rectangular area and echoes off a roof hidden by a halo of lights.

Dorothea beams at her audience, both hands waving, and struts towards a raised dais in the centre. Tables covered in crisp, white linen and set for dinner fill the space between. Dorothea squeezes shoulders as she passes, bending to speak to a lucky few. Blake and I trail her like ducklings. The scrutiny of the massive crowd pools sweat in the small of my back.

What will happen if this many people turn into a mob?

I clutch Blake's hand tighter and fix my gaze on Dorothea.

She twirls and sweeps out a hand towards a small crescent-shaped table near the stage. "Please, Anita, have a seat. You're next to me. I'll be right down after the official opening."

"I'll just stand, shall I?" Blake says when she skips up the steps to the dais.

"Don't feel too left out. You can sit next to me."

He nibbles my fingers. "So generous to the poor, common

man."

Name cards mark each place, Dorothea on my right and someone called Tiffany on my left. I switch it for Blake's card on the end of the table.

There's no way he's sitting that far from me. I don't plan on letting him go.

MacKelter and Norris settle into their seats. With a huff of breath and a waft of roses, a surly faced woman throws herself into Blake's old spot. Her short, bronze dress brings out the honey of her eyes and the auburn in her hair.

Pretty, if you ignore the scowl.

She shoots me a glance before focusing on the stage.

Perhaps Tiffany will be one of the few unfriendly people in Inverness. Somehow, it makes me feel better.

Too many shiny, happy soldiers gets me wondering what they're hiding.

"My friends, welcome to the fortieth Gathering!" Dorothea says into a microphone at the edge of the dais.

She waits for the roars and applause to fade.

It takes a while.

"And, may I say, this is an extra special night considering the presence of our two new additions. I know you will give Anita and Blake a proper Alba gu Brath welcome."

The muted assent sounds louder than the thunder of a hundred guns. I force myself to breathe.

"Baby, you're crushing my fingers," Blake says.

I flash an apologetic smile and relax my grip.

What a tough soldier I am, scared of a few people only here to drink and have fun. No violence, no mayhem. No one appears to be armed.

God, I miss my Glock.

Dorothea launches into what we can expect from the evening—fine food, music, stories, dancing. She laughs with her captivated audience about highlights of previous Gatherings, the lengths her minions have gone to secure a spot.

Attendance is on a rota system for a seat in the stands. A personal invite or a purchase of credits secures a place at a table. Seats can also be traded for credits and it forms a bustling little economy. Those not invited or included on the rota watch the festivities from the screens in their barracks.

"And perhaps we can have a tale or two from our travellers. I know Anita has been inside five different factions, including ourselves. A record held only by her, I'm sure."

Six, actually, but our backstory doesn't include Unification Army.

And like hell am I getting up and speaking in front of all these people.

Dorothea gives me a secret smile. I muster my lips into a response and she seems to take it as acquiescence.

More fool her.

"But for now, let us eat, drink and dance!" She leans into the microphone, her eyes twinkling under the lights, her fingers lightly gripping the stand. "And may you all have a pleasurable evening."

She grins at the whoops, whistles and bawdy laughter. A waiter dressed in crisp white hands her a glass of amber liquid, the insignia of Alba gu Brath stitched in red on his uniform like a streak of blood. Others materialise around our table and fill every glass.

Dorothea raises her drink and everyone mirrors her.

"Here's tae us," she says, rolling her r's.

"Wha's like us?" bellows the packed stadium.

Blake cocks his eyebrow, his glass in his hand, mine cool against my palm.

"Gey few," Dorothea says, "and they're a' soon to be deid."

She tosses back her drink. Blake swallows half of his. I take a sip and choke, the spiced liquid burning my nose and warming my belly.

"Jesus Christ!" I splutter. "What is this, acid?"

"This is the best moonshine I've ever tasted and I like to think I know my stuff," Blake says, taking another swallow and sloshing it around his mouth.

Alcohol was banned in our original factions but Stig, Dylan's friend and the guy who stopped Wick from raping me, created a stomach-dissolving brew.

Having spent five days in his faction, I understand why he needed the hard liquor.

Cheers sweep Dorothea from the stage. She smooths the skirt of her dress and settles into her chair next to me. The waiters serve us steaming bowls of mussels in a garlic herb sauce and top up our glasses, bubbles coating the inside. Dorothea raises hers again, her body turned towards me.

Dammit, another toast.

"To your health, Anita." She clinks her rim on mine and drinks.

I steel myself but the second sip slides down and curls in my gut.

"What's in this, Morrighan? Whisky, allspice and"—Blake swirls another mouthful—"is that champagne?"

Dorothea's gaze rests on me for a second longer. "Sparkling wine made from gooseberries. And it's allspice-infused honey in the whisky. Sweet but potent."

"It's very good."

"Thank you, Blake. It takes a lot of time, care and attention but it's worth it."

"No wonder these things end in orgies," I say.

Dorothea's laugh tinkles louder than the scrape of cutlery around us. Conversations flow easily, helped, no doubt, by the tongue-loosening powers of alcohol. Later, the panty-loosening power will kick in but I plan on being sober and gone before that part.

Haggis-stuffed chicken follows the mussels then shortbread and ice cream.

It reminds me of Bursey's fancy dinner, with battle-hardened soldiers instead of politicians and not a single invertebrate to be seen.

People mingle after the meal, an endless stream of bodies coming to our table to toast our arrival, our health, the fucking price of bread. I finish my drink despite my tiny sips and the alcohol buzzes in my head. The glass is replenished before I can blink.

Different acts come and go on the stage—comedians, singers, musicians. A talent show in a war zone. A band sets up and the dreaded dancing starts, some tables swiftly moved to create a space. Dorothea disappears into the swaying couples with MacKelter. Several men invite me to dance but I politely decline.

Blake holds out his hand.

How can I refuse?

He leads me to the floor and the music slows. I concentrate on placing each foot, the whisky concoction not helping my inability to walk in heels. I grab onto Blake a little too desperately and he laughs. His hands glide around my waist to the small of my back, my arms around his neck, the top of his head level with my nose.

"You feeling the effects already?" he says. "Such a lightweight."

"I'd be fine if people stopped toasting everything under the sun."

His lips find my throat and curve in a smile. Desire evaporates the alcohol in a burst of heat. I unwind the straps from my calves and kick off my shoes. My arms slip around his shoulders, my fingers tangled in his hair, our faces perfectly level, his violet eyes enough to make me dizzy.

"Hey, baby," he says.

He chuckles at my goofy smile and kisses me—finally—but pulls away after only a second.

"You taste like mint."

"The lipstick has peppermint oil in it."

His eyes darken. "I like it."

He kisses me, hard. I arch into him, the slide of his tongue sending tingles to my gut.

At least I'm wearing underwear this time.

No embarrassing wet patches on my dress.

Blake's fingers cup my butt and I squirm against him, separated by frustrating layers of cloth. One palm skims over my hip, his thumb stroking my thigh along the split of my dress.

God, I want his hands, his mouth, everywhere. Screw the Gathering and the thousands of people itching to talk to us.

Oh, shit. The Gathering.

We break apart at the same moment. My face feels as red as my dress, my pulse throbbing to my fingertips. The band engages in a lively tune and couples swirl around us.

"How many songs have played?"

"No idea." Blake smiles and my knees melt. "You are terrible for my observation skills."

I scoop up my shoes and we weave back to our table, breathless as if we've danced a marathon. I flop into my chair and stop myself from swigging my drink before I put myself in a coma.

Not a jug of water to be seen.

No wonder everyone gets shit-faced and amorous.

"Here. You look parched."

The man from the Market stands behind Blake's seat and hands me another drink. I cock my eyebrow at the full glass on the table. Half of his mouth tilts in a smile, the paleness of his skin highlighting the blaze of his emerald eyes through the mop of his hair. I accept his offering and his cool fingers brush mine.

"Cheers."

He clinks my glass and swigs his own, his gaze intent on my face. I clamp my lips on the rim and pretend to swallow. The liquid smells sickly sweet.

"That was quite the floor show," the man says, crossing one arm on his chest and cupping his elbow. His charcoal-grey tuxedo hugs a frame slimmer than Blake's.

"And you are?" Blake says.

"Malachay. I own a stall in the Market. I thought I had the perfect outfit for Anita but, as usual, Morrighan knows best. She has a great eye for the finer things."

He stares at my bared leg, starting at the toes and working his way up. He stops somewhere around my breasts. Blake tenses but he stays in his seat.

If he punched every man who leered at me, he'd have a very

busy night. Or life.

Malachay manages to lift his eyes to my face. "Can I interest you in a stroll through the woods? I promise you, it will be quite pleasurable."

The liquid sloshes in my glass. "Are you asking me what I think you are?"

"Blake can come, too." He smiles, showing perfect, too-white teeth. "In fact, I bet we all will."

"We're good here."

"Drink more. You'll change your mind."

Malachay downs his glass. I place mine on the table.

He pouts. "Has Morrighan not explained how these evenings usually end?"

"She has. We won't be participating."

"There's no need to be shy. We all like to share. In fact, it would be rude of you not to." This he directs at Blake.

Hmm. Maybe I'll be the one who punches him.

"I don't share," Blake says.

"But—"

"Goodbye, Malachay."

"How about a parting toast?"

We glare at him and he sweeps his long body into a bow, backing away and disappearing into the throng milling about the stadium.

"Well, that was weird."

Blake huffs. "Guess I'm going to have to get used to it."

"What, strange men propositioning me while you're sitting right there?"

"Yup."

"You poor, poor thing."

He grins and my stomach flips. "Don't you mock me,

woman. You don't see the ladies rushing over to beg me for sex."

"Give it a few minutes."

More people approach our table. None have the indecency to proposition us but everyone brings a fresh beverage until I have a collection of glasses on the table, all full.

If I drank the lot, I'd throw up and pass out, never mind join an orgy.

"I have the feeling they're trying to get me wasted," I say when we're blissfully left alone for more than a second.

"Christ, can't they just go shag each other?" Blake runs his hands through his hair and it falls in messy layers around his face. "Come on. Maybe if we dance, they'll stop wandering over."

We sway around the floor, cheek to cheek, the music slowing as the night winds down. Many seats in the stands are empty, the patrons probably out humping in the woods. I hug Blake and breathe in the sunshiny-rain-forest smell of him. I slip my hands inside his suit jacket to stroke up the smooth heat of his back, the ridges of his scars palpable beneath his shirt. I grip his shoulder blades and cuddle closer.

"Try not to react," I say into the soft skin below his ear, "but Malachay appears to be spiking my drinks."

The muscles under my fingers bunch. Blake spins and dips me, his hair hiding the direction of his gaze.

"That rat bastard," he growls. He kisses me and pulls me upright. "It's not like I'm going to leave you alone for him to drag you to some corner. What do you want to do?"

"Let's play along. I want to know what he's planning."

We return to our seats and I scoop up a glass, pretending to drink. Malachay watches from the edge of the stands. I pour half of the liquid under the table, splashing my toes. Wrapping my hands around the glass, I fake another gulp and spill the rest onto the floor. I slam the empty down and slump in the seat.

"How long does stuff like that take to work?" Blake says, his posture casual but his eyes scanning the room.

"Not a clue. I've only been tranquillised, not roofied." I lunge for another glass, sloshing lukewarm liquid onto my fingers. "Follow me to the bathroom and I'll ditch this one there."

I stand quickly and stumble, slapping my palm on the table to steady myself. Blake's hands slide around my waist. I giggle and touch my fingertips to my head. He follows me to one of the tunnels while I weave and wobble on my heels.

Some of it is faked.

At the door to the ladies' bathroom, I fist my hand in Blake's shirt and tug him in for a sloppy kiss.

"Top-notch acting," he whispers into my mouth.

I giggle some more, like a brainless idiot, and blow him a kiss, half-falling through the door. The spiked booze gurgles down the drain.

Out in the gloom of the tunnel, Blake shoves away from the wall and puts an arm around me. We find Dorothea to make our excuses, Blake propping me up while I smile and blink.

A hiccup would probably be overkill.

"She hasn't had alcohol in a long time," Blake says to Dorothea. "I'll walk her back. The air should do her good."

Dorothea's dark gaze prickles on my skin. I paste a crooked smile on my face and stare over her shoulder.

"Don't be silly! You stay here, drink, enjoy the festivities. I'll take her in the car."

Blake's fingers tighten on my hip. "That's not necessary."

"But I would be happy to. Stay. Get to know your new comrades. The night is young! I can take care of Anita."

"I appreciate the offer, Morrighan, but I'd rather take her."

She smiles, more teeth than lip. "Very well. It's such a shame to cut your first Gathering so short but I'm sure you'll see Anita home safe."

Outside, the cool breeze caresses the tiny hairs on my arms and slithers through the split in my dress. Blake supports me as we follow the road between the trees, my heels loud on the concrete.

I fake a trip and whisper into his hair, "Can you see Malachay?"

"Not yet. Permission to batter his arse into the pavement when we do?"

"Granted."

Laughter trickles from the trees to our left. A mound of flesh writhes on one of the daybeds, moans spilling between the gossamer curtains.

"Jesus, Dorothea wasn't kidding," I say.

Blake nuzzles my neck and I trip for real.

"Maybe we could find an empty bed and see what all the fuss is about."

"Hell no. Half the population of Inverness would faint if they saw you naked."

"Only half?"

"Homophobic men and lesbians, they'd be okay."

Streets and buildings replace the woodland, the glow of lights tinting the landscape bronze. Muffled cheers come from within several of the barracks blocks, the residents having their own party. A hush settles over the rest of the encampment. I lean on Blake, enjoying the quiet intimacy and the peace of the evening.

Apart from some strange sexual proclivities—and possible world-ending nukes—Alba gu Brath really aren't so bad.

Two black-clothed men step into our path, their faces hidden by masks. Two other men cut us off from behind.

I guess I spoke too soon.

41

"How often is this shit going to happen to us?" I mumble at Blake then raise my voice and slur my words. "Hey! You guys are wearing masks—*hic*—are you doing—*hic*—fancy dress?"

Okay, so the second hiccup may have been too much.

The men in front close in, all bulging muscles and hulking intimidation. I drape myself on Blake and wave at the guys behind us, who haven't moved.

"We're not here to hurt her," one of the men says, "but you need to learn to share."

I don't recognise the voice but I haven't been introduced to a million of the bastards so it's not a surprise.

I bury my face in Blake's neck. "You take the ones in front."

He nods and I slip off of his shoulder, staggering towards the men behind us. One short and broad, the other tall and skinny.

Malachay?

Gentle hands hold me upright. I squint at the emerald-green eyes watching me from behind the mask.

The rapey son-of-a-bitch.

"Take your beating like a man and we can get on with our evening," one of the idiots says to Blake. "We'll only bruise your pretty face a little."

"Jealous?"

I can't see Blake but he is definitely smirking.

"Cut the talk. Let's get it done."

I fumble at Malachay's mask. He smiles softly and captures my hand. I jab stiffened fingers into his throat. He chokes and I punch him in the eye. He collapses to the ground, curling up like a dead spider. The second man raises his hands and backs away.

"She's not drugged!" he yells.

I risk a glance over my shoulder. Blake keeps the two brutes at bay, dodging their blows. He sinks his fist into one man's stomach and the guy doubles over with an, "Oof." The second man pauses mid-swing. Blake steps towards him. The man hauls his partner upright and flees. The remaining man yanks Malachay to his feet and drags him away, his boots scraping concrete.

"You know, I'm a little disappointed."

Blake cocks an eyebrow, panting a little. "You wanted a better fight?"

"Contrary to the events of my entire life, I try to avoid getting into fights but, no, that's not what I meant." I take his hand and we head for the castle, no need to continue our charade. "I was actually starting to think this was the only civilised faction left."

"You can't let a few arseholes sway your opinion."

I smile at him. "You said something similar when you were trying to get me to trust you."

"And I was right, wasn't I?"

I cuddle into his side. "You were goddamn spot on."

We nod to the guards at the castle and navigate the many stairs and corridors to our room, my heels muffled on the thick carpet. I unwind the straps and kick off the shoes with a sigh, flopping onto the bed.

"Are you going to tell Morrighan?" Blake sits on an antique chair of gleaming wood to untie his shoes.

"Probably, though I have no idea who three of them were. The skinny one was definitely Malachay."

"Jackass," Blake growls, shrugging off his suit jacket and folding it on the seat.

He pulls his shirt out of his trousers and unbuttons it, revealing the smooth planes of his chest, the perfect stomach muscles and the glorious lines disappearing into his waistband. The shirt joins the jacket. My fingertips ache to stroke the curve of his shoulders and trail along his collarbone.

His body makes me think of words like sleek and hard and golly-gosh-wow.

He unfastens the button of his trousers. "Anita?"

"What?"

"You're staring at me again."

His fingers slowly undo his zipper. My eyes track the movement.

"No I'm not."

He climbs onto the bed to straddle me on hands and knees, his hair falling across his forehead. The warm metal of his dog-tags settles on my heart.

"Nothing fazes you, does it?"

I force myself to look at his face—no less stunning—and cajole my brain into forming words.

"No, because you'll never hurt me." My fingers cup his cheek. "And I know as long as you're here, I'll always be safe."

42

Dorothea's war room contains a table shaped like Scotland, the screen embedded in the surface showing an aerial map, too zoomed out to see if there are normal towns and greenery or craters and scorched earth. Ten people stand around the edge, turning as Dorothea and I enter.

I recognise several faces from the night before, particularly Tiffany of the bronze eyes and perpetual scowl. No MacKelter or Norris.

No Blake.

He's shadowing MacKelter after volunteering to be part of the guard detail. It increases the chance of one of us accessing the control centre, either alone or accompanying Dorothea.

She has to go there sometime.

Dorothea sweeps to the head of the table at the northern coast. "Thank you all for coming in so early after our festivities. I know I'm not the only one with a sore head."

Her advisers laugh and herd close to her, leaving me a space at the border with England.

I told Dorothea about Malachay and the attack on our short walk down to the war room in the basement of the castle. Her face darkened and she said in a tight voice, "I will take care of it." I left it at that.

Hopefully, Blake and I won't be in Inverness long enough for the asshole to try something else.

"Most of you should know Anita by now," Dorothea says, "but even if you don't, I've promoted her to adviser."

Glances dart around the table but no one whispers dissent. I note the people who frown—Tiffany, a couple of older men standing next to the east coast. The rest accept me with a nod. I return the gesture and lean on the table, the surface cool and slick under my palm. The whole image zooms in to a blur of brown and grey.

I snatch my hand back. "Shit. Sorry."

Dorothea smiles and swipes her finger across the table to fix the view. Tiffany's scowl flows into a sneer.

If I were a less confident person, I might be embarrassed.

"Is this an old image?" I say, powering through the silence. "The People's Republic tried to use the satellites but all we got were blurred images."

What a good liar I am.

To anyone other than Blake.

Dorothea shakes her head. "This is real-time footage. You have Soldiers of the Lost to thank for your blurred images. Buxton may think he was being clever to jam the whole country but I know everything that goes on in my borders and on this coastline. We have one jamming tower near us that I periodically disable. Just for fun, of course. I bypassed the jammers years ago to reach the satellites. They can't see me but I can see them."

My heart thuds hard but I keep my face blank.

Did she see us on the *Queen Elizabeth* or exiting the *Sea Shadow*?

I find myself stroking the purple pendant and force my arm

to my side.

The British Army can't help if she chooses this moment to shoot me in the head.

"The resolution isn't strong enough to track individuals or small groups"—cue relieved exhale—"but I can monitor vehicle movements, advancing armies and see what encampments are still standing. Priceless for planning my attacks, which brings me to the subject of today's meeting—our next steps. Anita, I believe you have valuable information on the faction currently at the top of my list."

Ten faces swivel my way, some hiding their scepticism, some not so fucking much.

I clear my throat and attempt to appear intelligent. "I've been in so many, you'll need to be more specific."

Her laughter tinkles and her black eyes sparkle like lit coals. Several advisers offer a polite chuckle. Tiffany screws up her face.

Was she in a relationship with Dorothea and resents the loss of attention in favour of me? It won't be the first goddamn time. My past is a hideous cycle of repeats and violence and death.

"Soldiers of the Lost is who I mean, Anita." Dorothea folds her arms across her chest, the loose sleeves of her deep-purple top flapping over her hands. "Tell me of your time with them. Buxton deserves a reckoning for the number of bombers he's sent into my encampment posing as refugees. Before I perfected my security systems, of course."

Was that the thing smelling of metal and oil when MacKelter asked us to step out of the jeep?

I tuck my fingers into my armpits to keep from fiddling with the table. "They accepted me into their faction after I delivered the ultimate weapon I'd stolen from Nationless."

The other advisers shuffle and mutter, their eyes flicking to Dorothea for reassurance.

"And what, pray tell, is the ultimate weapon?" she says, cocking her brow.

"It was a mechanical, almost indestructible, dragon machine."

"Was?"

"A woman set fire to the inside."

"Could anything be salvaged?"

"The fire destroyed her computer system but Buxton spoke of trying to replicate the material she was made from in other vehicles. I left two days later."

"Because of the woman?"

"Because they initially blamed me."

The self-righteous bastards.

Dorothea paces at the head of the table, one finger tapping her chin, her black heels loud on the polished floor. "Do you think Buxton can reproduce this material? Have a platoon of indestructible tanks ready to release on the rest of us and declare himself victor?"

"It's possible. He has a strong team of scientists and engineers."

Hand wringing and murmurs ripple through the gathered advisers.

Dorothea stops. "This is disquieting news but invaluable, as I knew it would be."

Tiffany scowls harder. Dorothea quizzes me for more information over the next thirty minutes. What's the material like? What is it composed of? What other defences do Soldiers of the Lost have? I answer as much as I can, not burdened by loyalty, though I hope my information won't result in Emily's death, my only friend there.

I have to tell Dorothea the truth of how the war started before she does something drastic. She's an intelligent, pragmatic woman. She'll realise there's no more reason to fight.

We can pick up the debate on who should lead our independent nation like we never left it all those years ago. Maybe we'll invite Soldiers of the Lost, though they deserve it even fucking less than the last time.

Dorothea claps her hands to conclude the meeting.

"This has given me a lot to think about. Thank you for your input today ladies, gentlemen. I fear we will have to act decisively on this." Her black eyes zip to mine. "And soon. Very soon."

43

I breach the inner sanctum of the control centre the next day.

The lift sails upwards, my stomach dropping at the height. Dorothea checks her perfectly applied make-up in the mirrored walls and smooths a finger under one eye.

She's wearing a burnt-orange chiffon dress, the material floating around her figure as if she's moving underwater. I feel pretty drab next to her in my dark-green t-shirt and combats, hastily purchased from the market since the clothes Dorothea gave me showed way too much chest and leg.

I made a point of stopping at Malachay's stall. A smudge of violet circled a bloodshot, swollen eye. He stiffened at my approach.

"How did you get the shiner, Malachay?" I said, smiling pleasantly.

He folded and refolded a royal-blue shirt. "Walked into a door."

I waited until he looked at me. My pleasant smile morphed into something darker.

"You should be more careful."

He mumbled about counting inventory and retreated through the curtain at the back of the stall, his reedy neck bobbing as he swallowed.

I hope whatever Dorothea does to punish him hurts as much as my fist in his eye.

The lift slides open onto a square lobby, silver flecks sparkling in the polished, black floor, a double metal door opposite us. Dorothea nods to a stern-faced woman guarding the empty space and flings the doors wide. Sunlight spills into the lobby, refracting into a million tiny beams that dance on the pale ceiling.

"Now, this is my second favourite place," Dorothea says, beckoning me forward. "Not many people get to see it."

The walls and roof are tinted glass, offering a panoramic view of Inverness, the Moray Firth to the right, the River Ness and Merkinch directly ahead, and the sprawl of the encampment to the left. A beautiful blue sky caps it all. I find myself closer to the main window, a huge control panel of blinking lights, dials and switches preventing me from pressing my hand to the glass.

At this height, the interior of the secret, walled area is laid bare, filled with flat, round structures of concrete and metal, a white number painted on each hatch.

Twenty. Twenty goddamn silos.

"Are those for nuclear missiles?" I say, my voice a little higher than usual.

"Good heavens, no. Nothing as crude as nuclear. I want to rule over the country, not a radioactive wasteland."

I close my eyes for a second and ease out a breath.

I can't sacrifice her faction to Lamb and Bursey if all she has are regular missiles like the other factions. Maybe once Scotland is united like it was supposed to be a decade ago, she can communicate with England, start peace talks.

Everyone will get what they want.

Dorothea joins me at the console and flashes a teasing smile. "Just don't touch any of these controls. It's a lot more sensitive than my satellite table. Who knows what you might trigger?"

I curl my fingers at my sides and slide back a step. "So this is the epicentre of your whole operation—power, defences, weapons?"

"Yes, Anita. This is where the magic happens." Her smile softens and her dark gaze drifts from my face. "Though you have yet to stay in my bedroom, where a different kind of magic happens."

Shitting hell. How am I supposed to respond? The fact she's a woman makes it more difficult. If she were a guy, I'd tell her there was no fucking way it was happening.

Does that mean I'm sexist?

I clear my throat and manage not to squirm but my cheeks heat, the room already warm from the humming panel. "Do you not need a team of people to monitor the controls? Keep it functioning as it should?"

"Oh, Anita, are you all work and no play?"

"I play just fine, Dorothea." I raise my chin. "With Blake."

A shadow passes across her face but she blinks it away, a small smile twisting her lips.

"Ah, yes. Blake."

I wait for her to say more but she holds out her wrist, a shiny fingernail slicked in red tapping the surface of her watch. The rectangular face unfolds into a larger screen the size of a keycard. Numbers scroll, replaced by coloured graphs and a scale, a tiny needle bobbing in the green bar in the middle.

"The system is highly automated but I can monitor it remotely with this. An alarm will sound if it ever needs my attention."

The screen snicks shut. Dorothea leans over the control panel and pushes a couple of switches. The hum deepens and vibrates in my belly.

"What are you doing?" I say.

Her head stays bent over the controls, her fingers typing on a huge, crescent-shaped keyboard covered in letters and symbols. Lights pulse faster and words scroll on several screens dotted throughout the expanse of the console.

"I didn't just bring you up here for a tour. I thought you might like to watch."

"Watch?"

"Following your information on Buxton and his threat level, I've decided to act." She tucks her hair behind her ear and twists a dial. "I've procrastinated long enough, somewhat distracted by the outside world, I'll admit. You were the encouragement I needed."

Movement in the walled area far below catches my eye. An orange beacon spins near the top left corner, the hatches next to it painted with a white number one and two. The hatches rise and expose circular maws of blackness.

"Dorothea," I whisper, my stomach clenched tight, "what are you doing?"

A dainty fingertip flips the protective plastic bubble clear of a red button. She finally raises her head and grins at me.

"Welcome to the inaugural launch of *my* secret weapon, Anita," she says, and flicks the switch.

44

Dirty grey smoke billows from the silos, fire flaring in their depths. I stare, unable to breathe, Dorothea prattling on in the background.

"Two should be enough to start with. My scouts will tell me how effective they've been then I can plan how many more I'll need for the other factions, though I suspect the threat of them will be enough once they see the aftermath. It's quite chilling for something that kills without carnage, and that's only from testing on animals."

Two squat rockets blast from the silos in a burst of light, marring the perfect sky with trails of cloud. They dwindle to a couple of specks in seconds.

"It's quite ingenious, really." She moves around the console, typing on the keyboard, the hum powering down to a low whine. "They work by detaching the molecules of non-chlorophyll containing biological organisms in the blast radius. No radioactivity. No mess. Just piles of dust that used to be people."

My head turns slowly, my lips numb. "Call them off."

"What are you talking about?"

"Bring them back, abort, whatever."

"Are you all right, Anita? You look a little pale."

"You're going to vaporise everyone in Soldiers of the Lost," I say, my voice rising, "of course I'm goddamn pale!"

She cocks her head. "This is a strange reaction for someone who left voluntarily, betrayed by her own people."

I force myself to calm down, a pulse thudding in my temple. A deep, steadying breath coaxes my heart rate towards normal.

"I have a friend there. One I'd hoped to meet again."

Oh, god, Emily. My actions will lead to the annihilation of an entire faction just like before.

"We've all lost friends, Anita."

"Then you should know how few we get in this place. I will protect the ones I have."

A delicate shiver runs through Dorothea.

Not fear. Oh, no. Warrior goddesses feel no fear.

She's fucking enjoying herself.

"This is the part of you that captivates me the most. The strength. The *heat*. It's really quite breath-taking." Her gaze sweeps me from head to foot and leaves nothing out. "Of course, you're also built like an Amazonian so that may be a contributing factor."

"Could you focus on the unwarranted death of thousands instead of my tits, please, Dorothea?"

She swallows what sounds suspiciously like a laugh. "Unwarranted, how? Buxton has slaughtered far more than I. We will be his next target, unless we strike first. I hoped you of all people would understand."

"Buxton didn't start this war. Only one faction did." I huff out a breath. "*My* faction, Dorothea. Marshall and his cronies slaughtered everyone in the debating chamber, including my sister. He tricked us all. Why should we keep killing for his lies?"

"You're Ailsa Carmichael's sister? I recognised the surname, of course, but it's common. How did I not notice you back in the day?"

Again with the top-to-toe scan.

"You're missing the point," I say through gritted teeth. "Soldiers of the Lost didn't kill your party leader. They didn't kill any party leader."

"Oh, I'm sure I know far more than you on what Soldiers of the Lost have done. Buxton showed me his CCTV footage."

"What? When?"

"About four years in."

"Why the hell did you keep fighting if you knew the truth?"

Dorothea's eyes glitter. "Did you never wonder why we only quarrelled with Soldiers of the Lost? At first, I was convinced it was Simmons and Buxton who assassinated Nicole. Then Buxton showed me the video. Not to make amends. Oh, no. To bask in his self-righteousness. Our party was second to your sister's in demanding they be banned from the debating chamber and he's never forgotten. Buxton holds a grudge better than a woman."

Another thing I already know.

"So why didn't you tell any of the other leaders? We could have allied to force Buxton to surrender. We could have been at peace."

"Your naiveté is quite sweet for someone who has experienced the other factions. When Buxton finished gloating, he swore he would not rest until my faction was ash. He may not have started this war but, believe me, he has much to answer for. This is his reckoning."

Hard to argue there. Still.

"Call off the rockets, Dorothea."

"I cannot."

"Can't or won't?"

She raises a perfect brow in challenge. "Won't. I intend to win this war, Anita."

"Where's the triumph in being queen of the dust?"

"Dust cannot kill my people, whereas Buxton can."

It makes sense. If she does nothing, Buxton will eventually attack, the smug, self-righteous asshole.

Fight or die—the mantra of the war.

Pity every time I fight, I get hurt.

Dorothea taps a button and the satellite image of Scotland flickers onto a screen. I examine the multitude of switches, dials and keys on the control panel.

Maybe I can abort the rockets.

Knowing my luck, I'll launch the rest and bring on the apocalypse.

My hands clench and unclench.

I don't have a weapon. Dorothea doesn't appear to, either, but attacking her would play our hand too soon. It might save Emily but not the rest of the world. And not Blake.

That's if the guard beyond the doors doesn't just shoot me and allow the rockets to continue on their merry way.

I can't stop the slaughter, only watch and deal with the aftermath.

Story of my fucking life.

The image zooms into the west of the country, to the large sprawl of an encampment nestled in the hills. Tiny vehicles move in the streets, squadrons of people scurrying to and fro. I swallow hard.

I'm sorry, Emily.

"The missiles will hit in approximately ten minutes. I

anticipate a slight cloud but nothing more. You are welcome to watch."

My head is shaking before Dorothea has finished speaking. "I've seen enough death, thanks."

I pivot for the door, my stomach twisted and bubbling, bile burning the back of my throat.

"It will get better after this," she says, softly. "You have my word."

I pause, my hand clenched on the cool metal door handle. "Maybe. Or maybe we'll be the only ones left in the dust."

45

I suck in air tasting of hot concrete, my hands on my knees, my butt pressed to the rough wall of the control centre, out of sight of the guard in the lower lobby.

Wouldn't want to ruin my tough woman image by letting him see my panic attack. Or my frustrated-shock-at-my-own-powerlessness attack.

The sun bakes my scalp, the sweat slicking my skin more to do with horror than the heat of the day.

What did I expect—a bloodless end to the war? Dorothea's rockets may be a radiation-free method of destruction but the worst is yet to come.

She will never surrender Inverness without a fight.

I straighten and pull the purple pendant on its silver chain from under my t-shirt, along with my dog-tags. Stroking Blake's name soothes my cramped stomach and frantic pulse.

One sharp tug and Lamb's necklace sits in my palm, an inert rock, the delicate links of the chain sparkling in the sunlight. I twist the ends of the stone and pull, a panel sliding to reveal a tiny button in the centre. My thumb hovers over it.

Dorothea has rockets. She seems content to use them on the other factions but that could change. Eighteen people-to-dust missiles could turn the cities that survived the Nuclear War into ghost towns.

And what's the other scenario—stay and see what happens? If anyone in Soldiers of the Lost survives, they will retaliate. Lamb will keep throwing men at Inverness, desperately trying to infiltrate. Any of the four surviving factions could attack, spooked by the disappearance of everyone in Fellhill and the sudden increase in particulate matter on the wind. Or they surrender, as Dorothea predicted, leaving her as Queen of Scotland. A force to be reckoned with for Bursey and the other world leaders.

And if they don't do what she wants?

Dust in the wind.

My thumb refuses to move.

"This doesn't make you a traitor, you goddamn moron."

Thankfully, the control centre runs parallel to one of the many warehouses containing the electrical generators so there's no one in the narrow alley to hear me growling at myself.

But throwing Alba gu Brath to the mercy of Lamb and Bursey sure feels like a betrayal. Once more, I am the traitor, sacrificing one faction for another, leaving a trail of death and destruction in my wake.

I lean my head against the brick and stare at the sky. My hand falls to my side, the stone loose in my fingers.

I can stop the war with the push of a button. The British Army will storm in and subdue a weakened Alba gu Brath. There probably won't be enough people left from Soldiers of the Lost to mount any resistance. The rest of the factions will roll over.

Apart from Rebel State. Those crazy bastards would rather die screaming than surrender.

A bloody end to a bloody war we should never have begun.

What would Ailsa think if she could see me now? My intelligent, loyal sister who thought every battle should be fought with words, not weapons. What was she trying to say to me before she died? She managed one word: don't. Don't start a war over this. Don't let revenge blind you to the truth and imprison you in a nightmare for a decade.

Don't kill everyone.

Dorothea can also stop the war with the push of a button. Her way is painless, bloodless, clean.

If you don't mind dusting the powder of millions of people off your windows for the rest of eternity.

In the end, the decision is easy.

Dorothea threatens the people I love.

Emily has minutes to live. My parents are in New London, an obvious target. Blake isn't safe in the middle of a war zone, despite the comforts of Inverness.

I will die to protect him. Kill to protect him.

I shove away from the wall. My thumb mashes the button and I drop the pendant in the dirt.

It's time to get the hell out of Scotland.

Again.

46

We have approximately four hours to disable the defences before the British Army get in range. If we don't, it will be a massacre and Bursey probably won't invite us to any more of his fancy dinners.

It takes up almost half that time to find Blake in the south of the encampment, walking the fence line by the hydroponic farms, joking with a group of guys I don't recognise.

The humour dies on his face. He murmurs a few words to the men and hurries towards me.

"What's wrong?"

"Dorothea has rockets. Not nuclear, but she fired two a couple of hours ago."

"Who was the target?"

"Soldiers of the Lost."

He pulls me into a hug and kisses my hair. "I'm sorry, Anita. Maybe she'll be okay. You said she lives in the basement of the hospital."

Emily won't have been in her rooms. She'll have been tending her patients, soothing them with her cool hands and no-nonsense demeanour.

Is she now a small pile of lavender-scented dust?

I hug Blake tighter, my nose buried in his neck. "It's my

fault. I should've pushed the button earlier as soon as we saw the secret, walled area. We'd be in England right now. Emily would be alive."

"It wasn't enough. You were right, we needed to be sure. Did you tell her about Marshall?"

"Yeah, but she didn't care. Some beef with Buxton. But now Soldiers of the Lost are gone, Alba gu Brath will soon follow. I'm a walking fucking disaster zone. Name one faction I haven't ruined."

"Revolutionary Front."

I laugh a watery laugh. "Goddamn John Anders."

"Amen." Blake smiles and wipes a tear from my cheek. "You okay?"

I scrub my face. "I will be. We need to get to the control centre. We have less than two hours to ruin more shit."

"At least life with you is never boring."

"Wait until we're back in the normal world, twiddling our thumbs. No guns, no threat of imminent death."

"Sounds like heaven." He takes my hand, his thumb stroking my knuckles. "Let's go fuck shit up."

I shiver and he grins.

"Really? Still with me swearing?"

"You make it sound so erotic."

He slings an arm around my shoulders and turns us towards the watching men. "Afraid I have to go, lads. Morrighan wants us."

"I'll bet she does," one guy says, giving us an appraising look. "I bet she wants a lot from you pair."

I roll my eyes while the men laugh and slap themselves on the back. Blake steers us away. As soon as we're out of sight, we break into a jog.

"Any idea where we can get something to bash in the control panel?"

Blake settles into a quick, easy pace beside me, his hair flopping into his eyes. "Vehicle depot. What about the guards?"

"They saw me go in with Dorothea this morning. I was hoping I could sweet-talk my way past them."

"Not that I doubt your skills, but if it doesn't work?"

"Guess I'll have to bash more than the control panel."

Reaching the vehicle depot eats up another hour, the vanishing time sending a prickle down my spine. If Dorothea's intact defences slaughter the British Army, she'll retaliate with the rest of her disintegrator rockets.

Blake and I won't have a normal world to return to.

The vehicle depot looks exactly like the one in The People's Republic—concrete bays infused with oil and sweat, an air wrench whining from the depths of an enclosed garage. We saunter around, nodding to the overall-clad mechanics, stopping short of whistling casually with our hands in our pockets. I scoop a crowbar, Blake grabs a spanner. We slip them into our waistbands and stroll out. There are no incredulous shouts or running feet but the weight of capture settles on my shoulders.

Events are in motion. There's nothing we can do to stop it now. If we fail, thousands—millions—more people will die.

Hell, we could die, waiting to be rescued.

Cheery thought. I bet Bursey would enjoy awarding us with posthumous medals to keep his word.

That's if the goon squad managed to disable one of Buxton's jammers to let our signal through. If they screwed that up, too, we have no reinforcements.

And what we're about to do will get us executed as traitors, despite Dorothea's infatuation.

The rectangular monolith of the control centre casts us in deep shadow. We slow to a walk and pass the dropped pendant. Blake cocks an eyebrow.

"Didn't want to keep it on me and set off any scanners if it's live. She's probably got them in every building."

"Good point."

The cool air of the lobby dries the sweat on my skin. The guard straightens, his fingers on his rifle. A bulky bulletproof vest stretches his black uniform, an earpiece dangling loose from a wire disappearing into his collar.

I curl my lips into a smile and try to appear relaxed. "Hi. I was here this morning. I think I've left my necklace upstairs. Damn chain keeps breaking. Do you mind—"

"Wait here." He slots the microphone into his ear. "You can't go up without Morrighan."

My smile freezes in place. "Is she at the star?"

"No. No one's down there." He touches a finger to his earpiece, his chin tucked to his shoulder.

I angle my body, the pointed end of the crowbar scraping my thigh as I draw it out. "Excuse me, sir?"

He raises a hand. "Give me a minute to radio MacConachy. She'll check for you."

"Do you want to have a threesome?" I say.

His head swivels movie-slow, his mouth agape. I rap him on the forehead with the crowbar. He continues to stare for a long, heavy second then his eyes roll back. Blake catches him under the armpits before he clatters to the floor.

"You certainly have a way with words," Blake says, smirking at me.

"I was desperate, okay?"

I push the button for the lift to the star. The doors slide open and Blake drags the guard inside, lowering him into the recovery position. I take his rifle and check his pulse, his breathing. All steady.

Hopefully, he'll wake up in a few minutes, his head aching and groggy but with no lasting damage.

I select the button for the lower level and step out. The doors shut and spirit the guard into the bowels of the earth. Blake calls for the second lift. Inside, the space is hushed, no music to break the tension.

How close are Lamb and his men?

If they're coming.

Thirty, forty minutes, tops? Did his itinerary factor in the range of Dorothea's defences? Maybe we only have ten minutes before they start to die.

I dance from foot to foot, the slow climb of the lift grating through my bones, the crowbar pressed to my leg. Blake touches my arm.

"After everything we've been through, this is easy."

I nod, perhaps a little too rapidly. "I know. The second guard is a woman so you may have to turn on your charms."

"How narrow-minded of you. She could be a lady-fancier."

A laugh bursts out and I clap my hand over my mouth.

He cracks his neck. "No matter. I'm all about the charm."

"The poor woman. Try not to turn it on too much, I don't want her disrobing."

The lift slows. Blake and I share a lingering glance. The doors open. The woman's eyes widen and the barrel of her rifle swings towards us.

Too late for charm.

I throw myself at her and we hit the floor in a tangle of limbs, the hard muscle of her body like landing on concrete. The rifle and crowbar slip from my grip but I need both hands to keep her arms pinned. Blake kneels at her head, her brown hair pulled loose from its clasp and shot through with grey.

She curls her lip. "You'll die for this, *traitors*."

The spanner thunks into her temple and she goes limp. Blake takes her rifle, sliding the strap over his shoulder, and I pat her down. We drag her to the lift and use her belt to tie her hands behind her back, her body sprawled between the doors to keep them from closing.

She'll get a little jostled but she's sturdy enough.

The only way up is the emergency stairs and they'll take a lot of climbing. We'll hear the cavalry panting before they get anywhere near us.

We pause at the threshold of the control room and steal a second to enjoy the view of a tranquil Inverness still bathed in sunlight.

It won't last long.

Blake motions towards the control panel with the barrel of the rifle. "Should we shoot it?"

"Keep the ammo. We might need it."

I heft the crowbar.

47

Smoke spills from the control panel, sparks spitting in the divots left by the crowbar. Buttons flash and dials spin, their needles quivering in the red.

I guess it is a delicate system.

"Christ, I hope the star doesn't blow up and bury us all in a crater," I say.

Blake shuts the double doors but the edges seal flush. No handles for wedging a crowbar through.

"The blast doors should keep it contained," he says. "I hope."

I peer out the glass. A flow of people rush through the streets and the alleyway of grids connecting the warehouses, converging at the base of the control tower.

"We're about to get company. In twenty million flights of steps. That should tire them a bit."

Blake settles his shoulder against mine. "I don't really want a shootout with these people. I like most of them."

"Me too," I say on a sigh.

"You both have a funny way of showing it," Dorothea says behind us. "Drop the rifles. And the crowbar, Anita."

I stare at Blake for a frozen moment, his eyes locked on mine, my heartbeat louder than the panicked control panel. Blake twitches.

"If you turn before you've dropped your weapons, I'll shoot you. Do not test me."

The rifles and the crowbar clatter to the floor. We raise our hands, facing Dorothea and her Glock 17. She still looks spectacular in her burnt-orange dress and heels.

How the fuck did she manage to run up all the steps and sneak in on us? She isn't even sweating.

"What was the outcome of your inaugural launch?" I say, my voice only wobbling a little.

She seems more bemused than angry, her black eyes flicking between me and Blake. "A success surpassing all my expectations."

My heart clenches.

No more Emily.

"What are you planning to do with the others? Eighteen seems a lot for subduing one small country."

I need to keep her talking and pray Lamb is amassing on the horizon with the British Army.

"Well, now that you mention it, Queen of the Universe has a nice ring."

"World domination, that's what you want?"

"Come now, Anita, don't be naive. Show me someone who doesn't."

I wave my hand. "Right here."

"Then you are not as intelligent as I thought."

Ouch. Lucky the opinions of psychopaths mean nothing to me. Or maybe she's more sociopath than psychopath.

Dammit. Why couldn't she have been one of the good ones?

The gun shifts to Blake. My heart leaps into my mouth.

"Who are you really? Spies from Soldiers of the Lost? Is that why you reacted so strongly to me targeting Fellhill? You don't feel like Revolutionary Front."

"We're factionless, like we told you," I say, quickly. "We just omitted a couple of details."

The barrel aims back at me and I ease out a breath.

"Go on," she says.

"We didn't travel north. We escaped the country from Unification Army and ended up in England."

A smile tugs at her lips. "Just how many factions have you conquered, Anita?"

"I wouldn't say conquered. But I've been inside six, including yours."

"Amazing. Is the great Prime Minister Bursey as pompous as he sounds?"

"Worse. He's also a bit of an asshole."

She laughs, flashing her teeth. "And yet, here you are, spying for him."

"He has an unsurprising fear of further mass destruction. I'd like to live in a free world. And he may have threatened me with prison for war crimes."

"You could have trusted me with the truth and I would've protected you."

"Yeah, my bad. I have a problem trusting people, especially if all they want to do is get in my pants."

Her gaze rests on Blake and a delicate sneer twists her features. "Apart from him. Sure, he's lovely to look at but what power can he offer you? Men are *weak*."

The thunder of boots shivers through the soles of my shoes, worried voices yelling for Morrighan.

Come on, Lamb. Where the hell are you?

"I don't want power. I want to be safe. Loved. I want to get out of this shithole of a country and have a real life."

"You disappoint me, Anita. You're a warrior and yet you're settling for some ridiculous fairy tale. Would you really miss him if he were gone?"

I bare my teeth. "You hurt him and I'll fucking kill you."

She chuckles. "See? This is what I'm talking about. *So fierce.* But your dependence on him suffocates your potential. You and I could've been great. When you realise that, maybe you'll forgive me."

"Dorothea, don't—"

She points the gun at Blake and pulls the trigger.

48

Despite fighting in the war for the past ten years, I've only been shot once—a bullet to the shoulder courtesy of an ex-friend. I have no desire to relive the experience but I'm moving before the echo of my words fades in the shininess of the control room, Dorothea's intent clear in the sparkle of her black eyes and the smirk on her Egyptian-princess face.

I dive in front of Blake.

The round hits me in the chest, a smack of heat between my ribs. It doesn't hurt as much as I remember—

Oh. Motherfucking. *Ow!*

Pain explodes from the heat. I slam to the floor on my shoulder and blink at the dusty tiles beneath the smouldering control panel. The room fills with shouting, banging, ringing. An alarm wails.

Why do they all sound the same?

"Morrighan!" a man barks. Possibly MacKelter, though I can't turn my head. "There's an army approaching. Air, land and sea. We can't tell what faction—"

"It's the British Army," Dorothea says, her voice cool and calm despite the tumult surrounding her.

Is she looking at me? It feels like she's looking at me.

When did I last take a breath?

"Oh, Anita," she says. "After everything you've suffered to survive, why would you sacrifice yourself for him?"

Because he's worth dying for.

I meant to say it aloud but scalding liquid swirls in my mouth and I swallow it down.

"Morrighan, we have to go."

"I know, Norris. Rally the troops. We'll give the English a worthy battle like old times."

"What about them?"

Is Blake still held at gunpoint? I'll take a second goddamn bullet for him if I have to. A third, a fourth. As many as possible so he can live.

I command my body to leap to its feet and shield him.

My leg twitches.

"This must be killing you," Dorothea says.

Well, duh. I have a bullet in my lung.

But she isn't talking to me.

"Your soulmate bleeding and my little gun stopping you from going to her. Shall we watch her die together? Both unable to get what we want? You should've left her with me at the Gathering then I wouldn't have sent my men after you."

She told Malachay and his goons to attack us?

"And what if I'd let you have her?"

Oh god, his voice, so tightly controlled but the anguish leaks through.

I want to see his face, hold him, breathe him in with my last breath.

My eyes burn, the need to touch him more agonising than the bullet burrowed in my chest.

"She just needed to relax, lose the inhibitions. Once I started, she wouldn't have asked me to stop. I'm quite skilled."

306

A snort. "Oh, yeah. I'm sure she wouldn't care it was rape as long as you were good at it."

"Perhaps. She is stubborn. Was it worth it? Weakening yourself for her?"

"You love her, too. You tell me."

A delicate sniffle.

The great warrior goddess crying over me? Surely not.

"Love is worthless."

"Morrighan, we have to—"

"Quiet, Norris, I'm almost done."

"No, we are done," Blake says, a soft growl in his throat, "because if she dies, *I'll* kill you. So you might want to fucking run."

Boots squeak on the polished floor.

"I meant what I said! You touch her and I'll shoot you!"

The warmth of Blake caresses my back, the fresh scent of him soothing some of my aches.

"Dying beside her is better than living without her. Maybe one day you'll realise that. So shoot me, *Dorothea*."

"Don't," I manage to wheeze. "I'll rip you—the fuck—apart."

My hand curls into a pathetic fist. The effort of talking bubbles fluid past my lips and drives a spike of agony deep in my chest. Blake leans over me, the dark shape of him in my peripheral vision, and places his hand on mine. I tangle my fingers in his.

"Even dying, she defends you," Dorothea says. "I hate you for that."

"I know."

Explosions rumble in the distance, accompanied by the sharp staccato of gunfire. Jets roar nearby, not quite overhead but close. The alarm shrieks. Inhaling feels like sucking fire through a straw. A huge struggle for a lot of pain.

Who needs oxygen?

"Morrighan, please…"

"All right, Norris. I've seen enough." Footsteps shuffle and pause. "If she dies, come find me."

"Count on it."

Bitch. I would've added a 'bitch'.

The trudge of boots fades. A wave of shouting carries the last queen of Inverness to safety. Blake rolls me onto my back, slow and gentle but it still drills the bullet further into my lung. His shaking fingers touch my mouth and come away red.

His breath hitches. "Woman, why did you do that?"

"Saved your life," I croak.

"Always protecting me. When are you going to let me save you?"

Christ, his eyes are so beautiful, even raw with pain and fear. The paleness of his face brings out the violet.

"You saved me the second you said 'I love you'."

He bows his head and presses his hands to my chest, my t-shirt sodden around a tiny hole in the material. I bite back a moan.

That side of my torso seems heavy, full. No space for air.

I lay my hand on his, no energy to help him stem the flow of blood.

"It's better this way." I choke on the taste of metal. Soon, talking will be impossible but somehow I'm not afraid. "You're stronger than me."

"Baby," he says and his voice breaks, "where did you get that idea?"

He cries then, soft sobs trembling through his shoulders, his blood-slick hands trying to hold me together. The cacophony of war hushes as if in sympathy, everything hazy-edged. Each inhale is shorter than the last, the rattle more pronounced.

Drowning from the inside out.

Blake raises his head and his despair wounds me worse than any bullet.

I always hurt him.

"I love you," I whisper.

"Please, don't leave me."

He kisses me, as tender as the first time. I brush the tears from his cheek and leave a smear of red on his perfect face. He captures my hand. My heartbeat stutters.

"You promised," he says.

I did.

And I try.

49

Blake

The anniversary of her death hits me harder than I thought it would.

A hidden path along the cliff edge leads to her grave, the shush of the sea below. The marble stone shines in the sun, flanked by splashes of colour—poppies, violets, daisies. I kneel and trace her name, my fingers brushing away the sand.

Her body isn't here, her ashes scattered to the wind, but she would've liked the spot. It's peaceful. A nice view of the ocean stretches to the horizon.

I stand, wiping the dirt from my hands, and touch the cool marble.

"Miss you, Mum."

She killed herself the day I returned to Scotland. Seems the women I love can't bear to live without me. It's a bit of a twisted ego boost. Though, in my mother's case, it was more a wounded protest at choosing Anita over her. But there was no choice.

I'd follow Anita anywhere.

Arms wrap around my waist. She tucks her chin on my

shoulder, her hair tickling my cheek and surrounding me with the intoxicating scent of cherries. Her lips nuzzle my throat and banish the sadness.

I lost all of my family but I found a new one.

"Hey, baby," I say, and smile, "or should I say wife?"

She bites me over my pulse. "I like baby better. Wife sounds funny."

"You not proud to be my wife?"

"Unbearably so."

I turn, her hands dropping to my arse, and I can't help but stare. A wild tumble of golden hair, the curve of her lips. Protective and loyal and mine.

My beautiful warrior.

She wore a green dress the same colour as her eyes to our wedding. It hugged her figure and flared at the bottom, her arms and shoulders bare, panels of flower-patterned lace giving tantalising glimpses of chest and leg.

No underwear.

I didn't even try to hide my stunned adoration.

The woman sees right through me.

We had four guests—Anita's parents, Felice and the tiny Chinese woman, Xia something.

Apparently, I have her to thank for my recent dress-and-no-underwear fetish.

The media begged us for attendance but we refused. Bursey and Lamb sent flowers and messages of congratulation.

Lamb's were a little too effusive.

He hung around for longer than necessary in the hospital, watching Anita as if he'd never seen her before. He didn't try to touch her so I let him be.

Falling for her happens like that—all at once after she shoves your misconceptions down your throat.

I pull her closer and kiss her. She does the moaning, trembling, eager thing I love. The same response when I finally got over myself and kissed her the first time. Like my touch is heaven and she never wants me to stop.

I'm always happy to oblige.

"Speaking of wife," I say, "when did you last perform your womanly duties?"

She smirks.

And she thinks mine is devastating.

"About an hour ago," she says.

"Ages then."

I take her hand and we stroll along the path to our house, the long grass swishing against our legs.

We live in an eco-friendly palace of wood and glass, nestled on the cliff and surrounded by trees. A gate, twelve-foot-high wall and fancy security system keep out the gawkers, stalkers and fans. It's no particle beam boundary fence but safe enough for our faction of two.

The O'Riley-Carmichaels. Or Carmichael-O'Rileys.

We're an equal opportunities group.

We wrote a book about our experiences and it's being made into a movie trilogy. The royalties are enough to live on but we still receive our stipend from the government, as agreed. We send Bursey photos of how we spend it—a hot tub, champagne spirited through the Channel Tunnel, a home entertainment system to rival any cinema. We even bought a seed crop of edible invertebrates for five families in Poland on Bursey's behalf.

We posted him the certificate.

He was re-elected. The man who stopped the Faction War

and prevented a second nuclear (or close enough) holocaust. Landslide victory.

David Brokenshire has his work cut out for him, though. There may not be many people left but those who are, are pretty feral. Only parts of Saorsa and Unification Army survived Dorothea's rockets.

And John-goddamn-Anders, the cockroach.

He came to our gate three months after the war ended and declared his undying love for Anita. She was the only woman to survive his blade, which clearly meant she was his soulmate. She pinned me to the ground to keep me from marching outside and pummelling his smug face. It was enough to distract me and we did something much more fun. She called the authorities on him afterwards.

He might not be jailed for how he treated her during the war but they have some questions on his human rights violations.

Like burying a hundred people sheltering in a bunker.

The British Red Cross and Lamb's rescue team dug them out four months to the day but they were three months too late.

We reach our house. The walls are immaculate. No cracked windows, rotten wood or bullet holes. No sleeping on the hard ground to wake up covered in a layer of frost.

Anita leads me to the bedroom, our huge bed a mound of pillows and a million thread count sheets.

Recycled, of course.

Above the bed is a painting of the pool in the trees I took her to when she was my prisoner. White sand, sunlight glittering on the water and blazing in the petals of a lily.

She's painting now that we have hobbies again. I like to cook. We keep some paintings for ourselves—the farmhouse where she finally surrendered to my irresistible charms, the river where she realised she loved me. The others are bleak and dark, shadows in shadows and the gleam of eyes.

We sell those.

She says it helps to put our past on canvas, stops it from poisoning her inside, but she still has nightmares. Her torture, me dying. I hold her in my arms until the shudders pass.

I tease her from her clothes, my light strokes enough to make her tremble, her eyes already dazed.

God, she is perfect. Slender but muscled, miles of creamy skin and curves. The scars only add to her perfection.

Strong but vulnerable.

I trace the ones between her ribs and her breath catches.

"Blake, please."

She's always so quick to beg for me. It never stops being awesome.

Dorothea's bullet almost killed her.

The scramble to get her medical attention when Lamb's men conquered Inverness nearly killed me.

Her pulse was weaker than the beat of a butterfly's wing when they finally found us and airlifted her to the *Queen Elizabeth.* Her heart stopped, and mine did, too.

That's what my nightmares are about—Anita bleeding in my arms, the horrible rattle in her throat as she struggled to breathe, her lovely eyes glazed.

Dorothea was captured trying to escape the encampment through a tunnel under the Moray Firth. She didn't get far since most of it collapsed when the star imploded.

She'll spend the rest of her life in jail.

Anita visited once to tell her she would kill her if she ever got out. Ten years from now, fifty years from now. If Dorothea isn't in a cage, she's dead.

My baby holds a grudge, too.

I lay her on the bed and press her hands to the covers, our fingers entwined. She arches against me, all velvet skin and dazzling heat.

The only woman to ruin my self-control.

I slide inside her and it's like coming home.

Let Me Know What You Think!

Thank you for reading my book! I love hearing from my readers so please leave me a review.

Can't wait to hear from you!

For a free prequel to *The Faction War Chronicles,* you can also join my mailing list at nadinelittle.com/free-prequel by scanning the QR code below:

What's Next?
Oh, just dragon-shifters, an angel apocalypse and humanity struggling to survive on a planet called Verdana.

Love Blake? Read the Novella: *Nationless Will Fall*
Discover how Blake survives the annihilation of his faction and what he really thinks when he first meets Anita.

Also By Nadine Little

The Faction War Chronicles
The Beginning (free prequel)
Nationless Will Fall

Hunters & Dragons
Who The Monsters Are
To Tame a Monster

The Warrior Angels
We Are Not Angels
We Are Not Broken
We Are Not Conquered

About the Author

Nadine Little lives in Scotland and is an ecologist with an interest in botany. She writes science fiction and fantasy in her spare time when she's not reading or playing *Fortnite* on her PlayStation.

The year 2020 seemed the perfect time to publish her debut trilogy *The Faction War Chronicles* since it all went to hell. Sometimes she worries that people will look at her differently.

But not really.

You can connect with me on:
- https://nadinelittle.com
- https://twitter.com/Nadine_Little_
- https://www.facebook.com/nadinelittleauthor

Subscribe to my newsletter:
- https://nadinelittle.com/free-prequel